A Journey With Poppies

A Story Set in the Mid Twenty-First Century

By

John L. Moore
&
David John Eagleton

ISBN: 1-4107-6247-5 (e-book)
ISBN: 1-4107-6248-3 (Paperback)

This book is printed on acid free paper.

1stBooks - rev. 11/10/03

ACKNOWLEDGEMENTS

We would like to thank and acknowledge the invaluable contributions of David M. Cornell and Kristen M. Kniest, each of whom served as proofreader, critic, inspirer, and co-visionary throughout the latter stages of the writing. A special thank you goes to Mary Ann Renken, who did the final proofreading and grammar correction.

iv

DEDICATION

This book is dedicated to:

- ❖ My wife, Sharon, for her tolerance during wee hours of the morning rewrites and for her pedagogic expertise in proofreading and grammar correction.

- ❖ My family, for their inspiration.

- ❖ My grandchildren, who in their zest for life, rekindle fond memories and a renewed spirit in their grandfather.

- ❖ The adventurous spirit of teenage boys everywhere and anyone who has dared to dream of times not yet come to pass.

John Moore

DEDICATION

My great-grandfather, Lewis M. Brantley, was not only a great man, but he was also a great friend. I called him Great Papa. He lived in California, but we still kept in touch, and he would always ask me how I was doing. He was very special to many people, but when he died, it was his time. Great Papa, I dedicate this to you, for everything that you did, because everything you did was great. We all miss you.

D. J. Eagleton

Editor's Note

D. J. Eagleton's great-grandfather, Lewis M. Brantley, read the final draft of this book from cover to cover just before he died at age eighty-nine. It was the last book he read as he passed from us on April 21, 2003.

PREFACE

Futurists have existed since man began to conceptualize time as having a past, a present, and a future. One does not need to be a futurist to imagine the future. But to do so with credibility is the real challenge.

Nostradamus, H.G. Wells, Robert Heinlein, and James Orwell are among those who have astounded us with their ability to see events that lie ahead in time. Who among us has not tried to envision the future? We recall the past and marvel at the changes that have been made in the past fifty or one hundred years. Then we try to extrapolate and envision what the next fifty or one hundred years will bring. While few of us can speak with certainty about the future, there are some who can predict with plausible credibility what might, indeed, take place.

This book is about the future. The story is the recollection of a teenage boy who, while growing up in the mid twenty-fifties, experienced several years of danger, excitement, and adventure. It is told from the perspective of David John Eagleton III—that teenaged boy—in the year 2055, as he looks back over the previous three and one-half years of his life.

x

INTRODUCTION

The year is now 2055. Looking back on all that happened and the way it happened gives me feelings of amazement and pride. It also gives me goose bumps. I am proud of myself because I played a small role in a venture to reclaim part of America that was under siege from a totally new type of warfare. But mainly, I am proud of my grandfather who saved me from danger many times, who helped me grow up, and who spearheaded the movement against an enemy few others recognized.

I call my grandfather, Poppies. I suppose it is because that is what he called his grandfather a few decades ago. But now, in 2055, it seems a bit old fashioned. Still, it has become a family tradition, and though I just turned eighteen, I would be honored if someday, perhaps, my grandson will call me Poppies too.

Our journey began on April 2, 2052. I was fourteen years old.

Signed:
David John Eagleton III

CHAPTER ONE

THE ESCAPE

Tuesday, April 2, 2052
Walnut Creek, California

Poppies called me on my newly embedded microcom at 7:00 a.m. Poppies typically was up and out of the house he and I shared before I awoke, so it wasn't unusual to get an early morning call from him. He frequently called to make sure I was ready for school, but today he spoke hastily and I caught the urgency in his message. "We've got to get across the border soon," he said.

I was already awake, but I wasn't ready for his microcom call, and my tooth vibrated with the sensation created by the new device. Microcoms had been around for over ten years, but this was my first really good one. I could receive and send verbal messages just by activating the "tooth phone" that had been embedded in my large upper molar. The voice-activated transmitter responded to my verbal command in a code known only to me. By voice commands, I could initiate a call, answer a call, send a call to voice mail, etc. Plus, it was a totally "hands free and instrument free" operation.

As I learned to master the new device, I thought how much of a drag it must have been to carry around a verbal communication device such as a cellular phone back in the first decade. Even the miniaturized wrist phones of the twenties had to be an inconvenience. I read once that those had to be dialed and the transmission quality was sporadic.

With the current state of the art, I could send a verbal message by microcom anywhere in the world just as easily and clearly as I could by talking to someone face-to-face. Further, since all transmissions were based on verbal commands, and number destinations were already programmed in Microcom Central, all I had to do was verbally activate the "tooth phone," say the name of the person I wanted, and start talking. Tiny speakers also were embedded in my Eustachian tubes so every message I received was crystal clear.

I wondered what the hurry was, but if Poppies was concerned, then I had better be too. He told me what to pack and that he'd meet me at the old pax train station at 8:00 p.m. that evening.

Back in the early twenties, Amtrak had taken over all the rail lines in America, including metro-area transit lines. Even that merger didn't help. The entire passenger rail network folded in the thirties. Ever since passenger trains stopped running in America, Amtrak stations had become havens for derelicts, but this one was in such bad shape, even the hobos and street gangs avoided it.

As I went off to school, I wondered what Poppies was up to. He had not been his former self ever since Grammy went away.

I was a little early for our rendezvous and, at age fourteen, I felt uneasy about going into the station after dark. Nevertheless, there was a strange feeling of human presence in the station. Perhaps it was the ghosts of all the riders who had passed through the station in years past. I had read in my history books that Amtrak never really caught on and had to be subsidized by the government for many years. Even in the years preceding the Petroleum Wars, when fuel for other modes of transportation was scarce, travel by rail did not flourish.

The station reeked with the smell of garbage and sewage. There were still remnants of drugs, alcohol, and marijuana going back to the days before legalization. This was the congregating place for the scum of society who had lost themselves in the mind-numbing world of narcotics when it was still illegal to use them. How ironic, that once legalized, the crack houses disappeared and the sidewalk junkies did likewise. I guessed that the principle of removing the prohibition, once again, removed the lure.

Drugs were not a problem in 2052. However, crime and oppression were, so it was with considerable trepidation that I sat there in the dwindling twilight of the station lobby. I was breathing quickly and sweating heavily as I brushed away the cobwebs and imaginary spiders I thought were crawling down my neck.

Poppies came up behind me and his "Pssst" about made me wet my pants. He motioned for me to follow him, and I stayed close as he took me down the frozen-in-time escalator to the track level. We walked along the track bed for about two hundred meters until we came to a tunnel that had been sealed. Somehow Poppies knew that some of the bricks had been knocked away, creating a small hole in the barricade.

I looked to my left and saw a dilapidated sign that read, "Walnut Creek Station." We slipped through the opening quickly and, without another word, we were on our way down the tunnel.

It was pitch dark, but Poppies seemed to know where he was going, so I reached out to touch his climate coat that was already warming him to counter the cold and damp of the tunnel. It was April and already quite warm, so my climate clothing was packed in my bag. The bag was strapped over my shoulder like the backpacks of old. The difference, of course, is that backpacks of the mid twenty-first century were made of air buoyant fiber and their weight was almost negligible. The climate suit weighed less than a kilo and my air-spring shoes even less.

That was all Poppies told me to bring, but I did bring my cyber bracelet that had been a gift from my mom.

That was about all I had left from her and I couldn't bear to leave it.

Even though Poppies hadn't said so, I had a premonition we weren't coming back.

In a few minutes we were outside the tunnel. The track bed was overgrown with brush and weeds, and dirt had blown over most of the track. As my eyes adjusted to the partial light provided by the moon and the few city lights that penetrated the smog, I saw what Poppies had in mind. He pulled a tarp off a pile of boards and other debris to reveal a Harley-Davidson hybri-cycle.

Motorcycles had been quite popular during the Petroleum Wars because of their fuel efficiency. However, even getting 80 kilometers per liter, they were soon replaced by the hybri-cycles that could easily go 250 kilometers on a pellet of fuel. The advanced cadmium battery was the reason. Petro-fuel pellets were only used for acceleration. Once the hybri-cycle was at cruising speed, the batteries took over and a state of near perpetual motion existed.

Poppies sat me on the back and showed me where to hold on, as I had never ridden a hybri-cycle before. Curiously, the propulsion cell made little noise, even when petro-fuel was being used. And once battery power was in charge, there was no noise, except the air blowing across our windshield.

5

Even though I knew little about hybri-cycles, I did know that a propulsion cell had replaced the internal combustion engine that once was used to power motorcycles. This cell used a concentrated petro-fuel pellet to both accelerate the cycle and to generate electricity for the battery. The battery could be charged from a separate source, but once fully charged, the battery and the petro-fuel combination would take the hybri-cycle a thousand kilometers before needing to be replenished.

He started the cycle and off we went. I was concerned at first that he had no lights to illuminate our way. He explained later that we needed the cover of darkness, and he had traveled this route many times by day and knew every bump and turn. Plus the night-vision goggles he wore shielded him against the wind and illuminated his field of vision. After a while I became accustomed to the whole situation and relaxed on the back of the hybri-cycle.

I looked for signs in the moonlight that would tell me where we were going. I only knew that we were headed northeast out of Walnut Creek along the line that had once been part of the Bay Area Rapid Transit System called BART. BART, under Amtrak, had been extensively expanded through the twenties, but had fallen into disuse after the start of the Petroleum Wars. I didn't recognize anything until finally I saw a familiar sign. Sacramento River, 1 Km.

We rode parallel to the river for several kilometers and only left the roadway when we approached populated areas. We slowly and deliberately skirted the town of Walnut Grove by staying on the river's edge, but Poppies stopped the hybri-cycle completely when we got to Locke. As we pushed the cycle along the mud bank, Poppies quietly explained that this might just be the most dangerous part of our trip.

I learned later that Locke, California had been the first and only settlement in the United States built by Chinese for Chinese. Built in 1915, it had been a thriving haven for Chinese workers who emigrated to work in the gold mining camps of Sutter's Mill fame and others along the Sacramento and Feather Rivers. That was between 1850 and 1880. As the gold rush excitement began to dwindle, the Chinese workers were recruited to build the transcontinental railway. When the railroad was completed in 1869, they returned again to Northern California to construct levees in the Sacramento-San Joaquin River Delta.

Just prior to 1915, a group of immigrants from China's Kwangtung Province was living in Walnut Grove while they worked to build the river levees that would shelter the rice paddies of the fertile Sacramento Valley. When a devastating fire burned their entire enclave, the Chinese leaders sought permission to rebuild elsewhere.

California state law prohibited the Chinese from owning real estate, so a wealthy landowner, George

Locke, leased the land to the Chinese and they built a complete town for their workforce. It was mostly boarding houses for the male workers, but it also had a general store, two restaurants, and three houses inhabited by ladies of the evening. However, by the end of the twentieth century, Locke had degenerated to a near ghost town of about one hundred people, of which less than ten were Chinese.

In 2052, the situation was entirely different. The twenty-first century Chinese had chosen Locke as their new congregating place and had rebuilt and restored much of the old town, while adding an entire new section. Its proximity to the capital at Sacramento and its historical heritage were probably the reasons Locke was selected. Whatever the reasons, the Locke, California we were passing by contained 2,500 Chinese, none of whom were levee workers.

They were the new Chinese aristocracy who were spearheading the movement to capture the power centers of California. So far they were doing a pretty good job.

As the lights of Locke faded in the distance to the south, Poppies started the hybri-cycle and we proceeded up the Sacramento River Road. Little did we know how much the Chinese of Locke would impact our lives in the days to come.

After about half an hour, we pulled off the track bed and into a large, covered, concrete culvert. It was about two meters in diameter with a trickle of water running through it. Poppies turned the cycle around so we could make a quick getaway if necessary. Then he found an old wooden pallet and placed it over the dampness at the bottom of the culvert.

We were adjusting to the darkness inside the culvert when we heard a noise from the other end. Poppies grabbed his laser pistol and put his fingers up to his lips to shush my babble. From the far end, we heard a cough, a loud thud, and some swear words. As I followed along, Poppies slowly edged into the culvert until he had reached the midpoint of the forty-meter-long pipe.

At the far end, we could make out a form. It was a human slumped against the side of the culvert. He was covered with mud and crud, and Poppies got to within a couple of meters of him before the man opened his eyes.

"What the hell?" the startled man screamed.

Poppies quickly replied. "Take it easy, sir. We were just wondering if you are all right. We heard a loud noise and thought you might have fallen."

The man had regained enough composure to respond, "Well, I'm cold, tired, hungry, and beat to hell, but other than that, I'm peachy. Are you cops?"

Poppies and I both laughed out loud. "Not hardly," Poppies spoke up. "We have a few rations we are willing to share, but I'm afraid we all are going to share the cold and damp here in this culvert. My name is David Eagleton and this is my grandson, D.J." Poppies extended his hand.

Reaching out from his slumped-against-the-side-of-the-culvert position, the man replied, "And I'm A.J. Hamilton. I used to be somebody, but now I'm a homeless, hopeless wretch."

Mr. Hamilton looked to be about sixty, but his shoulder-length hair, scraggly beard, and the dirt-caked face made him appear much older. Beneath his disheveled appearance were two darting, yet sad, eyes, not unlike those of a frightened and exhausted puppy that had been abandoned by its owner. He was totally helpless and I felt sorry for him.

Mr. Hamilton was wary of everything and everyone, including us. It took us over an hour to convince Mr. Hamilton that we were not police, nor were we associated with the government in any way. He was obviously and understandably cautious. His survival depended on his vigilance.

Poppies began talking about a lot of seemingly mundane things—sports, weather, and life in California. I'm not sure whether Poppies sensed there was more to Mr. Hamilton than met the eye or whether he was just being genuinely compassionate, but eventually the barriers between the two men began to break down. Poppies compared their two situations by saying how ironic that they should meet in the dank, dark culvert. But these were desperate times and, as such, sometimes men were driven to desperate actions. As he continued to speak, Poppies' genuine sympathy was obvious.

Finally, Mr. Hamilton began to show signs of trust. He asked if we had any food. Handing him a concentrated sustenance capsule (CSC), Poppies asked what had brought him to this culvert.

"Well, since I gave you my name, if you had been police, you would have arrested me long ago. So I'm going to trust you. I have been living here for about a month, I guess. Up until a year ago, I had been the assistant general manager of Livermore Laboratories. Perhaps you have heard of them?"

Poppies nodded that he indeed was familiar with the prestigious Livermore operation that performed highly sophisticated research in a number of significant areas.

"How did you get from there to here?" Poppies inquired.

"As you may or may not know, Livermore was the research lab for the embedded-chip program used nationwide for personal identification. We not only created the chip that was eventually used, we also created a number of other chips along the way. Part of the research process, you understand. One of those additional chips was designed for people suffering from autism. The chip would send out nerve and brain signals to counteract the abnormal signals being generated in the brain of an autistic person. Unfortunately, it had some unwanted side effects. It frequently would be too dominant, and the patient would not only overcome his or her autism, but would become docile and submissive.

"The lab abandoned its efforts and actually banned the chip from further research. But after Governor Luis Santiago was elected, we were told to reinstate the program and to include testing on non-autistic subjects. That was when I first came to blows with the administration."

Mr. Hamilton paused and looked off in the distance as if to visualize that time of his life.

"What happened then?" Poppies was more than casually interested.

"Well, we were given a direct order to complete the test phase and get the chip ready for production. I fought against it using every bureaucratic roadblock I could devise, but eventually the chip was developed and tested. We found that it had a finite lifetime of about a year, and once embedded in a human, that human became submissive and feckless for about that long. Once we turned the research data over to the State Department of Health and Human Affairs

(HHA), we were out of it and they were free to do as they wished."

"And what was that?" Poppies asked.

"What they did was criminal. They mass-produced the so-called autism-chips and began implanting them in the citizens of California. Do you remember the free physical examination Governor Santiago advertised? Well, that was a sham to get people to come in. Part of the exam included a check of their identity chip. While that was being done, the additional autism-chip was embedded as well."

Poppies was shaking his head slowly from side to side.

Mr. Hamilton continued, "I didn't find out about it until a member of my own family came home from the physical exam. My daughter had changed from an enthusiastic young woman into a veritable zombie— overnight. She had been active in politics and had helped in the campaign against Governor Santiago. After the physical, she was amenable to anything the administration put forth. I don't know what else they did to the chip during production, but it was now able to sway people away from any form of dissent and toward the party line."

Poppies had grasped the significance of what Mr. Hamilton was saying more quickly than I.

"So it was the chip that was causing it?" Poppies' voice rose as if he had been given a revelation. "I wondered why so many of my friends and colleagues had become so wimpy. It couldn't have been anything but those damn chips!"

Mr. Hamilton was warming up to the interest Poppies was showing. Then he said, "I went to Sacramento. I argued with the Department of HHA until I was blue in the face. I went to legislators, the governor's staff, and even tried to get an appointment with the governor himself. Behind every door, I found the Chinese. They were at the bottom of this program, and the governor and his departments were no more than stooges."

Mr. Hamilton paused for so long that we thought he had finished. But he had not. He was just getting warmed up.

"Because of the inherent secrecy of the lab research, I was one of a very few who even knew about the autism-chip. I found out later that those who worked to develop it mostly turned up missing. Then one day, I came home and found my family gone. My wife, my daughter, and our Labrador retriever—all gone." He seemed to be reliving the dreadful moment.

"When I went to the police to report the situation, I was arrested. I was held incommunicado for over two months with no charges ever being brought. One night I was able to get out of my cell by feigning illness. They thought I was unconscious so I was taken to the infirmary. They left me alone on a gurney for a few minutes. That was all I needed to make my escape. I have been on the run ever since," Mr. Hamilton concluded.

"How is it that the authorities haven't tracked you down by homing in on your identity chip?" Poppies asked.

A. J. Hamilton smiled for the first time since we met him. "Do you think I didn't learn anything about chips and how to disable them while I was at Livermore? That was the first thing I did and it has enabled me to escape, evade, and survive this long."

Poppies had connected all the dots by this time. He went over to Mr. Hamilton and told him how sorry he was for his situation. Then he explained that he and I were not in much better shape. We had managed to avoid the physical examination (and the autism-chip procedure) because I was too young and Poppies disliked physicals. But we too were on the run and we would be moving out at first light.

Mr. Hamilton said he understood completely and sank back against the culvert wall. In seconds, he was asleep.

Poppies covered him up with a piece of canvas that was lying just outside the culvert. Beyond that there was nothing we could do, so we returned to our end of the pipe. Poppies motioned for me to sit down, and he produced some more concentrated sustenance capsules (CSC's).

The water in the culvert was far from potable and we needed to ration our canteen water, so we used the moisture extractor Poppies had brought in his pack. That was a neat device that had been invented by a friend of Poppies to pull water out of the air for drinking. It had been incorporated in gas masks during the Petroleum Wars so that there was no need to remove the mask to get a drink. It even filtered out radioactive particles, if any were present. Actually, it only extracted a few cubic centimeters per minute, but scientists found that a few cc's on a continuous basis provided moisture to the human body more efficiently than by drinking larger quantities every few hours.

Poppies whispered that I should put on my climate suit, lie down, and sleep because we had a long journey ahead of us the next day. I lay back on the unyielding wooden slats of the pallet and began thinking. I wasn't sure what was going to happen next. Heck, I wasn't even sure I knew what had already happened, but as my mind raced from thought to thought, I reflected back on my fourteen years of life.

I was born in 2038—just eight years after the Petroleum Wars had come to an end. I had been an incubator baby because that was the way my mom wanted it, and because babies conceived, nourished, and born in incubators, called synthewombs, were healthier than natural-born babies. Their mortality rate was almost zero.

A few mothers still used the old way, called natural birth, but mostly they were women in backward parts of the world. In the United States, what had begun as test-tube babies at the turn of the century, had become commonplace. I learned in science class that an incubator baby is where the entire gestation process takes place in a synthewomb and the mother and father are involved only as much, or as little, as they wish.

My emergence from the synthewomb was in Palo Alto, but my parents took me to their home in Walnut Creek after my physical and medical introduction to the atmosphere had been completed.

Mom was a computer programmer for Astronet, which was the largest communication network company in the earth-lunar-space station environment. My dad, David John Eagleton, Jr., was a physician in the California Medical System (CMS) specializing in oncology research and was on the team that developed the cure for cancer in the mid thirties.

I was very proud of both of them even though they never married. They stayed together for the first six years of my life, and we lived in the old home my great-great-great-grandparents had built a century earlier. Unfortunately, after the Petroleum Wars, the government needed the talents of both my parents, and they were conscripted to work elsewhere. Mom went to Space Station Altair and Dad went to Rochester, New York.

From the age of six, I was pretty much raised by my grandparents, Poppies and Grammy. The Cal State school system kept me occupied ten hours a day, six days a week so, except for a four-week vacation each summer, there wasn't much time for frivolities. Nevertheless, Poppies was always ready to take me to a zoo, ball game, or to Disney's new Space World Theme Park in Southern California. That was until the Chinese took over the state a year or so ago.

Poppies had come to California as a young man of eighteen when he earned a scholarship to Stanford in 2007. He actually earned two scholarships—one for academics and one for baseball. Poppies was an outstanding player as a catcher and third baseman throughout his early years and, even though his throwing arm had been hampered by a thoughtless accident at age thirteen, he still could zing the ball down to second base to cut down would-be base stealers.

He finished Stanford with a degree in civil engineering and would have gone into professional baseball, but he saw the handwriting on the wall. The sport was self-destructing. Over the years, the greed of both the players and team owners had driven the price of a ticket to a point where the ordinary family could no longer afford to go to a ball game.

The competition provided by other sports and venues added to baseball's demise. Probably it was the popularity of extreme sports in the twenties that turned fans away from baseball and toward the exciting, life-threatening aspects of extreme polo, extreme bungee jumping, slam ball, and others.

In any event, Poppies worked as a bridge designer for Bectel Engineering and was the lead engineer for the Golden Gate II, a parallel suspension bridge spanning the San Francisco Bay. He devoted himself to excelling at his work for several years until he met Grammy. Her given name was Jennifer, but most folks followed Poppies' lead and called her Jenny. They married and Grammy had my dad, David John Eagleton Jr., barely nine months after the nuptials. Their wedding was quite a ceremony as Grammy's family had a lot of money and put on a reception party at San Francisco's Fairmont Hotel ballroom. Afterward, they honeymooned on the SS Omega, one of the first space stations to accept civilian guests.

Grammy and Poppies lived at various locations in the Bay Area for several years, finally settling in the house that, at that time, had been in the family for over sixty years. They later shared space in that home with my mom and dad, when they were not out of town.

I grew up in that home enjoying the same roses, oleanders, and hibiscus planted by my great-great-grandfather, the original Poppies. The grape arbor, that had been planted several decades earlier by my great-

great-great-grandparents, still bore grapes and had given our family decades of shade and enjoyment. The house at 14 Sharmar Court had been a safe haven to five generations of our family, and I hope one day I will return to be the sixth.

Poppies shook my leg to wake me just after dawn. It was Wednesday, April the third. Every muscle I had ached from the bouncy ride and from the hard night's sleep on the wooden pallet. Still, I stretched and yawned and accepted one more concentrated sustenance capsule that Poppies had offered. He pointed out that we would need to ration our supplies of sustenance capsules because he didn't know how long it would take us to reach the border.

He said, "If we run out, we might even have to resort to plain old food from the fields and forest, if there's any left."

I had tasted food several years ago, but I much preferred the sustenance capsules that had become the norm in the early forties. I popped the CSC into my mouth, followed by a drink of water from our canteen on the hybri-cycle, and felt much better.

Poppies said that we only had enough containerized potable water to last two days. We had the moisture extractors to use as a backup, but there is really no substitute for a cold drink of water. However, in two days, with any luck we would be clear of the H_2O Contamination Zone. Once we were in aquifers above

1,800 meters, the water would be safe to drink. Each year the Water Contamination Zone was shrinking as the leaching process took place. Scientists estimated it would take another thirty years before all residual contamination was eliminated. The anti-radiation serum developed in 2033 was only effective on airborne radiation, so drinking the water could be lethal.

It was hard to imagine a world where water was free and clean. I read in my science book that before the Libyan terrorist contamination incident in 2029, water plants captured water from lakes and streams and, with minimal treatment, allowed the water to flow through pipes to people's homes. However, when the radioactive seed particles were introduced to many American aquifers by rogue elements of the Third World, over half of the sources of potable water were contaminated.

Fortunately, the half-life of the radioactive elements used was about ten years, meaning that they would be at negligible concentrations in fifty years. The combination of dilution and half-life degradation was working, but the cost to civilization to generate this life-essential commodity was phenomenal.

Desalinization plants sprung up to harvest seawater. It was easier and cheaper to purify water with salt than water with radioactivity. There were also great strides made in the large volume ambient extraction process whereby water was taken from the air. Unfortunately, sometimes the particles contained trace radioactivity, so that method was discontinued.

At its peak, the price of a quart of pure uncontaminated water was twenty dollars, but now it was under three dollars. It was hard to believe that this precious commodity had once been so plentiful and so inexpensive.

Poppies and I walked the forty meters to the other end of the culvert to check on Mr. Hamilton. He was still drowsy and huddled under the canvas. We left him one more ration of CSC's and said our goodbyes. We wouldn't see him again.

I slid aboard the hybri-cycle and we were off. Poppies explained that we couldn't take the usual freeway route east of Sacramento because Chinese robots called humanoids were patrolling it. He said he knew a route that would take us parallel to the usual way but it was a few miles north and not heavily traveled.

We ran out of track bed shortly after leaving our culvert near Sacramento. Turning east, we paused to rest and stretch along a river that Poppies said was called the American River. He mentioned something about that river having great significance in our family history, but that was all he said. He seemed to be in a hurry to move on, so I thought I would save that story for another time.

Poppies was a great storyteller. Not only that, he knew a lot about almost everything. I never ceased to be intrigued by his explanations and his stories, even the ones I knew to be tall tales.

We continued on what had been a bicycle trail along the American River for a little while and then, without warning, Poppies pulled the cycle to a halt in a wooded clearing at the side of the path. Shutting the cycle off, he motioned for me to be quiet. I didn't know what to make of the situation but then I heard it.

My ears picked up the distinctive sound of the gyrocopter before I saw it. The copter sounded like a hissing cobra I had once seen in an Oakland zoo. I had been quiet before, but now I froze. I knew this was a Chinese aircraft and they were looking for unauthorized travelers.

Travel by Californians had been placed under strict control some six months earlier, under the guise of saving fuel. Travel had to be pre-approved and was strictly limited to specific routes and times required to continue essential service and commerce. Individuals had to provide strong justification and formally apply if they wanted to travel to and from essential destinations such as work, service centers, and even homes of friends and family members. Any deviation from the approved routes was banned and schedules were strictly enforced.

It may have saved some fuel, but everyone knew that the real reason was to keep us under control—their control.

Poppies had detected the oncoming gyrocopter on his modar. He continued to use it to monitor where they were going.

Several years ago, Poppies showed me how to use a modar and explained the technology behind it. Modar was an acronym for multiple object detection and revelation. It combined the capabilities of radar, sonar, infrared, global positioning system (GPS), motion detection, and a few others to tell you just about anything you wanted to know about a man-made moving object as far away as 10,000 meters. Instantly, it gave you size, type, speed, etc. and most importantly, IFF—which stood for "Identification, friend or foe."

Poppies continued to stare at the modar. I looked over his shoulder to see what he was learning. He pointed to one obscure bit of information streaming across the screen. The gyrocopter was not manned. It was "roboted."

I was about to ask Poppies what we were going to do when I heard the rush of air from the gyrocopter's nuclear propulsion nacelles. I was scared but I tried to remain calm.

I had studied nuclear propulsion and wrote a report on it back in the sixth grade. Years ago, engineers were unable to harness nuclear energy for scaled-down uses. Back then, it was used to run giant electrical power plants and even power submarines of the last century, but the thought of using nuclear power for aircraft or land vehicles was unheard of.

At least two obstacles had to be overcome. The first was size. Compression of the nuclear reactor size and weight didn't occur until 2026 when the first self-contained nuclear power plants were developed for trains. Even then, they weighed several thousand kilos, but the technology continued to evolve, and now a good self-contained nuclear power plant weighs less than one hundred kilograms.

The second obstacle was radiation. Great advances had been made in light-weight shielding technology, but even more importantly, self-contained plants are now equipped with fail-safe rods that activate to shut the plant down and neutralize the emission of radiation if and when the containment mechanism is compromised.

Also in 2033, Dr. David J. Eagleton, Jr. was part of a team that developed an anti-radiation serum. That serum countered most types of radiation poisoning and became part of the standard panel of inoculations given to all Americans. Thus, the way was cleared for the widespread use of nuclear energy in vehicles, buildings, and even homes. It was a good thing because the Petroleum Wars had decimated the supply of fossil fuels.

The copter was directly over us. I was sure we were going to soon be guests of the Chinese. But I underestimated Poppies.

He told me later that he wanted to be sure the crew was robotic for two reasons. First, there wouldn't be any need to destroy a human being and second, as good as they were, robots were still no match for a crafty human. Poppies was that. Before the copter could fully settle down, Poppies had taken his hand laser pistol from his pack. With deadly accuracy, he aimed at the "Intel/Com" port on the copter's underbelly. He knew that this computer pod governed the flight controls, landing characteristics, and general flyability of the craft. What I didn't know was that he knew exactly where to direct the laser to wreak havoc.

Suddenly, the copter lurched upward to about a hundred meters, spun around several times, and then nosed down into the rocky terrain below. It made a thunderous noise as it crashed, and afterward, the only sound was the last few gasps of air from the propulsion jets of the nuclear engine as it was still trying to supply thrust. It was like one giant bowel movement, followed by short bursts of gas. Then silence.

While I was standing there in awe of what happened, Poppies had started the hybri-cycle.

"If we don't roll 'em now, you're going to meet some live Chinese and real soon. I don't know how long it will take them to determine the cause of the crash, but eventually they will, and we will then be their prime target." Poppies' tone was bordering on solemn.

Up until now I had looked on this as a game, albeit a serious one, but now I knew it was life or death. We had thrown the fat in the fire. Now we had to run or fight for our lives. I was scared but also I felt great confidence in Poppies. He had gotten me through my first fourteen years and I wasn't about to change horses now.

I watched as Poppies mounted the hybri-cycle. Although he tried to appear unaffected, I could tell he was a little shaken. He paused for just an instant to look back at the crash site. His expression told me he felt more than he wanted to show.

Although, over age sixty, Poppies had kept himself in great physical condition. He was still ruggedly handsome, and he carried himself with pride and a bit of a swagger. His once-brown hair had turned a silver gray, and his previously taut muscular arms and torso had sagged ever so slightly. His above-average strength may have come from good genes or from his early years of weight lifting. Poppies stood over 183 centimeters but his stocky build made him look somewhat shorter. His expression was as intense as his eyes when he focused on something or someone. In all things, from his days as an athlete to his job as an engineer, he was highly competitive. I respected him totally and I loved him unconditionally.

Poppies guessed that we had about four hours before the Chinese determined that the gyrocopter crash was caused by outside intervention. The data stream from the copter's "info box" was already being received and analyzed by their safety people. As precise as Poppies' laser shot was, he couldn't completely hide the cause of the crash.

In the past, the predecessor to the info box was called a "black box," and it had to be physically recovered from a crash site to be useful. But, by the mid twenties, computerization had become so omnipresent and combined with high frequency transmission, that data previously stored in the black box was constantly fed to multiple land-based receiving stations. At any time, these stations had current flight and other data about every flying object in their sector, including a three-dimensional record of surroundings, both on the ground and in the air.

The only reason Poppies thought we had four hours leeway was that the Chinese were not as sharp in analysis as our guys were, plus their egos refused to let them believe they could have been even remotely to blame for the crash, so they would be looking for an "act of God" cause.

The crash site and the American River were miles behind us. Our hybri-cycle sped along the curves of the mountain road as fast as Poppies dared. I found it better not to look when we came near the edge of drop-offs that exceeded five hundred meters. One slip on his part and we wouldn't need to worry about the Chinese.

Up the incline we went. Occasionally we would see a sign of life such as a house or trailer, but mostly what we saw were signs where life had been. Windowless houses, burned-out trailers, abandoned vehicles, and an occasional deer or rabbit carcass framed the scene. Up ahead, we saw the first sign of civilization since the crash.

We had reached the town of Graniteville.

CHAPTER TWO

GRANITEVILLE

Poppies slowed down and began scanning the desolate streets for something, but I didn't know exactly what. Finally, he pulled up next to an old motel. Poppies said we would hide the hybri-cycle and hole up here until we were convinced the Chinese had lost our trail. He explained that to continue on would be the worst thing we could do, as their modar would find any moving object. I asked how he knew their modar hadn't already tracked us.

He looked at me with a grin and said, "Because if it had, they'd be here waiting for us."

I presumed he was counting on the time needed by the Chinese for crash analysis to get us a few kilometers away from the crash. Now that we had used that up, we had to resort to another tactic. Poppies looked at the town with amazement and a hint of nostalgia.

"This place hasn't changed much since ought six," he stated. "The last time I came through this stretch of California was as a lad younger than you are. I never thought I'd be back and certainly not under these circumstances."

The old motel still had electrical power and water. Poppies went to the utility shed down the road and threw the main switch. Then he turned the water valve to the "off" position. He wheeled the hybri-cycle into the motel lobby and down the hall to room number 16. It was the last one before the emergency exit. It had two beds and a small table.

"We will have to make this home for a few hours or perhaps days," Poppies said.

"Okay, but why did you cut the water and the power?" I asked.

"Why do you think?" he replied.

I thought for a moment and then it came to me. "Because any consumption in a previously unused system could be detected and they would know someone was here using the utility?" It was a half answer, half question.

"Exactly," Poppies exclaimed. "We don't want to do anything that will make them think this abandoned town is not still abandoned."

I felt a little smug, but not for long. The door to room number 16 swung open and a female voice demanded, "What gives you the right to cut off our water?"

She looked to be about forty, was quite attractive though dressed in jeans and a sweatshirt, but the laser pistol in her hand told us she meant business. Poppies stepped in front of me in a gesture of protection.

"Ma'am, we meant you no harm," Poppies began. "We had no idea there was anyone around and we just needed a place to stay for the night."

It was not totally true, but he didn't want to give her too much information. In the California of 2052, you were never sure whom you could trust. The Chinese had infiltrated virtually every social and economic strata of the state and many native Californians had been won over or had been brainwashed, with or without the autism-chip.

"Well, if you just wanted a place to bunk, why wouldn't you want lights, heat, and water?" The lady was nobody's fool.

Poppies sized the situation up quickly and decided he had better level with this woman. "Are you here alone?" he asked.

"No, I live here with my daughter, Zell, on the other side of the motel courtyard."

"You mean to say there are only two of you living here. How long has that been?"

"Going on a year now," she replied, "but getting back to my question, what are the two of you up to?"

Poppies evaded the question. "Do you know what has happened in California?" he asked the lady.

"Well, I know the damn Chinese have either taken over everything or run everyone off, or both," she spit the words out. "But I don't know how it happened or to what extent things are screwed up. We moved up here to get away from the Chinese influence two years ago, and you are the first visitors we've had since the rest of the town left eight months ago."

"Would you like to know?" Poppies asked in a hushed and sympathetic tone.

"Very much," her words and her attitude softened and she laid down the laser pistol.

In the late afternoon light, I got a better look at the woman. Her round face and warm smile contrasted, what I thought to be, sad eyes. She probably had been a real knockout in her twenties, as hints of her beauty could be seen in her high cheekbones, chisel straight nose, and ample lips. Her dark brown hair, cut straight just above her shoulders, showed streaks of gray when it caught the sunlight. I guessed that the tiny crows-feet at the corners of her eyes were recent, as were the two creases across her brow. Although I was never terribly observant about such things, it was easy to see she wore no makeup.

"Okay, let's start over," Poppies motioned for her to sit down.

Just then another voice called out from down the hall. The door opened and the late afternoon sunset rays revealed the most beautiful girl I had ever seen. It was Zell.

She was about my age and had long flowing auburn hair. She also wore no makeup and was dressed simply in jean shorts and a top that revealed her midriff and a small bit of cleavage that was intermittently hidden as she swished her hair back and forth. I was dumbstruck.

Poppies continued, "I presume this is your daughter."

The woman nodded.

"Well, my name is David John Eagleton and this is my grandson David John the Third, also known as Deej, and we apologize for breaking in on you and for any inconvenience."

The woman spoke, "No need to apologize. We have been wondering what was going on and why no one came back, but we were afraid to investigate for fear we couldn't stand the answer. Incidentally, my name is Olivia. Would you care for something to eat?"

Olivia invited us to move to a room adjacent to the motel lobby. In a few minutes, she brought out some real food. It was quite different from the real food I had eaten years earlier and tasted much better. However, I think I still preferred the CSC's. Neither Olivia nor Zell wore climate suits. I presumed they didn't need them because, at the higher altitude, temperatures were really quite comfortable. I took mine off and rarely wore it after that.

After the meal, Poppies began to tell Olivia and Zell about what had happened in the rest of the state. I thought I knew, but after he had finished, I was astounded at how little I had really known. Perhaps I was like a lot of other Californians who had been lulled to sleep or blindsided by the clever and insidious way the Chinese had infiltrated our institutions, our businesses, and our lives.

"It started over ten years ago," Poppies began. "After the Petroleum Wars had ended, people were disorganized and undoubtedly vulnerable. The Chinese had not been as deeply involved in the last Petrol War as the United States had been. So while our attentions were directed toward the war, China began to move their people in position.

"They already had immigrated some five million people into the state. They trained these immigrants in blending in and in becoming prominent in every avenue of influence and power we had. They proceeded to get their people elected to local and state offices; they ran the utility companies; they became police chiefs and police officers; they ran the lotteries; they took over small, medium, and large businesses; and so forth. What's more, they did this without the rest of the state's population having a clue as to what was in store."

Olivia was nodding her understanding of what Poppies was saying. Zell also sat listening in rapt attention. I watched her out of the corner of my eye and hoped she didn't notice.

"You mean to say, they have taken over?" Olivia asked.

"Lock, stock, and barrel, I'm afraid," Poppies said with a hint of bitterness in his voice.

Olivia's face showed a sign of both comprehension and concern. "I think I know what happened to my parents, then," she mumbled. "The Chinese took both of them away from the retirement home, under the pretext of relocating them to a better location, but I was never allowed to know where that was or what happened to them. I haven't seen them since. Can you explain that?"

Poppies paused for a long while and the silence fell on all of us with an uneasy pall.

"I can't be sure," Poppies said, "but I will tell you what happened to many senior citizens in the area we lived in. There were several large complexes that had served seniors for many years. One of those was called Rossmoor. I had several old friends who lived there, either under the nursing home or the assisted-living condition. About eighteen months ago, they began to disappear. No funeral, no burial, no explanation."

Olivia was aghast. "How can they do that?"

"We made it easy for them," Poppies continued. "Back in the mid twenties, the first laws were passed to allow euthanasia for humans. They were enacted with the best of intentions and with strict rules. Their premise was to give dignity to the many, many elderly people who had outlived their ability to enjoy life, yet were living to age 120 and beyond simply because medical science could extend their physical lives that long. The financial drain on the economy, along with the truly deplorable existence that many had, seemed to justify the laws. However, as time went on, these laws evolved. Restrictions and rules were relaxed over the years, and the strict oversight that had existed before the Petrol War fell victim to the dip in the economy after the war."

Olivia was paying close attention to Poppies' every word.

He went on. "The Chinese first used the laws to exterminate the non-productive elders that were nothing more than a drain on society and the economy. They soon expanded their program to include the old guard diehards who opposed their methods and rise to power. I guess their belief was, 'Once they were dead, they didn't complain nearly as much.' I found myself in that category and I feared for my life. That is why Deej and I are here. We are on our way out of

California." Poppies waited for what he had just said to sink in.

Zell finally spoke. "So that is what happened to Grandma and Grandpa? The Chinese killed them just because they were old. But how could the middle-aged and the young people of California allow that to happen? If we had known, we would have done something." There was obvious despair in her voice.

"The Chinese were very sneaky," Poppies went on. "We recently learned that many Californians were given a special chip that was implanted in their necks to make them submissive.

"For those without the chip, there were other pressures. For example, your mom couldn't do anything because she had to be concerned for you. It was not hard to look the other way, not that she did. But many others did.

"The Chinese bribed the more youthful populace with cash, fringe benefits, and promises. Once in power, they broke the promises. Even my peers, who knew better, were powerless to stop them. Technically, for the most part, the Chinese were within the law—the laws that our generation had enacted."

Olivia was almost numb by the time he finished. Perhaps she had guessed that her parents were dead, but she had apparently been in denial until that point.

Zell, broke the silence, "So what are we to do?"

"That question needs to be addressed immediately," Poppies got back to business. "You were in danger just being here, unregistered, and unaccounted for by the Chinese. Now that we are here, you are in even more danger. The reason we stowed the hybri-cycle, cut your utilities, etc., was to evade the Chinese who are after us."

Then he briefly explained what had happened back down the slope with the gyrocopter.

"We are sorry to have added to your predicament, but it was totally unintentional, I assure you," Poppies hoped they would understand, and not be angry.

Olivia finally came out of her trance. "Well, since we were consuming utilities before you came, and now we aren't, won't that be a deviation that will be noticed by Cal Utility Central?"

She had a point. Any change, no matter how slight, normally triggered an inquiry and perhaps a maintenance action. That was standard practice, and it had become so efficient that utility outages of any kind were unheard of. That was the good news. The bad news was that any blip in the detection system called for an investigation. Right now the four of us wanted to remain as inconspicuous as possible. Poppies agreed that the utilities should be again turned on, consumed at the previous rate, and we would hope that the turn off would be recorded as just a pause in normal usage.

He was guessing and we were all hoping.

CHAPTER THREE

ZELL

When Poppies and Olivia left to restore the utilities, Zell and I were left alone. She politely asked what school I attended, where I had grown up, and what type of music I liked. I gave her the answers willingly and began to feel more at ease with this very pretty girl. She seemed unaware of her beauty and did not seem to be stuck on herself the way many of the attractive girls in my school had been. I liked her immediately.

After we had exhausted the small talk, she asked if I would like to take a walk around the town. She explained that there was a beautiful waterfall and pond a few blocks away and we could see it before the sun went completely down. It seemed harmless enough so I eagerly agreed. We left a note for Poppies and Olivia.

The walk to the waterfall took only five minutes and I felt like I was lighter than air as we glided along. Once there, she pointed to a ledge that was just about halfway up the waterfall so we could see water coming down from above and then splashing on the rocks below. The scene of trees and vegetation all around appeared as if a landscape decorator had worked a lifetime to create it. It was a lush oasis in what had been a complicated composite of my existence since

43

we left Walnut Creek. I sat down and looked at the beauty around me, but mainly I looked at Zell.

I had been studying this girl since the moment we met. She moved with the nimble grace of an impala, yet she was athletic and not fragile at all. Beneath her naturally wavy hair was a face unlike any I had ever seen. Her cerulean blue eyes shone as bright as any gemstone. Her nose and mouth rivaled her mother's and she had inherited Olivia's high cheekbones, but Zell's cheeks had a twinge of pink that radiated warmth to everyone, especially me.

There was one noticeable difference between Zell and Olivia. Instead of sad eyes, Zell's were like sky blue pools of sparkling artesian water that one could dive into. I was in awe.

"What happened to your parents?" she asked.

I proudly told her of their expertise and how they were called to serve the government. I looked down at my cyber bracelet.

"This is the only thing I have to remember my mother," I told her. "It not only is a beautiful piece of jewelry, it is quite functional. It is a timepiece, a compass, a locator, a computer, a voice recorder, and a few other things that I haven't mastered yet."

"It's beautiful," Zell said with genuine admiration.

Zell gazed wistfully into the pool of water below, just beyond the white churning froth where the waterfall impacted the ledge.

"You are the first boy I have seen in almost two years. I have read about love and romance plus I have seen romantic programs on holovision when my mom lets me, but I wonder what it's really like. Have you ever been in love?"

I about fell off the ledge. The question came so quickly and so easily from her. I had had fourteen years to think about it, but I never did, and I certainly wasn't ready for it. I stammered, "Not that I know of."

She smiled. "Well, perhaps I'll be your first," she said teasingly.

Then she leaned over and kissed me gently on my lips. It only lasted a couple of seconds but I would remember it forever. It was like nothing I had ever experienced or dreamed of. I wasn't sure what to do next, but I didn't really care. I felt great!

The most exquisite moment of my life was brought to an abrupt halt by a voice from the path.

"Deej, Zell, get back here right now! Don't you know that Chinese sensors might be scanning?" Poppies was pissed.

Back in the motel, Poppies and Olivia took turns at reading us the riot act about what we had done.

"We used every bit of stealth we could muster in restarting the utilities," Poppies began.

"Meanwhile the two of you are out in the open giving off infrared and motion signals like nobody's watching," Olivia chimed in.

Zell and I both expressed regret and admitted we had been thoughtless to take the trip to the waterfall. Secretly and deep down, I felt that whatever risk was taken, was well worth it.

As night closed in, Olivia and Zell said their goodbyes and went back to their room. Poppies and I prepared to turn in. We had agreed not to increase the consumption of utilities, so we kept the lights off and did not shower even though we were both caked with road oil and dust. After the waterfall fiasco, we just couldn't take the chance.

I slept fitfully on the small bed with thoughts alternating between the Chinese copter incident and the waterfall kiss. What a contrast, I thought. Poppies finally dozed off with his modar set to alarm him if any approaching object should be detected.

Poppies was up early the next day. He let me sleep because we weren't going anywhere unless we were forced to. Our best chance was to maintain a low profile until the Chinese gave up the search. The only problem was that we had no idea how long that would be. I heard Poppies go out the exit door next to our room. I wasn't sure how long I had dozed, but I awoke to hear Poppies and Olivia talking outside. I really didn't want to eavesdrop, but the sound of their hushed voices penetrated the thin walls and open window of the motel room.

"You never said what happened to your wife?" Olivia was asking.

I knew this would not be easy for Poppies so I listened more intently.

"My wife went to work one day and never came home," Poppies answered. Seeing the question marks on Olivia's face, Poppies went on. "I had been active in speaking out against many of the injustices perpetrated by the Chinese in our town and in Contra Costa County. I never guessed they would get back at me by doing something to her. She was my wife, and the love of my life, and I would have never said a word if I had thought it would lead to her harm."

"Do you have any idea what happened?" Olivia inquired.

"None whatsoever. It happened over six months ago and I have been distraught ever since. D.J.'s folks are out of the state and not allowed back in so I have been responsible for him. In fact, my wife and I have raised him since he was about six. When I found that I was powerless to do anything to help my wife or to assuage the iron grasp of the Chinese, I decided the only thing to do was get away before it was too late. I bought the hybri-cycle on the black market and plan to use the mountain pass roads to get to the Nevada border."

"I see," Olivia said.

"There are three problems to deal with now. First, the Chinese want us because I knocked out one of their robotic gyrocopters yesterday. Second, if we do reach the Nevada border, we have no idea whether there is any sanctuary there or not."

Olivia waited for Poppies to finish his thought, but he must have been distracted.

"So, what's the third problem?" Olivia queried.

Poppies seemed reluctant to respond, but eventually he said simply, "It's what to do about you and Zell."

Olivia was quick but she admitted she was not sure what he was getting at.

"Zell and I will be just fine here as we have been, thank you," Olivia bristled.

Poppies went on to explain that as long as the four of us were together, the Chinese would not make any distinction between those who destroyed their aircraft and those who didn't. At best, Olivia and Zell were harboring criminals. At worst, they were co-conspirators. In either event, we were all in way over our heads. I was impressed by Poppies' concern for Olivia and Zell for I felt that way myself, particularly for Zell.

"Well, what is your plan?" Olivia had processed the information Poppies had given and was moving on.

"We have no choice but to remain immobile for the time being. Their long-range modars and other detection equipment would pick us up in a heartbeat if we were on the move. If your holovision works, I would like to monitor it for a day or so to see what is coming out over the media. When we think we can move, we will. I believe we can reach the border in a few hours with a little luck. I have heard that they may have taken Nevada also, so we are prepared to go as far east as necessary to get back to America." Poppies summed up our predicament most succinctly.

Olivia said nothing for some time. Finally, she spoke. "David, you are welcome to stay as long as you like. Thank you for your concern for our safety. If the Chinese come, they come. We'll deal with the situation when and if. While you are here, you are free to dial up our holovision as much as you like, but as you know, most of what is on, is garbage. They have done a great job of putting out sanitized news broadcasts that distort the truth and lull the masses into acceptance. Zell and I would go with you if we could; for I believe what you are doing is right. However, without any transportation, we are rooted here."

Olivia paused again and Poppies did not respond.

I was about to get up when Olivia spoke once more. "If you get out, do you think you will return to California?" she asked. I thought I detected more than idle curiosity in her voice.

"I don't know," Poppies said. "I would like to think we can do something to turn this invasion around, but I will have to see what conditions are in Nevada or wherever we end up. Right now, I'm just trying to keep Deej and me alive." Poppies had been quite candid with Olivia, I thought. There was nothing to do now but see what might be on holovision about the crash.

Holovision was the twenty-first century answer to television of the twentieth century. It evolved from the flat screen, high-definition TV technology of the early 2000's, and ultimately became the three-dimensional portrayal via articulated hologram technology that was perfected in about 2030. It was strange to imagine an entertainment media that was not totally realistic as the three-dimensional holovision was. What was even more difficult to imagine was a time when television was only in black and white. Nevertheless, we were interested in information, not 3-D holographic technology, and we looked intently at the holovision screen in Zell's compartment.

National news coming from the nation's capital in Chicago had been phased out months ago. In its place, local newspeople who looked like Californians, who sounded like Californians, and who previously were Californians, now acted like Chinese. But that didn't always come across to the uninitiated.

The holovised news anchors, Bob Sheppard and Li Ying, gave local, national, international and space news. It sounded quite similar to broadcasts of a decade ago, with one exception. It was managed. More accurately, it was slanted, distorted, and fabricated to influence all viewers that the current regime and all related agents in business, industry, etc. were highly efficient and working in the people's interest.

They had preserved the interaction features that had been developed in the late teens and viewers could interact with the media just as they had in the past. Again the difference was, the viewer was given a line of propaganda, albeit credible, but propaganda nevertheless. We knew that, going in, we were not likely to get straight answers regarding the gyrocopter crash. But we had to try.

The first night there was no mention of any problem with any government aircraft. We took that as a good sign and that they were still trying to sort out what had happened. The same was true for the second night. Poppies thought they should easily have come up with the answers by now. After all it had been over seventy-two hours since the incident.

The third night, Bob Shepard reported, "In local Northern California news, a government gyrocopter carrying a robotic surveillance team of three crashed in the mountains just east of Englebright Lake. A controls malfunction is the suspected cause. Officials have removed the debris to Sacramento for further analysis."

We were both excited and dismayed to get the report. Poppies speculated that perhaps they did believe it was a simple controls problem and that we were in the clear. But after more reflection, he thought it was more likely they had already completed the analysis, knew that it had been shot down, but had not located the shooter. This was their way of trying to make the perpetrators overconfident and think it was okay to come out of hiding. At best, they were still working on the analysis and just hadn't come to that conclusion.

Whichever, our prudent move was not to—move, that is.

Two more days went by and we took turns monitoring the holovision. Not a word about the copter crash was said. That night Poppies said we had better stop the twenty-four-hour-a-day vigil because we were depleting the energy in the hologram power source, and the electromagnetic force field being generated, however weak, created a possible anomaly in the characteristics of Graniteville and just might be picked up.

The oversight and surveillance of all citizens and activities had risen to where they knew who you were and what you were doing virtually all the time. Of course the data was processed and analyzed by computers, which had been programmed by humans. Sometimes the program tolerance limits would overlook activity. It just depended on whether the computer analysis was focusing in on that spectrum of activity at the time.

We were beginning to enjoy our stay in Graniteville. I spent a great deal of time with Zell. Later I learned that Olivia and Poppies had observed our obvious attraction for each other, even though we were shy and uncertain about it ourselves. They were proud and pleased at the way we conducted ourselves, but also wary of the impetuousness of puppy love. Moreover, they knew these were desperate times, and they wanted to enable the two of us to savor the joys of youth and young love as they had both known them in better times. So Zell and I were frequently left alone to experience our newfound emotions, but not for too long.

One day the four of us were particularly bored from the incessant rain that was blowing in from the west. We had grown weary of playing cards but I was still surprised to hear Olivia ask about things I thought she should have known. Perhaps she was doing it for Zell's benefit; I could never be sure.

Out of the blue, Olivia asked Poppies, "You know I have never understood how or why we Americans stopped eating food. I ran a restaurant and raised a garden and I always thought food was better than CSC's."

Poppies paused for a minute and then started what I had come to know would be a comprehensive coverage of the subject—a true engineer.

"Well, maybe it boils down to laziness," Poppies began. "If I recall correctly, by 2045, the majority of Americans had stopped eating food. The exceptions were a few diehards who lived in the wild and who had not yet adopted the proven concept that the human body was healthier and would last longer when fed by a variety of liquid concoctions and tablets. Scientists had been working on a better way to provide nutrition for several years, mainly due to the increasing tendency toward obesity exhibited by Americans across all classes and economic levels."

"Were people getting sick from food?" Zell asked.

"Not really, but years of dining on junk food and excessive portions had made Americans extremely fat. By 2018, the dining out/dining in ratio was 80/20. Americans were too busy and/or too lazy to cook. Affluence had purloined them out of the kitchen and into the restaurant."

"So what changed their attitudes?" Olivia inquired.

"Fear of dying, I suppose," Poppies replied. "The fact of the matter is, in 2020, ninety-eight percent of all Americans were overweight and half of them were categorized as obese. The solution was not to provide diet pills as had been explored early in the century, but to provide nutrition tablets that would give the body all the energy it needed and to provide fiber tablets that provided the bulk needed for absorption of the digestive track acids and for peristalsis."

"Ugh," Zell said as she wrinkled her nose.

"You undoubtedly remember the highly refined water and liquid nutrition drinks that began to supplant harmful drinks such as soft drinks and coffee. Gradually, Pepsi, Coca-Cola, and other major soft drink companies migrated to developing and selling nutrition drinks. Restaurants and fast-food places, so popular in 2010, began to founder and were soon replaced by nutrition bars and lounges. Alcohol was still in use but most upper-class Americans had been taught to use the safer, government-sponsored "hallu" drinks (short for hallucinogenic) and, other than the mind-altering effects that lasted for brief periods, these drug-filled drinks had no long-term adverse effects."

Poppies was warming up for his finale.

"The net result was that Americans were living longer, enjoying better health, and had more time for work and leisure since the typical nutrition 'meal' could be consumed in a minute or so. Projections now call for boy babies born in the year 2060 to live to age 134 and girl babies will live three years longer."

Olivia and Zell were frozen in rapt attention. I guessed both had underestimated Poppies' knowledge on the subject, and most certainly his gift of gab.

"Well I had no idea you were so knowledgeable about the history of food and CSC's," Olivia commented with sincere appreciation.

"You know, I have always meant to ask my mom about this but I just never did. What I want to know is—what happened to smoking?" Zell interjected. "I see old films on holovision that show people smoking cigars and cigarettes in public, but not anymore. What happened?"

Having had a captive audience on the subject of food, Poppies willingly stepped to the plate for an oration on smoking. It was one of his favorite subjects to condemn. Many years ago, one of his close friends had died of lung cancer, a consequence of heavy smoking.

"Well, if you really want to know, I'll tell you." Poppies was on a roll.

"In about 2023, one by one, the fifty states began banning smoking tobacco. Both medical agencies and the government acknowledged that smoking added nearly a trillion dollars to the country's health costs each year. In addition, the growing disdain by non-smokers, led to legislation which increasingly restricted places where smoking could take place. In many cities, the ban on smoking in public was so popular that anyone in violation could be incarcerated for months. In a few cases, violating smokers were subjected to physical injuries by mobs of objecting non-smokers. Even before that, taxes that were ten times the cost of the product made the cigarette a prohibitively expensive luxury item by 2019. Smoking refuges still could be found for those who could not escape the nicotine addiction, but they were few and resembled the leper colonies of the early twentieth century."

"Well, I guess I'm glad I never had the opportunity to try it," Zell said. "Still, those old movies on holovision sure make it look inviting."

We looked out to see the rain had stopped and a rainbow was forming at the west end of town.

Zell and I were becoming more comfortable with each other as each day passed. We spoke about our past lives and how strange it was to be thrown together as we were. For the first time in my life I began to think I had found a true friend. Zell was more than just a pretty girl. She was very bright. She had lived most of her life away from the unsavory influences of the twenty-first century. As a result, she was extremely curious about the world she had not experienced.

One day we were exploring each other's family history. That is when I learned that she knew a lot about Olivia's side, but nothing about her father or his family. Even so, she only had a sketchy memory of her grandfather and grandmother who had disappeared, courtesy of the Chinese. Her whole life was focused around Olivia. Of course, I could easily see that the reverse was the case, as well.

I suspect the absence of grandparents in her life made her more curious about mine. She asked about my parents, and about my grandparents. I told her the story of how I was raised by Grammy and Poppies, my grandparents on my father's side. I also explained that both of my mother's parents had died in a plane crash in 2021. It was one of the early un-piloted transports that crashed on landing when the nose gear collapsed. Nothing about the cause of the crash was attributed to the automatic pilot, just a mechanical malfunction in the nose gear assembly.

Of course commercial aircraft continued to demonstrate that they were ideally suited to un-piloted flights and they paved the way for the computer-controlled airships of all types today. The last bastion of aviators to resist the move to removing the human pilot from the cockpit was the military. It was particularly objectionable to those who flew in air-to-air combat aircraft. However, in the later stages of the Petroleum Wars, the un-piloted airplane invariably won dogfights between the piloted and the "computer-in-the cockpit" aircraft. Those airframes could turn tighter, pull more "G's," and perform in ways that would overstress a human being.

Zell asked if I had any brothers or sisters or any other living relatives. I was about to say no, but then I remembered about Poppies' parents. His mother and stepfather were still alive, living in the Colorado mountains. His father had recently died at the age of ninety-nine. I was pleased and flattered that Zell showed so much interest in my family and me.

It was the thirtieth day after our journey had begun. Poppies announced that it would be okay to resume normal activities as long as we were cautious about being out in the open and disturbing the environmental factors typically being monitored. Such things as power consumption, communication use, physical motion, etc., were the most prominent features that had to be guarded.

Zell and I had played more cards, checkers, and Monopoly games in two weeks than I had during my entire childhood. We had become bored with the regimen of watching holovision, playing board games, eating and sleeping. Each time I looked at her, I recalled the evening at the waterfall and longed to return. But, I couldn't ask her without getting Poppies' permission and I didn't know how to do that. Plus, what would I do if she said no?

CHAPTER FOUR

THE DISCOVERY

Saturday, May 4, 2052
Graniteville, California

It was a beautiful morning in the High Sierras. The crisp spring wind helped balance the warm rays of the sun that shone brilliantly across the mountain sky.

Ever since the ozone cover had been depleted back in about 2025, the sun warmed the earth much faster than had been the case in the century before. Average daily temperatures had risen about fifteen degrees and humidity levels had gone up markedly due to the partial melting of the ice caps. The efforts to artificially replace the ozone had only marginal success, but at least the depletion had been stopped. Regardless, the temperature at 2,100 meters elevation, where we were, was already in the sixties and would top seventy-five degrees by mid afternoon.

Zell met me coming out of the motel and asked, "Would you like to do some exploring? I've already cleared it with Mom and your grandfather."

I wondered why I hadn't thought of that. Exploring! I could have suggested that without saying I wanted to take Zell to the waterfall, and Poppies could have agreed without admitting he knew I wanted to take Zell to the waterfall. Oh well. I hated feeling that I wasn't as clever as I thought I was.

"What did you have in mind?" I asked with as much innocence as I could muster.

"There is a section of town that we have never investigated," Zell began. "We always thought it was someone else's property and they might return, so we never entered the buildings. As time went by, we lost our curiosity, I suppose. I think it's time we got curious."

I wondered if it was the buildings, or perhaps something else, that she was curious about, but the excitement of doing something besides playing cards overcame me and I readily agreed to the venture. Zell had packed a lunch of real food and was already out on the street before I could ask anything more. I ran down the steps and caught up with her.

"Where is this unexplored area, I asked?"

"Oh, it's about a kilometer from here, but we will need to take a circuitous route so we will avoid being in the open. All told, it will be about a kilometer and a half— if you're up to it, that is?" she teased. I was up to the challenge and I bounded out ahead of her.

"Come this way and stay behind me," she ordered.

We started through back alleys and around buildings and other structures to avoid having to cut across vacant lots or parking areas. We passed an old supermarket that must have been built before the turn of the century. "Safeway" was the name on the front and it had most of its glass front shattered on the sidewalk. Empty shelves and racks could be seen through the spider webs, but there was no food. Zell pointed out that they had scoured all the stores for supplies several months ago, but the departing citizens of Graniteville had already looted them.

Past the old supermarket was a fueling station that had once been a gas station when gasoline was still available. The fueling station had gone out of business well before the demise of Graniteville. Any fossil fuel still available was far too expensive and they certainly weren't shipping it up here.

We continued to walk in the alley behind the desolate buildings because we thought the narrower alleys would afford us greater protection than the street. Zell admitted she had never been this far. We had stuck our heads in most of the buildings but some looked like they could fall down on us and others were totally void of anything. It was like a vacuum cleaner of the old days had sucked away all the furniture and furnishings.

One of the buildings had what appeared to be a patio at the back. As we walked around the side, we could see it had once been a restaurant. "The Crystal Slipper" sign still hung on the marquee above the front entrance. The door was locked and, peering through the window, we didn't see anything worth breaking and entering for.

"Let's have lunch on the patio," Zell suggested.

She opened the sealed container of real food and produced two sandwiches, a tomato, and some cheese. A thermos of water with two cups rounded out the contents.

"I hope you like wild greens salad," she said hopefully. "I made it especially for you."

I would have gushed over Tasmanian lizard salad if she had made it. "Sure, I love wild greens," I tried to sound as appreciative as I really felt.

"What are kids like down in the Bay Area?" Zell asked after we had polished off the lunch.

I wasn't exactly sure what she was asking but I wanted to be responsive. "To tell you the truth, I don't like what is happening to kids in the urban areas. I don't mean to come off as 'holier than thou' but I think our generation is going too far."

I paused for some direction, but getting none, I continued. "For example, girls' fashion has become absurd. Do you know that half the girls in my school come to class wearing nothing but a sheer climate cover over a thong? Admittedly, the temperatures get to 100 degrees on many days, and the humidity levels necessitate the use of climate covers, but there is no reason they have to be transparent."

Zell did not respond.

So I continued. "Further, I don't particularly like the fad of hair changing. Both guys and gals have permanently recessed the hair follicles on their head and wear multi-colored hairpieces all the time, often changing them between classes. I didn't mind some of the colors, but some of the chartreuses and mauves, not to mention the spikes and other hair substitute materials just don't do anything for me. I think the hair God gave me is just fine."

"What's a climate cover?" Zell had not gotten past that part of my oration.

I thought it strange that Zell didn't know about climate clothing. She should have worn climate clothes before she and Olivia came to Graniteville. I would soon find out the answer to that puzzle. But for the moment, I brushed off my concern and continued.

"They've been around for years, actually. Climate suits, climate jackets, and climate covers all came about when global warming threatened to wipe us out. I guess it didn't have as much effect on you up in the mountains as it did on us down near the coast."

Zell still seemed interested.

"Anyway, these are outfits that are lightweight, waterproof, yet contain multiple tiny computer cells that sense your body's temperature and moisture and generate a miniscule amount of heat or cooling to maintain that area at levels ideal for you. They do the same for humidity. Way back in the past, people had something called heat pumps that would provide either heat or air conditioning to their homes. The principle of the climate cover is similar except everything is miniaturized. Essentially, spaced at every few microns around the climate suit, are tiny heat pumps that serve a small area of body cells. The pumps work to keep the few body cells they are responsible for at the right climate. No more need for bulky coats and other garments. I'm surprised you have not heard of them."

As soon as I said it, I thought I should have phrased my last comment better. However, Zell did not seem to be offended by my remark.

"That's not the only thing I am unfamiliar with," Zell continued. "I have never really understood why Mom and I had to come to Graniteville in the first place. She told you and your grandfather that we came two years ago, but really it was much before that."

This was something I wasn't prepared for. Zell was revealing a family secret to me that I was sure her mother would not appreciate.

"What do you mean?" I asked innocently.

"When I was little, we moved around a lot. I never really knew my father, but many times I was left with my Gram and Gramp while Mom went off to work or whatever. Sometimes, Mom came back to get me and we would go to cities and live in hotels for a few weeks. We went all over. We were in Reno when I was about seven years old, and Mom got me out of bed late one night and carried me to an air taxi. All my toys and clothes were left in the hotel so it must have been a real rush. The next thing I remember is being here in Graniteville. I think we have been here ever since."

The revelation Zell had given me was astounding. First of all, it told me that Olivia obviously had something to hide about her life before coming to Graniteville, and, secondly, it made me wonder if whatever it was had any impact on our situation now. What if she was wanted as a criminal? What if the Chinese wanted her? What kind of job could she have had to make her move around so often? These and other questions began popping into my mind.

"So when did the other people in Graniteville really leave?" I probed Zell's story.

"They really began leaving about two years ago just as Mom said," Zell said candidly. "We have never known why, but we suspect it had something to do with the Chinese."

No doubt, I thought.

"Before they left, Mom worked in one of the few restaurants still around. She started out as a waitress, but worked her way up to manager. She ordered the supplies, hired the staff, kept the books, and handled the money for the owner. He was a man from Sacramento who rarely came by. As long as Mom deposited proceeds in his account each month, he was content to let her run the business. It was a good deal for both, because he really didn't have the interest, and Mom needed the job. She thrived on it," Zell said proudly.

"Further, she was smart and I'm sure she squirreled a little extra away for herself. The other advantage was that she could see the handwriting on the wall as Graniteville citizens began to sell out and move. So, she began hoarding both food and CSC's."

"But isn't the stuff we have been eating fresh?" I asked.

"You bet," Zell replied. "Several years earlier, she had started growing vegetables and other food items in something called a garden. Those were quite unique and gave the restaurant a niche. People would come from as far away as Reno and Maryville to sample items that had been grown in her garden."

"Oh," I said.

"We have been living on the stuff she hoarded as well as food from the garden ever since. We even have some cold storage units all over town filled with perishable foodstuffs. You have been eating some of that too. Did you know?"

Zell had explained what I had been wondering about ever since that first dinner. Where did the food come from and how come they just didn't eat CSC's like everyone else? Now I knew.

"What was your mom running from?" I returned to that part of the revelation.

"I really don't know. Whenever I bring it up, she changes the subject," Zell pursed her lips in clear disappointment. "Well, what do you say we continue our adventure?" It was an obvious and abrupt attempt to leave that painful subject matter.

I agreed and we left the patio as we had come.

We wandered down alley after alley looking for anything of interest. We found a tavern whose name sign was still flashing—at least the part that said "Tavern" was. I presumed that this and similar other uses of electricity had continued on after the departure of Graniteville's populace. I wondered who was paying the bills. Cal Utility was usually quite sticky about unpaid utility bills. Either, they had a big glitch in their system or someone was paying the bills.

Our next stop was at the Graniteville United Parcel and Mail Service building. The door was wide open so we peeked inside. Ever since the United States Postal Service had been disbanded in 2012, packages and non-electronic communications were sent via private companies, such as UPS, which later was called UP&MS. Actually, because of the popularity of electronic mail, letters and other correspondence previously sent by U.S. mail essentially disappeared in the first decade of the twenty-first century. That led the U. S. government to reinvent the postal service several times before finally realizing that it could no longer be competitive with private carriers. By the time it was dissolved, the cost to mail a letter had risen from three cents in World War II to two dollars and forty-five cents in 2011.

There were still some undelivered packages lying around the building. I wanted to rummage around more and even open some parcels, but Zell said it wouldn't be right. While I thought she was being unnecessarily concerned, I admired her integrity. Of course I was finding there was not much about her that I didn't admire.

After nearly three hours of poking our noses in one door and then another, we came to an ominous-looking fence. Vegetation had grown up all around and over the fence so it was almost impossible to see past it. Zell asked me to boost her up so she could peer over the top. I was happy to comply.

It had been several days since I had last touched her in any meaningful way. Her feet on my knees and my arms wrapped around her upper thighs, evoked thoughts in me that didn't have anything to do with what was on the other side of the fence. My chin was against her back, just above her waist, and I could smell the fragrance of her perspiring skin as her shirt rose up. I was fully engaged in enjoying all the senses triggered by our physical proximity when Zell let out a scream.

"You've got to see this," she was excited.

I was excited too, but not for the same reason as she. She jumped down from my boosting position. Much to my dismay, she was in no mood for anything but the pursuit of the unknown behind the fence. I was much too heavy and too macho to allow her to boost me up so we searched for another way.

After a few minutes, Zell came up with a long steel bar. I used it to pry the gate open a crack. It was not locked, but rust and overgrowth had given it powers of stealth. We wedged a brick in the opening and pried a little more. Eventually, we wore down the vegetation barrier and could slip inside the crack in the fence.

Inside was every piece of equipment you could imagine from military campaigns of the past. There were tanks and guns from all three world wars. There were manned aircraft from the wars we lost—Korea and Vietnam. There were unmanned aircraft from the

Religious War campaigns and laser weapons from the Petroleum Wars. There may have been other wars represented, but I couldn't be sure. I guessed that this site had originally been a war museum but had apparently been abandoned several years ago.

At one time, the items had been arranged according to some plan, but now they looked as if they had been all shoved together. It was like a giant cupped hand had moved them from a ten-acre site to a two-acre site. The growth of weeds, shrubs, and trees added to the eeriness of what we saw.

At the back of the lot was an old barn. As we gingerly stepped through the bits and pieces that had been strewn around, we headed for the barn. Again, Zell tried to peer through one of the windows, but she admitted she had not been able to see much through the dust and cobwebs. We went back for the pry bar. With surprising ease, the door to the barn came open. Perhaps I was just getting good at this, I thought, as the door swung 180 degrees. There it was. As the sunlight of the mid afternoon choked out the dark of the barn, we both gasped.

Sitting there in mint condition was a military Humvee, all gassed up and no place to go. The inspection tag on the hood said this was a 2008 Humvee, but it only had 800 kilometers on the odometer. The exterior appearance seemed to validate this low usage.

We took turns getting in behind the wheel and crawled in the back. I peered under the hood and checked the fuel tank for any sign of fuel. Full. It was as if this vehicle had been left there in readiness for a need that never surfaced. I checked once more for any signs of additional fuel. I didn't know much about these forty-year-old relics, except that they were very durable, were shell and laser resistant, and could go over almost any terrain.

As if by fate, Zell and I found ourselves in the rear seat. Before I could say a word, Zell had leaned against me and put her arms around my neck. I looked down to see her mouth coming toward mine. I closed my eyes.

CHAPTER FIVE

EXIT FROM GRANITEVILLE

Zell and I ran all the way back to the motel. Both of us were out of breath, so we took turns telling Poppies and Olivia what we had discovered.

"I'm sure it can be driven," I blurted out.

"It has all kinds of room. We could go too," Zell gushed with enthusiasm. I thought I caught an endearing look from her when she said it.

Poppies and Olivia agreed that there were possibilities, but I detected misgivings from both of them. I wondered why.

The four of us gathered some items, including Poppies' modar, and headed for the war museum. Our first task was to drain the fuel from the Humvee. Poppies explained that fuel in those days was something called diesel and would congeal over time. It would have to be drained and replaced with fresh fuel. He found some supplementary tanks that had been pressurized all this time so that fuel should be okay to use.

By mid afternoon the four of us were cruising down the main street of town in the Humvee. There were all kinds of gear stored inside and the fifty-caliber machine gun mounted on the top gave me a feeling of superiority even though we had no ammunition. The trip, although risky, was necessary to check out the vehicle, according to Poppies. I suspected it was also because the little boy in him wanted to see just what it could do.

We started out on the flat and drove at speeds befitting a parade, but it didn't take long for Poppies to find a small hill and he took the Humvee up the incline to give it a test. The ride was bumpy, even bumpier than riding on the hybri-cycle, but it was fun. Zell and I bounced around in back and I held on to her to keep her from falling out. (At least that's what I told her.)

The ride was over much too quickly, and Poppies returned the Humvee to the museum building. "We shouldn't do any more to risk detection," Poppies explained.

The walk back to the motel was quiet, but Zell and I were bubbling with questions by the time we arrived. They all boiled down to one thing. Why can't we take the Humvee across the border?

Olivia had remained reticent during the ride and the walk to the motel. We congregated in the lobby and Zell and I jumped up on the office counter. As she and I were bombarding Olivia and Poppies with questions and ideas about the Humvee and our departure from Graniteville, Olivia interrupted. "Zell, there is no way we can go with them in the Humvee."

She was quietly emphatic. It was that placid firm response that kids hate to hear, because one knows no amount of begging will change the answer. Zell was struck dumb. We had gone from discovering the best to hearing the worst, all in the space of a few hours. Zell slowly got up and headed out the door. Her blue eyes, darkened to azure, were about to spill liters of tears. I wanted to run to her, but I was so surprised and angry that I was frozen to the counter.

We didn't speak of the Humvee or leaving Graniteville the next day, or for three days afterward. It was as if we had never found it.

Friday, May 10, 2052
Graniteville, California

At first I thought I was having a bad dream when Poppies woke me by saying, "Get your stuff together. I think it's time to head for the border."

Deep down I knew that day would come, but I had been in self-inflicted denial. I acted as if I had never considered the possibility.

"How can we leave so soon?" I asked. "What about the Chinese? Won't we be leaving Zell and Olivia in danger?" But mainly, "How can I leave Zell?"

Zell knew immediately what was up when she opened the door. In the past few days, we had gotten to know each other's moods quite well, and we could sense them by the expressions on our faces. I told her what Poppies had said and suggested we approach Olivia once more. She said she had done so every day since we found the Humvee so it would be of no use. She said Olivia had given her lame excuses about it being more dangerous for Poppies and me if they tagged along and that Olivia simply couldn't impose on us to take them.

Olivia's excuses simply didn't satisfy me, so I told Zell I would come back later in the day to say goodbye. Then I went back to confront Poppies.

"Why don't we invite them to come with us?" I pleaded.

Poppies was busying himself with gathering the necessary items for our trip and was loading the hybricycle he had made ready several days before.

"Sit down," Poppies said quietly. He stopped packing and looked me straight in the eye. "Olivia and Zell cannot leave Graniteville because Olivia is a wanted criminal," Poppies spoke directly.

Without waiting for my response, Poppies continued. "She told me that, a few years ago, she had lived with a man named Rodney who was Zell's father. He got her involved in a gambling scheme in Reno. Apparently, Olivia's role was to befriend a mark they had singled out. Being particularly attractive, Olivia would have no trouble guiding the mark to Rodney's backroom poker parlor. There, Rodney and a few other locals, who were confederate players in on the scheme, would cheat the mark out of his money in a high stakes poker game and split the proceeds among themselves. Olivia would continue her shill role until the mark was fleeced and left the game.

"After that, she would see to it that he was further entertained and assuaged until she felt it was safe to send him on his way. Most of the time, that involved getting the mark drunk, returning him to his hotel room, and slipping a sleeping pill in his drink just in time to avoid any further involvement. Virtually every time, when the mark awoke the next day, he was groggy, embarrassed, and uncertain of just what had happened. He would leave town never to return."

I was in too much shock to say anything.

"Unfortunately, on one occasion, they picked the wrong mark," Poppies continued the story. The man Olivia escorted into the poker game was Nick Medici, a member of the East Orange, New Jersey mob. He was in Reno incognito on an assignment to purchase a share in Harrah's Casino in downtown Reno. While the purchase amount would be handled through foreign banks, Nick had been given a substantial amount of cash to wine and dine the decision makers of Harrah's, plus enough to bribe one of their advisors.

"Nick's judgment was as bad as his ethics because he had all of the money on him when he entered Harrah's that night. After watching him lose a few thousand at blackjack and craps, Rodney and Olivia picked Nick to be their 'pigeon du jour.' They had no idea who he was, why he was there, that he was connected to the New Jersey mob, or that he was betting with their money.

"Olivia had picked him up and, without too much urging, the two of them went to the back room. Nick took a seat at the table with Olivia at his arm. They normally played pot limit, table stakes with a minimum buy in of ten thousand dollars. Nick peeled off fifty grand from a roll in his pocket that he delighted in showing to Olivia.

"After a couple of hours, Nick had gone back in his pocket twice more and his roll was all in chips, most of which were in front of other players. Rodney and his co-conspirators had plucked some wealthy pigeons before, but this eclipsed anything they had ever done. By eleven o'clock, Nick had transferred over a quarter million of the mob's money to the game. Nick was apoplectic. Moreover, he was mad. He accused Rodney and the other players of cheating and demanded they return the money. Of course he was right, but whether he knew or was guessing was immaterial, because the format was set. Olivia's job was to soothe the loser's mood and escort him from the game, after which the booty would be divided, and the game disbanded for the night.

"That night would not go according to script. Nick had used his microcom to summon his bodyguards who had watched the whole episode play out, prior to Nick's entering the poker room. Nick had previously told them that he might need some help, so they were spring-loaded to the respond position.

"They brandished hand lasers and mind stoppers. Rodney was the first to be hit. The first ray from the mind stopper reduced him to a blithering idiot. The other players were scattering but two were dropped with laser shots. Olivia had hit the floor when she first saw the goons. She might have gotten out of it all right, but Nick had caught one of the confederate players. He spilled his guts and fingered Olivia as the shill. Nick rewarded his forthrightness by applying a mind stopper to the side of his head.

"Olivia would have been next, but just as Nick turned toward her, Harrah's security guards and the Reno police arrived.

"Nick had to use up all his chips with Harrah's managers and police to buy his way out. Corruption had become commonplace in America and particularly in locations where gambling had been legalized. Indicative of the extent to which things had deteriorated, Harrah's preferred charges against Rodney and all the players, dead or alive. Nick was allowed to return to East Orange without so much as a warning ticket, and Olivia, the remaining living player, went to jail.

"When the mob boss found out what had happened, he was enraged. Nick had not only lost their enticement money, he had cost them five hundred thousand more to buy his way out of trouble. But his biggest screw up was that he had queered the deal with Harrah's. Two days later Nick stepped into his private gyrocopter and was never heard from again.

"Olivia had three big problems. First, she was being tried for a list of crimes too long to recite. Second, the mob felt she owed them big time. And third, her little daughter had lost her mother. Fortunately, Olivia knew where Rodney had stashed the considerable proceeds they had collectively 'won' over the years. She made some calls, some arrangements, and for just under a million dollars, was able to buy herself out of jail. It really wasn't a jailbreak, because the sheriff let her go, but when he was explaining it to the press and others, it became a 'flight to avoid lawful prosecution.'

"Olivia's only recourse was to gather her daughter up and 'beat feet' away from Reno. And that's how they got to Graniteville and that's why they can't leave."

I concluded that Olivia had solved one of her three problems, but the other two were still very much alive. She wasn't sure which was the greater threat, the law or the mob. But she was in no position or disposition to find out.

"I'm sorry that you have to hear this because I know how you feel about Zell and how you'd like to take her with us," Poppies concluded.

I was astonished and chagrinned, but I understood. Zell had no idea of the plight they were in and I couldn't tell her. That was Olivia's call. I had to find a way to say goodbye without giving away what I knew. We had grown so close that I wasn't sure I could do that.

Zell and I knew where we wanted to spend our last few minutes together. The waterfall glistened brightly in the mid afternoon sun. Sparkles of white and turquoise bubbled up from the deep blue water beneath. Cascading sprays played across the worn rock shelves, singing a sweet and soothing melody. At least that's the way I remember it. Zell leaned back against the same rock where we first kissed and where we had returned many times since.

"I want to remember this place," she said. "It's the most beautiful place I can imagine and I love it because of that and because of you."

I was overcome by her words and her sincerity. "I'll always remember this waterfall too and when I do, I will think of you," I mumbled. I wished I had been more poetic.

With that, Zell pulled me closer and gazed directly into my eyes. "I think I love you," she precisely, but softly, said the words.

Before I could respond, we kissed. Then, without a word, she slid down the rock and was gone. I had wanted to say I would come back for her. I had wanted to say I shared her love. I had wanted to say so much. But it didn't happen. I hoped she knew.

The muffled swoosh of the hybri-cycle brought me back from my daydream. Poppies was slowly coming down the path toward the waterfall. I didn't want to share my feelings, my memories, or my love for Zell with anyone. I ran out of the glen and jumped aboard. In minutes we were out of sight.

CHAPTER SIX

WEBBER PEAK

The hybri-cycle cruised easily up the slight incline toward Webber Peak. The road was surprisingly smooth but tunnels and hairpin turns kept Poppies' attention focused on the road. That was fine with me because I was still savoring my last moments with Zell and thinking how painful it was to leave. I silently swore that one day I would return to Graniteville and Zell. The wind cooled as we climbed higher and higher toward the summit.

When we were about a kilometer from the top, Poppies pulled over for a break. I thought this was premature for we had not been on the road more than an hour. Then I saw what he had seen some two kilometers before. Down in the valley was a campsite. There were about a dozen air cushion homes (ACH's) and a couple of old time motor homes. All seemed to be immobile and it looked as if they had been there for a while. Ahead, the hairpin curve told us that our route would take us directly by the camp.

Poppies steered the hybri-cycle into the campsite. The fact that they had barricaded the highway and routed the road through their camp gave me the shivers. But Poppies seemed to know what he was doing, so I tried to put on my game face. He drove up to one of the ACH's and switched off the cycle. Without a word, he went up to the ACH hatch and passed his identity patch across the scanning bar. After a few seconds the hatch opened and out stepped a short stout man who looked like a fugitive from a bar fight.

"Hello, Art, remember me?" Poppies began.

"Of course. I saw your name and face on the biometric hatch scan and I said to my wife, 'That's old David John Eagleton out there. What in the world is he doing up here?' So what are you doing up here? The last I heard you were stirring up the Chinese down in the Lafayette area."

I learned some months later that Poppies had been keeping tabs on Art through a mutual friend in Walnut Creek. So he knew about Camp Resistance and he was aware of Art's involvement. But, in view of the lack of trust that was rampant in California these days, Poppies decided it was prudent to not make contact until we actually arrived. He did this for Art as well as for us.

I was still rooted to the cycle, but I could tell my grandfather knew this man well and had a deep respect for him also. After introducing me, Poppies quickly told the story of how we were headed out of California. Even though he left out a few details, such as the Chinese gyrocopter incident and our several weeks in Graniteville, this was the first time Poppies had extensively opened up to anyone about the journey and our attempt to evade the Chinese. Art Morris was a likable gentleman and he insisted we spend the night. Poppies agreed saying that they needed at least one evening to reminisce about old times.

Art looked to be about Poppies' age. He was shorter, fatter, and had less hair—a lot less. What remained was a speckled white and brown that somewhat complimented the moustache and short beard he wore. I wasn't sure if the beard was intentional or just a result of not shaving for five days. Art's unassuming appearance was immediately offset by his warm personality and jovial wit. He was extremely gregarious and I understood later when Poppies told me, "Art could sell iceboxes to Eskimos." He was an engineer, but an articulate and personable one, and he had drawn on that ability to organize the people in the camp.

Marla was Art's wife, or so I thought. In a few minutes, she produced a meal consisting of a blend of CSC's and fresh fruit, along with some cheese. After the dinner and the small talk had subsided, Poppies asked Art, "So what has brought you and the others to this place and how long have you been here? I've got a million questions. Why don't you start with when we last saw each other at the ribbon cutting of Golden Gate II?"

Art smiled as he reflected back on what must have been proud, and certainly happier times. "Okay, I'll give you the short version." I settled back because if Art was like Poppies, his stories had no short versions.

"When you and I were being commended for having pulled off the bridge project, I felt the need to try something else besides engineering. For reasons I still don't understand, I decided to get into politics. I went back to my old stomping grounds in South Laguna and began generating support and money to run for a seat in the California House of Representatives. The Petroleum Wars were drawing to a close, and I thought I could contribute to the rebuilding of our economy and restore some of the values that had been lost while we were struggling to win a war that had more fronts than we could keep up with.

"Anyway, I put together a campaign and was rolling along well I thought. That was before I discovered my opponent was being sponsored by the CPP, the Chinese People's Party. She was young, about forty, attractive, personable, glib, and totally brainwashed by the CPP. My slight lead was decimated by the tons of campaign funds provided indirectly by the CPP. After the election, I was so discouraged that I began to speak out against the party and the tactics they used against me.

"Then subtle little misfortunes began to hit. First, a total stranger filed a lawsuit citing me for professional malpractice. She contended I had caused her financial loss as a result of a Laguna Beach reclamation project I had designed years before. It was a totally spurious suit, but the combination of the election loss and the lawsuit hurt my feelings and my ego, not to mention my pocketbook, because I lost the lawsuit. After that, a lot of little things began to happen—things that hadn't ever happened before. Chairs would disappear from our patio and my mail would be interrupted. Microcom calls chided us for things we hadn't done, my professional engineer license was not renewed, clients went elsewhere, and so on. Ultimately, I found that the reason I lost the lawsuit was that the judge was on the CPP payroll. It took me a while, but I finally figured out that there was a vendetta against me and I had either better get used to it or 'get out of Dodge.' I chose the latter.

"The rest of the ACH's you see here are folks much like me. We've been effectively exiled from our communities. Damn Chinese."

"How do you think it happened?" Poppies had a very strong opinion that I had heard expressed many times, but I sensed he really wanted to hear what Art had to say.

"I think it was the Petroleum Wars that did us in." Art was indignantly defiant. "While we were absorbed with trying to save the world's dwindling supply of petrol, the Chinese were moving in. When they couldn't win an election, they bought it."

Art went on and on about the dirty tricks played by the Chinese both during and after the election. He and Poppies agreed on many things, were at odds on a few, but basically the old bridge engineers had followed similar paths and were now running for their lives.

Many others in the camp had had similar experiences. As a result they had banded together in a show of passive resistance and had elected their own officials (Art was mayor), and they were living away from the influence of the Chinese as free and unencumbered as possible. The Chinese seemed content to allow Camp Resistance to exist, at least for the time being.

I had been quietly listening to the conversation for some time, but my curiosity got the better of me. "How did the Petroleum Wars begin and how did they help the Chinese?" I asked.

Apparently I touched a nerve in both men because both immediately began to decry the war and the Chinese infiltration. Finally, Art prevailed. "The Petroleum Wars were really an outgrowth of religious wars that had begun shortly after the turn of the century. Arabs versus Jews, Muslims versus non-Muslims—it was something America should have avoided, but we thought our national interests were at stake, plus we had become peacekeepers for the world.

"Actually, our interests <u>were</u> involved because petroleum was involved. Many of the battlegrounds of the religious wars were in countries we relied on for petroleum. When war over religious issues broke out, oil shipments ceased, and America was so dependent on foreign oil that our economy and our standard of living took a severe hit. Quite frankly, we were not totally neutral and the Arab countries sensed that. Nevertheless, in many cases, we were pitted against enemies with whom we really had no argument. But, the radical terrorist factions, who wanted to destroy everyone that didn't follow the extreme religious tenets they believed, fueled the other Muslims. Our country was either fighting to keep the peace between Arabs and Jews, or we were fighting to defend ourselves from those who considered us infidels and just didn't want us in their sphere of the world, or anywhere else for that matter.

"Soon, the shortage of petroleum forced us to take over one or two nations with rich oil fields. However, that only made the other oil-producing nations more fearful and they quit supplying us with petroleum. It was a self-fulfilling prophecy. When we took over a regime to keep oil flowing, we actually lowered the net flow because five others would boycott us. To compensate, we stupidly thought our only recourse was to take over yet another oil-producing nation.

"The ultimate irony came after nearly twenty years of these conflicts from Iraq to Somalia, from Saudi Arabia to Venezuela, and even into the underground reserves of the Arctic Ocean. The oil fields and deposits were either consumed in the war or purposely destroyed by losing regimes. Ironically, the biggest losers were the oil-producing nations themselves, especially the Islamic nations of the previously economically powerful Middle East. When they lost their oil, their wealth dried up as well, and most reverted to their pre-World War II economic status."

"So, is there no petroleum left?" I interrupted Art's diatribe.

"Sure there's some," Art responded. "The Middle East has some, as does Venezuela, Sudan, and Canada plus there are still some off-shore reserves. But the cost of pumping it has increased a hundredfold. We still use it occasionally as a lubricant, but there are many other substances that are more economical to use as fuel."

"I thought that all lubricants were synthetic?" I continued to probe the issue.

"Well, actually most are, but some are composites of petroleum and other chemicals and there are still a few uses that are best served by petroleum even at its exorbitant cost. It's hard to believe that petroleum in the form of gasoline cost as little as a dollar a liter fifty years ago. Today, it's fifty bucks a liter, if you can find it! But back to the basic question—the real impact of the Petroleum Wars." Art was on a mission.

"So what began as a religious issue and a peacekeeping endeavor ended up costing the earth its petroleum natural resource and embroiled the United States in conflicts which had no value, as it turned out. In the meantime, the Chinese were sitting on the sidelines with their focus turned inward. They had five thousand years of mediocrity to overcome. However, their nearly two billion people finally turned the corner and made it into the industrialized world. Once that happened, there was so much momentum that it was impossible to stop. What's more, they were clever. They didn't launch armies to cross borders and capture territory by brute force. They launched infiltrators to join the ranks of the 'Overseas Chinese' already positioned in most of the industrialized and highly technical nations of the world. The United States, Great Britain, Japan, Canada— the list goes on.

"The object was to surreptitiously capture the hearts and minds of the people in each area so that institutions could be controlled and resources could be funneled back to help the billions of humans in China. A few areas have held out or the Chinese methods just haven't borne fruit yet. However, California was among the first to fall. We really don't know where else and to what extent. We suspect the East Coast is heavily infiltrated. That's one of the reasons the nation's capital was moved to Chicago a few years ago. The nuclear incident is the other reason, but that's another story.

"So that's what is going on and those of us such as your grandfather and me are powerless to stop it. In fact, we are lucky to still be around. A number of our colleagues, who thought like us, went to work one day and never came home. There are a great many more details I could relate, but I think it's best you turn in. I understand you plan to continue on toward Reno tomorrow unless I can persuade your grandfather to stay longer."

I went to bed on the makeshift cot they provided, but once they had energized the air cushion suspension mechanism, it was comfortable enough. I thought about what Art had said. He had voiced the same thing I had heard from Poppies over the years. Our country was in serious trouble. Our state was already lost and our lives were in jeopardy. Damn Chinese.

We didn't leave the next day. In fact we didn't leave for nearly a week. Poppies and Art spent a great deal of time together, sometimes talking quietly, sometimes arguing vociferously. I wasn't able to understand everything, but I sensed they were planning and plotting something important. They talked about something called the "Infiltration War." Just as America and the free world were pitted against terrorists in the early part of the century, Californians today were pitted against Chinese infiltrators. Just as America and its leaders had to find a way to fight a new kind of war—the War Against Terrorism—that began back in 2002, so too must our leaders today find a way to fight this new kind of war—the War Against Infiltration!

Art was of the opinion that it could only be won by eliminating the infiltrators, preferably by death. Poppies pointed out that this new warfare was totally unlike any seen before in that it was mostly non-violent. Further, he was convinced that a violent solution to a non-violent situation would be a hard sell. Look what had already happened throughout the state. Most of the people were sheep. As long as they were left alone, they were content to let others make the decisions, control the assets, and dictate lifestyles, even if it meant the real benefactors were the two billion people over in China.

I thought about what they were saying a lot. My initial reaction was to get the U.S. military to march across the border and kick the Chinese out of our state. Soon I realized that was totally simplistic. The idea that one could use brute force to subdue an enemy who had cleverly and stealthily positioned players throughout the fabric of our government, businesses, schools, courts, law enforcement, and virtually every other meaningful institution, was not realistic. It would be analogous to using bombs and napalm to attack the Viet Cong widely scattered in a Vietnam jungle. This was a new kind of war and it called for a new kind of strategy, tactics, and army.

While Poppies and Art were working on their scheme, I had lots of time to wander around. I tried to help Marla around the camp, but she said didn't need any assistance. I cranked up the hybri-cycle and drove it around the camp but never fast enough to get out of second gear. One day I began thinking about how Camp Resistance was able to remain hidden from the Chinese. I asked Marla and she said I should pay a visit to Jon-Ben Dennell. She said he was once the foremost person in the country on computers and he could explain it to me. That afternoon I paid Mr. Dennell a visit.

Mr. Dennell was an unseemly sort to have been a leading computer expert. With his disheveled appearance, stringy hair, and abundant growth of whiskers, he was totally unimpressive to look at. However, to talk to, he was mesmerizing. I began by asking him how they were able to evade detection by the Chinese.

"Well, Sonny," he began, "How much do you know about the embedded-chip program?"

I honestly replied, "Nothing," and he rolled his eyes.

"I guess you wouldn't, would you? You're too young," he said. "Well, it all began back in the thirties when the government convinced everyone that we'd be safer and more organized if people had a computer chip embedded in the back of their neck. The idea had its merits because, with that chip, each person's identity was known at all times. Further, it contained all sorts of valuable information such as blood type, allergies, medications, and so forth. So, if you were in an accident, the medics would know immediately how to treat you. It also contained certain coded information about your family history, your employment, your criminal record, and more. That information was to keep the wrong people from purchasing weapons, entering classified areas, and debiting someone else's bank account. All of these things seemed good at the time and they were sold to the American people as part of modern progress.

"The problem came when employers, governments, and other institutions began using information in the chips to control human behavior. They first set up a surveillance program to keep track of undesirable people such as criminals and suspected terrorists. That spread to the next layer of undesirables and ultimately extended to those with different ethnic backgrounds, different religions, and even different political affiliations. Pretty soon, there was no anonymity. They knew who you were and where you were at all times. Individual freedoms of choice and lifestyle began to be severely eroded.

"It all came to a head in the Sam Stanton case when Sam was arrested and convicted of second-degree murder even though he had nothing to do with the crime. It mattered not that Sam was blind and deaf, but because the computer/surveillance system had placed his chip (and therefore him) at the location, he was found guilty by the automated jury system in place in the State of New York at the time. That was the last straw. The people of most states rose up and struck down the embedded-chip system and the computer/surveillance system that had become 'Big Brother' to everyone."

"But if they threw it out, how are the Chinese able to monitor people in California?" I asked.

"A couple of reasons," Jon-Ben answered.

"First, California was one of the states that was slow in reversing the chip legislation. So, when the Chinese came into power, the system was still semi-active and most people still had their chips embedded in them. They did stop placing chips in young people though. For example, you are young enough that you didn't get one, but your father and grandfather did. Some features of the chip system were deactivated, but not nearly enough. Even though coverage was not one hundred percent, the Chinese saw it as a way to control the citizens of California.

"Second, there is a major contingent of folks in our state that believe there is value in the government knowing who and where people are. You saw the crime and corruption in the Bay Area. A number of law-abiding citizens are convinced that giving up a few personal freedoms are worth it if the state can keep the criminals and other undesirables under control. The problem is that the systems themselves are corrupt and certain people and certain organizations buy their way out of them. For example, there is an Asian criminal element involved in smuggling located in downtown San Francisco whose members operate outside the surveillance net. For that matter, so do we. The only difference is they pay big bucks for the privilege and we simply outsmart them."

"And how do you do that?" I inquired.

"Well, I know all the codes needed to break into the system and I can add or remove chips," Jon-Ben replied. "I have removed all of the chip identification for everyone in Camp Resistance. I did the same for your grandfather a couple of days ago."

"How do you know the code?"

"For openers, I invented it," Jon-Ben was neither smug nor boasting. He just answered the question.

Then he looked at me and asked, "Are you interested in computers?"

I replied that I was, but I thought it wasn't so essential to know about computers anymore. "Isn't that a dying profession?"

Jon-Ben bristled. "I should say not. Just because computers are everywhere these days, and just because voice activation has diminished the need for the average person to thoroughly understand computers, it doesn't mean that more progress isn't needed. We have come a long way but I predict the power of computing will continue to invisibly shape our lives indefinitely.

"You don't remember, but fifty years ago, every school child had to take computer courses. They all had computers that they used for schoolwork. Businesses used computers to handle transactions, perform analyses, and design everything from buildings to clothing. The old-time computers used

99

something called a keyboard to communicate between the user and the machine. The computing power that used to be contained in a top-of-the-line desktop machine is now in a device no bigger than your thumb. In accordance with Moore's Law, with each passing year, computers were growing more powerful and smaller.

"Then along came voice recognition and activation. Shortly afterward, the ultimate in miniaturization came along and the micro and nano-computers were developed. These incredibly small computers had a limited range of function, but whatever their purpose was, they could do it continuously and well.

"These infinitely small computers could be networked and placed on the surface of materials, in materials, and even inside the human body. For example, your climate suit has over two million computers laced throughout. They work in concert to detect environmental changes and then activate tiny electro-coils and micro-heat pumps in the fabric.

"Computers are integral to virtually everything you encounter these days, either in their production or the end product. Wireless chips costing only a few cents are embedded in nearly every object, and even some people. The result is that humans and computers are inextricably linked together in a single global network."

"Wow, I knew that computers were nearly everywhere, but I had no idea," I expressed my ignorance and amazement. "So, if you invented the computer surveillance system, you must have been involved in other areas as well?" I was probing for more information from Jon-Ben Dennell. He was very forthcoming.

"Probably my greatest accomplishment was to harness the computing power of virtually every computer on the Internet. Back in the twenties, we pioneered something called 'Grid' computing. By using the Internet access to millions of pieces of hardware worldwide that were under-utilized, we were able to spread massive computing tasks over many machines. Prior to that, machines sat idle while they could have been processing zillions of instructions per second. It didn't cost anyone anything and it enabled us to solve the riddle of the genome, to simulate the effects of earthquakes on cities, to calculate the number of barrels of petroleum in the earth, to allow biochemists to simulate a viral attack on the human body, and to perform a number of astronomical permutations and combinations that had previously been out of reach."

I was beginning to become overwhelmed, but I was enchanted by his knowledge and willingness to share it. "So, computers are nano-size and virtually everywhere we are. What about communication systems? Aren't they integral to computing?"

"You bet. As recently as twenty-five years ago, our communication systems became so highly developed that machines began talking to each other, making decisions, repairing their networks, etc. So, all humans have to do is occasionally tweak the systems. Another thing I forgot to mention is that in the last century, wired technology dominated the scene. Computer and voice networks were ninety-nine percent wired together by copper wire and fiber-optic cable. Then, shortly after the turn of the century, wired technology gave way to wireless technology so that voice, data, video, and holovision are now primarily transmitted in a wireless environment.

"All this, of course, led to impulse technology. Early in the century, man proved that by bombarding a receiver with enough impulses, the sensation of 'touch' could be produced. This seemingly impossible feat was honed to the point where today we think nothing of not only seeing an object or person that is many miles distant via computer, but being able to 'touch' them as well."

I was in total awe of Jon-Ben Dennell. I had no doubt that, whatever computer surveillance system the Chinese were using, Mr. Jon-Ben Dennell could defeat it. I slept quite well that night.

The next day, armed with the new knowledge I had gained from Jon-Ben, I cornered Art at breakfast. "I've been thinking a lot about what you and Poppies were saying about petroleum. If the Petroleum Wars eliminated oil, and oil was a primary fuel needed for heat and electrical power, why is it that we still have both?"

Art seemed both amused and impressed that I would pose such a question. "That is very perceptive of you, young man," he began. "The answer primarily is solar. The American technological community had been working for some time on using solar power. Of course, solar had been around forever, but it was never quite cost competitive as long as we had oil to burn. Naturally, reducing the size of nuclear power plants enabled designers to place them in such things as electrical substations and moving vehicles. Further, the use of hydrogen as a fuel source also came into play. But the main source was solar. It was on the verge of becoming cost effective anyway, and the obliteration of petroleum made cost competition a moot issue. Although there was one other significant development that still is being improved."

"And what is that," I asked.

Art leaned back as if to make a major pronouncement. "The tides," he said. After thousands of years, man has finally harnessed the tides. Would you like to hear about it?"

I nodded that I would.

"Well, with the removal of fossil fuels as energy sources, all countries were forced to look elsewhere for ways to produce or convert energy into a usable form. One of the age-old sources that man has endeavored to harness is the ocean tide. In 2038, a Danish company developed an underwater turbine that would rise and fall with the tide and direct the energy to giant storage batteries fixed beneath the surface. These batteries, in turn, could be tapped by on-shore power lines and routed to hydroelectric plants for transforming.

"At first, the cost of these giant apparatus far outweighed the value of the electrical energy generated. Therefore, their initial usage was in remote locations where conventional electrical networks did not exist. However, as the technology was refined, the cost came down and these 'free' power plants were placed offshore to supplement major metropolitan areas. They were ideal for confined areas and small islands where nuclear generation plants were unwelcome or where solar was inadequate to meet the need. The island of Hong Kong is seventy percent powered by tide harnessing. About two years ago, approximately five percent of the earth's electrical power was coming from tides and it is growing every year."

Art seemed quite pleased with his answer to my question and with himself. I dropped the subject and went out to find Poppies.

Poppies was busy looking at documents on the holovision screen when I found him. "I know why Graniteville was deserted," he said.

"Why? How did you find out? I asked.

"Art and his associates told me, plus the proof is here in these documents." Poppies pointed to the screen. "Apparently, the Chinese in Locke picked Graniteville as a staging point for their eventual move into Nevada. They began forcing the Graniteville residents to leave three years ago. Why they haven't moved their own people in is a mystery. Perhaps they have abandoned the idea or, more likely, the time just isn't right. That explains why the utilities are still activated, I suppose. The other question I have is whether Olivia knows about the plan or not. In any event, she and Zell are sitting on a time bomb."

I felt queasy as the impact of Poppies' words began to sink in. Zell was in more danger. The damn Chinese again—it was just a matter of time.

Friday, May 17, 2052
Camp Resistance, California

On the morning of our seventh day at the camp, Poppies announced we would be leaving that day. He and Art had finished transmitting their plan of action to the secure communication receiver Art had in the ACH. There were no long-range transmission waves involved, so whatever was downloaded to the receiver would be safe from any who did not know the entry code. My guess was that only Art and Poppies knew it.

Marla seemed genuinely sorry to see us go. I detected she had a special feeling for me as she would go out of her way to attend to my needs over the seven-day stay. She asked me about my mother and father and seemed to know them. She also asked about Grammy and said she had known her since they were young girls together in Alamo. She told me stories of how the two of them would race their horses across the yellow grass pastures of Northern California, up the hills, and then back down on their way to the barn. She said that Grammy was, not only the prettiest, she was the best rider. It was a statement of fact, not envy.

I learned that Marla and Art had never married. I think she regretted it but understood that she was caught up in a trend. She told me in great detail how marriages were failing so frequently at the turn of the century that young couples began to fear the consequences of commitment.

A divorce rate at the turn of the century of nearly sixty percent had grown to eighty percent by the early twenties. Despite incentives by the government, the number of marriages dropped dramatically and people who married did so much later in life. The net result was that, of the total number of adults in America in 2050, less than twenty percent of them were married in a ceremony. People still lived together as man and wife, had children, shared expenses, shared joy and sorrow, but they stopped going through the ceremony, the expensive wedding, and the legal commitment.

There was another reason contributing to the downturn in marriages. The women's liberation movement, begun over eighty years ago, had made women more independent. They stopped using their husband's last name, they stopped being homemakers, and when synthewombs came along, they stopped having babies. I thought it was ironic that men and women still sought each other's company on an exclusive basis, still remained committed to a single individual, still behaved in every way as if they were married, yet they were disillusioned with marriage as an institution.

I thought about my own parents. Having never married may have made it easier for them to part. I didn't know. I hoped not. I thought about Grammy and Poppies. I wished Grammy could be here to hear the stories Marla was telling.

It began to spit rain just as we pulled out of the camp. Marla had resupplied us with CSC's and a few other items so we were ready for the short trip to Reno. As we wound down the tight turns of Webber Peak, I could see the storm clouds approaching.

Once down the slope, we headed due east past Webber Lake. We scooted by several small caravans of vehicles. These were really old cars with some dating back into the thirties, when the hybrids and total electrics really came into use. I wondered where they found the batteries compatible with the power plants that came with those old cars. Not only were the cars old and unusual, so were the passengers.

As we approached the California-Nevada border, I wondered how Poppies intended to cross. No doubt there would be sentries or identification patch checking devices. I could see the border a kilometer ahead as Poppies slowed down and pulled off the road. Off to the right was another caravan of old people. We drove up to them.

"Is anyone in charge here?" he asked.

At first, I thought no one heard him as these old folks probably didn't hear very well. We waited patiently for a response. Finally, an old woman came forward. "What do you want, young fella?" I laughed to myself because she was addressing Poppies.

Poppies wanted to know why the several caravans of old people were scattered left and right along the highway for the past several kilometers.

"They won't let us cross the border," was her reply.

"Why not?" Poppies demanded.

"Because we are old people, we don't have a travel authorization (TA), and we would be taking assets out of the state."

The woman choked back the tears as she went on to tell us that all the caravans of seniors had been turned away. They had no place to go, so they just stopped.

Some had been there for several weeks but she had only been there four days.

"Why do you want to leave California?" Poppies softened his tone.

At first there was no response but after a most uncomfortable time, she spoke again, very softly. "They were killing us in the home. Every day, someone else would not wake up. We knew they must be putting something in our CSC's or our medications, but we didn't know what and we couldn't prove a thing. Then one day, I hid in the closet of my friend's bedroom. In the middle of the night, a medical technician came in and administered an IV to her. I thought it was just routine medical care, but the next morning before I could sneak out, two techs came back. One took her pulse while the other slipped on the body bag. The interesting thing is that the one with the bag started before the other was finished. That told me without a doubt that they knew she was supposed to be dead and the pulse check was just routine.

"We gathered up our personal belongings and those who could get out, did. I feel so sorry for the ones we couldn't take. But I guess now we have nothing to do but wait for the Senior Citizen Overseers to come for us."

We couldn't leave these people here to die. We had to do something. But what? Poppies told me to get back on the hybri-cycle. We headed for the border.

Black and yellow striped barricades between two layers of chain-link fence stood between Nevada and us. Most of that was for show because the real barricades consisted of visual and concealed laser beams. Some were for alarms and some were lethal. The lethal ones were supposed to be triggered by the alarm lasers, but one never knew for sure. Poppies got off the cycle and went up to the official at the barricade.

"What do we need to pass through?" he inquired.

The border-crossing official wore a state patrol uniform, carried a sidearm that I took to be a hand laser, and displayed an insolent look. "Unless you have a TA signed by the governor, you're not going to," snarled the official.

Poppies thanked him, although I suspected he wanted to punch him in the nose. Poppies had already "cased the joint" and determined that there were four humans and four humanoids guarding the gate.

CHAPTER SEVEN

THE BORDER

Back at Camp Resistance, the signal had been received. I didn't know how, but Poppies had set up some code with Art to communicate without being monitored by the Chinese. Art and three others at the camp had had military experience in the early days of the Petroleum Wars and they had cached a number of weapons for such an occasion.

Using all-terrain, high performance, one-man air-cushioned assault vehicles, called ACAV's, Art and his comrades headed for the border. They rode the rocket-propelled, air-cushioned vehicles like we rode the hybri-cycle, except they could go anywhere. Over land, over water, over marshland, it didn't make any difference as they were riding on a cushion of air generated by the powerful electro-nuclear power plants prominent on each vehicle. The rocket thrusters were at minimal power, yet the assault vehicles were able to glide at 75 km/hr across the windswept waters of Webber Lake.

Once they had crossed the lake, they looked for paths through the dense forest of pines and firs that dotted the California mountainside. Art was pleased that previous reconnaissance had mapped out a fairly direct route to the border. He wanted to get there before the border guards detected any movement coming out of

111

California. That way, they could cross the border and approach the guard station from the Nevada side. That was the plan. Art and Poppies wanted the Chinese to believe that the four vehicles had come from Nevada, a place where the Chinese had not yet become dominant.

Meanwhile, Poppies and I raced back to the old folks along the road. It was after midnight when Poppies told them they had to make a decision and do it fast. "In four hours the border guard station will be unmanned," he told them. "If you dare, you can cross into Nevada and scatter. If you hesitate…well, the Chinese are on their way and you will be returned to your old compounds."

We went from enclave to enclave of senior citizens spreading that message. At first, I thought no one was going to act. Then the old woman we had spoken with earlier stepped up to the plate. There were representatives from all of the small groups of voyagers at her trailer.

"The way I see it is that we can wait here like sheep and the Chinese will take us back to be slaughtered. Or we can hope this young fella is right, and scoot across the border. What's the worst that can happen? If the check point is not taken out, then we will be stopped and we'll be right here, on the California side of the border."

Her words were not immediately grasped by all present. Some muttered that it was foolhardy to think the guards would be gone. Others worried about recriminations if they failed or were caught. Still others couldn't bring themselves to believe that the decision was that time sensitive. They had no idea what Art and his followers were up to nor did they fully understand that the border guards would be replaced and reinforced within a few hours of whatever Art and company had in store for the current group.

Poppies saw that indecision was ruling the day. The old woman had done her best, but she had not been persuasive. Poppies took control of the meeting.

"I have just come back from the border guard station," Poppies began. "There are four humans and four humanoids on patrol. They will disappear in less than two hours. Trust me. There are people like you— people who want to extricate themselves from the Chinese and their influence, people who are risking their lives as we speak, for you. It is too late to stop their attack. The guards will be gone, but they will be replaced.

"When the window opens, this fourteen-year-old boy and I are going to cross into Nevada. All you have to do is follow us. You don't have much time. If you hesitate, the efforts of brave men fighting on your behalf will have been wasted. Moreover, you will be left here, sitting ducks for the Chinese who will either take you back or exterminate you right here where you stand. This is a 'no-brainer' folks. For those who want their freedom, we leave in fifteen minutes."

There was a hush and then a mumble. Then came a ground swell of affirmation. The old folks would take the chance. They headed off to their vehicles and their fellow travelers.

Art's group crossed the border and skimmed across the half-frozen terrain for about five kilometers before turning north to meet the road that led to the border crossing station. They had darted from shadow to shadow thus far, finding flat paths where possible and keeping their modar profile as low as possible. Art suspected they had been undetected or else the unmanned reconnaissance probes would have been launched. The low signature of the stealth assault vehicles had made them virtually invisible to the border detection system. Also, since the surveillance detection systems were directed toward the California side, the game plan was to come in from the east. Once on the Nevada roadway, they were traveling at normal approach speed, so if they were detected, it would register as normal.

On Sunday morning, May 12, at precisely 0450 hours, Art pulled over. They were ten minutes early. At attack velocity, it would take less than a minute to reach the guard station. He did not dare communicate with Poppies, although he was tempted to send one short coded message, signaling they were in position. Art was extremely pleased at their accomplishment but his warrior instinct won out over his temptation to boast.

The modar-like observation system on the ACAV's showed what Art suspected. Only the humanoids were activated. Stupidly, all the human guards were sleeping. Further, the humanoids were programmed to look west and that's what they were doing. Even their laser protection shields were pointed west. The only question was what to do with the humans. They could probably be taken alive, but the problem only compounded because there was nothing to do with them. Art had made his decision before they left Camp Resistance. The guards would have to be eliminated.

At precisely 0458, the ACAV's rolled.

Two of the vehicles were to head directly to the gate and eliminate the four humanoids on duty. Art and his friend, Jack Oakley, were to enter the compound pod, laser the hatch cover, and eliminate the humans before they could awake and send any meaningful alarm. Of course, the automatic detection equipment would trigger an alarm signaling there was a malfunction just as soon as the humanoids were made inactive. However, if the humans could be stopped before they alerted the Sentry Guard Command Center, that would give at least two hours before they would react.

The two ACAV's approached the gate guards with such speed and stealth that not one raised a weapon in resistance. All four were inoperable in 4.3 seconds after the attack began. The humans in the compound pod were not quite so easily disposed of. One of them had already awakened and was dressing in the pod anteroom. When the hatch mechanism was being lasered, he managed to awaken his fellow guards. The result was that two of the four had secured weapons and one was scrambling to reach the communication panel to sound the alarm. Art knew that if that happened, not only would Poppies and the senior citizens not make it through, but also automatic identification devices would deploy and he and his crew would be identified. If that happened, they were dead men.

With no precision whatsoever, Art lasered the communication panel and the approaching guard. He had not wanted to do that, because he didn't know what other automatic warnings that might send. But there was no option. His partner, Jack, turned his attention to the two guards with weapons. He lasered one but the other managed to direct a ray into Jack's shoulder. Jack fell to the floor of the pod, mortally wounded. Art glanced at his fallen comrade and, in a fit of rage and despair, brought the full force of his laser gun down on the guards. The job was completed but it was botched. Worse yet, there was no way to remove the ACAV that Jack had driven. Art picked up Jack's body, threw it across his vehicle, and withdrew to the agreed position. He quickly explained to the other two what had happened and called Poppies.

At 0505, we entered the guard station. I was wide-eyed at the devastation. I had never seen a human killed by a laser gun before. There wasn't much left. We rolled through the various barricades and detection pits and

Poppies cleared as much as he could for the caravan of seniors that was on our tail. About two minutes later the first vehicle arrived. It was the old woman.

"I knew you could do it,' she cried. "Never a doubt!" Then she headed up the road to Reno. Vehicle after vehicle, caravan after caravan followed. In all, more than three hundred of California's senior citizens had changed their residence to Nevada.

Poppies turned to me. "Think you can operate the hybri-cycle?" he asked.

I was surprised, but I had been playing around with it when we were at Camp Resistance. But riding around the camp was a lot different than on the open road. "I sure can." I didn't hesitate a second. The confidence of youth overcame any reluctance or inexperience that I might have had.

The call from Art had asked Poppies if he could take the ACAV out, for not doing so would allow them to be more easily tracked if it fell in the hands of the Chinese. Poppies agreed it was the least we could do and he prepared to operate this high-powered military vehicle for the first time. We were both on unfamiliar ground, in a great many ways.

As the last of the caravans came through, we acknowledged their waves and shouts of thanks and headed east toward Reno. My heart was still pounding and the adrenalin was still flowing as we came down the hill into the city. At eighty kilometers per hour, we flew under a sign saying, "Welcome to Reno, The Biggest Little City in the World."

CHAPTER EIGHT

UNCLE MAX

The first order of business was to stash the vehicles. Even in Reno, an ACAV stood out. Poppies seemed to know where he was going and didn't pause once as we passed the glitter and pizzazz of the city. I didn't have time to look around, but I was inwardly pleased at the way I had mastered the hybri-cycle.

Past the cluster of casinos, bars, and brothels of downtown Reno, through the thin layer of high-rise office buildings and apartments, and out into the suburbs we went. It was a good thing they didn't enforce the speed limit, because we didn't get under it at any time.

We continued through the outskirts of Reno as if we were on our way to a fire. After multiple twists and turns, we ultimately came to an open gate in the middle of a long fence. Poppies made a hard right and I followed. About a kilometer up a dirt road was an old warehouse. Poppies stopped at the door and waited for a few seconds. Just as I was about to dismount the hybri-cycle and ask what was going on, a grisly old man appeared in the personnel door. He gestured something to Poppies and the warehouse door opened. In a flash, Poppies had the ACAV inside and parked. He motioned for me to leave the hybri-cycle outside and come in.

The old man seemed more interested in the ACAV than he was in us. He looked at the rocket thrusters, the two mounted laser guns on each side, and the turret lasers on the front and back.

"I haven't seen one of these since we fought the Kurds in the thirties," he said.

Poppies introduced me to Gus and explained that Gus was an employee of my Uncle Max. Before I could garner any more information, Poppies said that we would be staying here in Reno for a few days to catch our breath and to let the commotion we had caused at the border, blow over. I wondered where we would be staying because the warehouse did not look inviting. I didn't have long to wonder because a sleek new gyrocopter was setting down a few meters from the warehouse. We gathered our few belongings from the hybri-cycle, turned it over to Gus for safekeeping, and boarded the gyrocopter. Sitting at the controls was Uncle Max. Sitting next to the controls was a double martini for Poppies and a sonic drink for me.

"Welcome to Nevada, Cousin," Uncle Max said warmly.

Uncle Max was charismatic and personable. Though he wore a loose-fitting flight suit, I could tell he had a lithe, athletic body. His curly brown hair betrayed his age, but I knew he was about the same vintage as

Poppies. It probably was a hairpiece, but it was a good one.

Without any more conversation, the gyrocopter lifted off and headed for the high-rise section of Reno. Uncle Max put the gyrocopter on auto-vector and the copter found the correct altitude and sector to fly. In five minutes we had landed on the copter-pad of the thirtieth floor of the Harrah Building in downtown Reno.

The apartment he had arranged for us was a short walk down the hall. Uncle Max showed us around quickly and then excused himself, saying he had an appointment but that he would join us for dinner that night. We made ourselves at home and, while Poppies took a nap, I looked around the apartment and the thirtieth floor.

Uncle Max showed up late but it didn't matter because I was enthralled by my new surroundings. The Harrah Building was eighty-five stories high. Every ten stories had its own gyrocopter pad. They were simply extensions of the floor slab and stuck out away from the rest of the building about forty meters, just far enough to safely takeoff and land a gyrocopter.

Individual air travel had become commonplace for those who could afford it in the mid thirties, and it was only logical that building construction would soon accommodate the need to move people from Point A to Point B with the least number of transfers. With the addition of forced air traffic control, both vertically and horizontally, auto-vectors took over and the need for a trained pilot was eliminated. Anyone who could drive a car of the twenties could operate a gyrocopter of the fifties. I had seen buildings like this in California, and on holovision, but this was the first time I had been in one to see it close up.

Uncle Max landed on the copter-port at six o'clock that evening. I met him at the door of the apartment.

One of the things that enchanted me about Uncle Max was his gyrocopter. "Where did you get it and how did you learn to fly it?" I asked.

With genuine humility, Uncle Max explained that this was a company gyrocopter, but it was at his disposal, sort of like a company car was fifty years ago. "It's no big deal to operate a gyrocopter," he added. "It may look difficult, but it's not."

I had not learned much about hover aircraft in school so the incident with the Chinese gyrocopter was an eye-opener for me. Now, being able to ride in one was an even greater thrill and I wanted to know more. "Tell me about gyrocopters, Uncle Max," I asked.

"Well, gyrocopters were the outgrowth of twentieth-century helicopters. While they look and perform much the same, they are quite different machines. Giant whirling fan blades that were energized by internal combustion engines, that are now obsolete, propelled the helicopter. The gyrocopter has no whirling blades. Instead, spinning gyroscopic wheels give the craft tremendous stability while volumes of air moving through its nuclear thrust engines propel it. Jet blast nozzles somewhat akin to the Boeing Harrier 'Jump Jet' of old give the gyrocopter vertical lift and horizontal thrust. But it is the gyroscopic technology that has made the aircraft so stable that it is simple and safe enough for a novice to fly. We'll go again soon, I promise."

Uncle Max had grown up in Oregon, but he had gone to college at Stanford. That is where he and Poppies got to know each other quite well. In fact, they roomed together for a couple of semesters. Poppies played on the baseball team and Uncle Max was a second team all-American flanker on the football team that was rated in the top ten at the close of the 2012 season. That was before college football had become too commercial, and before the National Football League had started using humanoids.

Still, the average lineman on Uncle Max's team weighed in at 390 pounds and the backs ranged between 240 and 280. Even the quarterback was 245 and Max, at 215, was the lightest member of the starting squad. But, he grinned as he quipped, "I was the lightest, so I had to be the fastest."

Steroids and other muscle enhancement products had become impossible to regulate and athletes had become a haven for abuse. The pharmaceutical companies touted their products as totally safe, but there was no long-term study to validate this. As we know now, virtually all of the performance-enhancing products (PEP's) had long-term effects on their users. It was like the smoking tobacco products of half a century ago. Scientists finally demonstrated that tobacco caused cancer and many other diseases and tobacco was outlawed. Nearly half a century later, scientists were still trying to prove that performance-enhancing products were just as deadly. As was the case with smoking, decades earlier, the popularity and profitability of PEP's made it difficult to declare them unsafe and illegal.

Uncle Max had gone to law school after graduation from Stanford, and he and Poppies drifted apart for several years. Max had met and married a girl whose last name was Harrah. That led him to his job as legal advisor and general counsel to Harrah Industries, whose business was mainly gambling.

Uncle Max pulled up a chair and turned to Poppies. "Okay, suppose you tell me the whole story of why you left California and why you blew into our town in a high-powered, illegal-to-own ACAV?" Uncle Max asked directly.

He had arranged for a catered dinner to be brought to our apartment on the thirtieth floor. So far only the hors d' oeuvres and drinks had arrived. I was prepared for a couple of hours of small talk before we got to this point, but apparently Uncle Max was not.

Poppies began, "Well, Maxie, I couldn't give you much detail and I had to be careful about what was being transmitted. Even though the communication networks claim to be secure, we know in California that it is far from the truth."

"I don't believe we have that problem here in Nevada," Max replied. "What makes you think your microcom call was monitored?"

"You really don't know, do you?" Poppies looked him straight in the eye.

"Don't know what? All I know is that California has adopted some strict travel rules, allegedly due to the fuel shortage, and that they kicked our butts out of Tahoe a few years ago so they could take over our business. Other than that, I have no use for your state—or your former state, whichever it is." Uncle Max was truly uninformed about the corrupt politics and foreign infiltration that had taken place.

Poppie's face exuded disbelief. "It has been going on for years. Are you telling me you don't know about the Chinese dominance? You aren't aware that they bribed or intimidated whomever they had to—workers, small businesses, and voters (mainly Hispanic Americans) to take over virtually everything of importance in the state?"

"I have no idea what you are talking about," Uncle Max responded.

It was at that point that Poppies said something profound, but it was almost as if he were thinking aloud.

"Now I understand how they have pulled it off. They have orchestrated the best smoke screen since Hitler convinced the Allies that the Jews were only being taken to the showers. By making it appear as if nothing had changed, the Chinese and their Hispanic and American puppets could precipitate the takeover, gradually strengthen their position, and not be challenged by any outside elements, least of all the federal government.

"Their initial weapon was the embedded autism-chip. Everyone who came in for physical exams was given an extra chip. This chip acted like a drug to induce an attitude of submissiveness in the recipients. The people inside the state who didn't get the chip were either bought off or killed off, depending on their stand. A few of us who sensed the truth could find little support from our fellow Californians. That was because the thirty-eight percent Hispanic population had already bought into the Chinese gambit, the twenty-four percent of the population that are Orientals were obviously on the inside, so that left the rest of the people in a minority. And most of them had been chipped. Even many of those who didn't get the autism-chip were intimidated or lulled into acquiescence. Some put their own life and standard of living ahead of everything else and are 'going along to get along.' As is invariably the case, many are on the take, and willing to sacrifice their principles for a few pieces of silver." (The analogy was not lost on either Uncle Max or me.)

"I'm sure there are still some who simply believe that there is no takeover afoot. And a few more who would rather remain in denial than to confront reality. Regardless, the fact of the matter is, California is no longer a free or safe place to live. People do not have the protection of the U.S. Constitution; they have lost the inalienable rights that had been fought for over nearly three centuries. And other Americans, folks right across the border, haven't a clue!"

It was infiltration war at its finest. Uncle Max was silent. I couldn't tell if he was aghast or in disbelief. He was about to speak when the main course arrived. We had been eating mostly CSC's since leaving Graniteville, so this was a real treat. Smoked salmon flown in from Norway, prawns from New Orleans, oysters from Apalachicola, Florida, and steamed crab from Bombay Hook, Delaware. This was a seafood feast, the likes of which I had never imagined.

Uncle Max turned his attention to the food. "I suggest we put the subject of California to rest for a while," he said. "It's been forty years since we shared a pizza at that little pizzeria just off the campus. Mama

Campisi's, wasn't it? I am honored that you have come to visit and I ask you to let me be a good host."

The aroma of the mixture of seafood delicacies, along with the continuous flow of two vintages of chardonnay wine, made it quite easy to agree to Uncle Max's request. Poppies dug in and showed me how to dip the prawns and crack the crabs. I balked at the oysters on the half-shell at first, but I didn't want to seem like a little kid, so I closed my eyes and let one slither down. I told them how good it was, but I guess my expression said otherwise because both Poppies and Uncle Max had a good laugh.

Even though I had been on a diet of CSC's for most of my life, I had learned that some interesting things had happened along the evolutionary road from eating food to consuming CSC's. For example, all seafood in 2052 was farm-raised under carefully controlled conditions of nutrition and purity. The same was true for vegetables as most were raised using hydroponic gardening.

Ever since the Animal Rights Party had successfully lobbied for legislation against the slaughter of animals and birds, it was a misdemeanor to possess meat products derived from these sources. Fortunately, for the minority that still wanted a juicy steak now and then instead of CSC's, they could purchase fairly good synthetic meat products derived from genetically altered soybeans. I should add that a vigorous black market existed for all banned products and much of what we were eating came from that market.

It was nearly midnight before we stopped picking at the crab legs and sipping the wine. Of course, my wine was non-alcoholic. I could have had the chardonnay if I had wanted it, but I thought it best to wait for another occasion.

During the meal Poppies asked about Uncle Max's brothers. Uncle Max was most complimentary of both Alex and Oliver. Apparently Alex, the older brother, had gotten the acting bug and parlayed his good looks into numerous acting jobs in Hollywood and in Europe. He had married a famous Italian movie star and was now living on the Italian Riviera. Oliver had followed his father in the television industry and was one of the first to recognize the future of holovision. He made a ton of money and also retired before age sixty. Uncle Max said one day Oliver just left the business and society, and was living with his fifth wife on a remote lake near Moose Jaw, Saskatchewan.

Uncle Max said he heard from his brothers each Christmas but, even though they lived far apart, time had not weakened the brotherly bonds that had characterized their youth.

We said good night without another word about California or our trip. The first question asked by Uncle Max had not been addressed. I found out later that Poppies simply didn't trust the security of that strange new place, barely out of earshot of the Chinese surveillance equipment, to give any more details about what had happened. When Uncle Max offered to cease and desist, Poppies welcomed the opportunity and was afraid that the martini and wine had loosened his tongue too much already.

We spent several days as thirtieth floor guests of Uncle Max. I was given a tour of Reno by one of Harrah's employees. She was about nineteen and was both pretty and pleasant, but as far as I was concerned, she wasn't Zell. Plus, she was way too old for me.

Meanwhile, Uncle Max and Poppies finished the conversation that had begun on our first night. It turned out that Uncle Max was familiar with the episode of a few years back when Nick Medici had come to buy a stake in Harrah's. Not only was he familiar with the incident, he knew the replacement for Medici who had ultimately come in from New Jersey. Sal Tesoro had shown up a couple of years after the Medici fiasco, seeking to mend fences and do a deal. The Harrah family was even more wary than before, but they weren't quite certain how to handle this new opportunity, or how to handle Mr. Tesoro.

Much to my chagrin, on May fifteenth I was placed in school.

Poppies started the process with the Nevada school administration but was running into obstacles because I had not officially withdrawn from the California school system. As he was trying to explain that it was not possible to request and receive transfer records from California, he encountered yet another example of total unawareness. The administrators in Nevada had no idea what had transpired in California and they were unwilling to permit my enrollment without transcripts, health records, etc. Even though all such records were stored in giant databases and supposed to be easily accessible, for some reason, they weren't. Poppies tried to explain that the system was broken; people were being denied the ability to change schools, to travel, to enjoy life, liberty, and the pursuit of happiness. The Nevada bureaucrats were as obstinate as they were ignorant. They simply did not, could not, believe anything we had said.

Of course, I had mixed emotions about returning to school. I was beginning to enjoy my freedom from studies that was now into the ninth week. At the same time I recognized that, for a fourteen-year-old, school was a necessary evil and I had better go back. Plus, I confessed to myself, I kind of liked school and learning. After three days, we had made no headway whatsoever with the Nevada school system. That's when Uncle Max stepped in. He made one phone call and I went to class the next day.

Poppies was frustrated. He had come to Nevada uncertain about what he would find. But, he never thought he would find indifference and ignorance so rampant. Everywhere he turned, it was like he had stepped off a spaceship from another planet. The experience we had with the school administrators was replayed virtually every time Poppies opened the subject. He approached businessmen, city halls, civic organizations, and he even went to engineering companies who knew him and his reputation. The result was the same. It was as if they didn't want to know the danger that lurked across the border.

Nevada, and Reno in particular, of the twenty-first century were unlike anywhere else in the United States. Over the years, the influence of gambling had penetrated all areas and all levels. Interestingly, the gamblers had taken on an air of respectability (at least on the surface) and the rest of society had dropped down several notches. The gaming business, as it was euphemistically called, had influence in politics, government, big business, and law enforcement. In that respect, it mirrored what the Chinese had done in California.

As Poppies went from agency to agency and from person to person, he shared the results with both Uncle Max and me. I could tell that Uncle Max was, at times, conflicted. On one hand, he was sympathetic to the plight that we had endured and had unveiled to him. Yet, on the other, he was part of the Nevada establishment. It appeared that the mission of everyone in the state was to make money.

Gambling was the "cash cow" and most everything else fed off of it. Prostitution had been legalized since the twenties. The few remaining states that prohibited gambling allowed their citizens to gamble "by wire" in Nevada. So, even though the loss of revenue from Californians was significant, there was more than enough gambling demand to go around.

Although smoking had been banned and drugs legalized, you could get a cigarette on the black market as easily as you could buy a joint fifty years ago. Even though red meat was prohibited, you could buy a steak in the private dining rooms of many exclusive restaurants, at an exclusive price, of course.

Reno was a wild place. People jetted in for gambling, sex, and entertainment. They didn't care about anything else and the locals didn't care about anything but the jet-setters' money. It took over six weeks, but Poppies finally admitted that Nevada was not the state to take on the War Against Infiltration. He would have to look elsewhere.

Uncle Max had been a good friend and a big help throughout. He got me into school and opened many doors for Poppies. The fact that people behind the doors were not receptive was not Uncle Max's fault.

CHAPTER NINE

THE BLUFF

It turned out that Sal Tesoro was a little smarter than Nick Medici, but he still did stupid things. One of these was to play in high stakes poker games where he invariably pissed everyone off. He wasn't a very good poker player, even in an honest game, and when he lost, he raised hell. Nevertheless, he invariably returned to the game that Uncle Max was responsible to set up and he came in well heeled.

This was just "nice to know" information until Uncle Max told Poppies that Tesoro was still looking for the woman who had survived the poker game blood bath that had queered the deal with Harrah's. Somehow Tesoro thought if he could find that person, he would be able to obtain more information about Harrah's involvement. The boys from New Jersey suspected that Harrah's management was well aware of what Rodney and Olivia were doing and was getting a cut. If that could be demonstrated, that would give the mafia some leverage to force a buyout. Actually, it was to be a "buy in," as they just wanted to get in on the action, not run it.

When Poppies heard this, he was glad he had not gone into the whole story about Olivia. He had told Uncle Max about their encounter at Graniteville, but nothing about Olivia's past life in Reno. As casually as he could, Poppies asked Uncle Max if he could arrange for him to play in the weekly poker game.

Casino poker was played a little differently in 2052 than it had been in years before. Modern technology had made the use of cards obsolete. Further, an electronic tote screen had replaced the physical placing of chips in the center of the table, and a player used a mini-mouse to indicate his bet. Resources to validate the bet were electronically drawn from the player's account and placed into the "escrow pot." When the player's stake in the escrow pot drew low, he could place more in or drop out. Pasteboard playing cards had been replaced by an encrypto dealer, which was a computer-driven device that shuffled, dealt, and displayed the cards. The cards "in a player's hand" were displayed on "heads-up" glasses worn by each player. If the game had common cards, they were displayed on a "common card screen" in front of each player. Other than that, the games were the same as had been played since the days of Hoyle.

Poppies arrived at the game early. While he had some familiarity with the equipment being used, he wanted an opportunity to check it out personally. Uncle Max assured him there was no way to tamper with the encrypto dealer. There was no reason for the "house" to do so because the house received a nominal cut of each pot, regardless of who won. This system totally eliminated dealing seconds, palming cards, or cheating by a player in any way. The stakes for the evening's game were pot limit, unlimited raises, table stakes with a minimum buy in of fifty thousand dollars, and a minimum escrow pot placement of one hundred fifty thousand. The house took one percent of each pot.

Sal Tesoro and two other players came in at the same time. Uncle Max made the introductions. He played it straight saying Poppies was his cousin visiting from California and looking for a little Nevada action. The other two players were regulars in the game. Soon three more players were escorted into the highly secure poker arena and outfitted with heads-up glasses and mini-mouses. These were visitors from Miami, New York, and Paris.

Poppies described Sal Tesoro as a quintessential Sicilian gangster. His pudgy arms were too short for his rotund torso and his fat fingers were invariably clinched in a fist. His straight shock of coal black hair crowned a face that appeared to have been injected with Botox. Two flashing, beady eyes set too close together rested atop a pug nose and ribbon-thin lips. His mouth, which was mostly open, spewed forth cuss words, insults, and cigar smoke. Other than his offensive body odor that reeked of garlic and sweat, he was a totally unattractive guy.

Poppies had two objectives. One was to win some of Tesoro's money, but the most important objective was to find out what he knew about Olivia and what he intended to do.

I didn't realize it, but Poppies was quite well to do. He had always been unassuming when it came to money, so I never assumed he had any. The truth was he inherited a considerable amount from a family trust and his engineering work had also paid well. He and Grammy invested wisely and his fortune was over ten million dollars when he entered the poker game.

The game began at 8:00 p.m. and ended promptly at 2:00 a.m. This was a house rule enforced by Max and Harrah's. After all, this was a legitimate game. The games played were five-card stud, seven-card stud, five-card draw, and five-card lowball. Nothing wild, no extra cards, it was just plain poker. Poppies had played poker since the seventh grade, having learned the game from his grandfather when they went on camping and ski trips. Also, he had been in some substantial stakes games in college. He always enjoyed the competition and had become pretty good. Still, he was in the company of pros and he wasn't sure how he would stack up.

Poppies tried to stay in the hands that Sal Tesoro was in. He wanted to make an impression on him by being the one to either beat him out of a pot or fold to him. As the evening wore on, sometimes the strategy worked and sometimes it didn't. The first fifteen-minute break came at ten o'clock. Everyone stretched, some went to the restroom, but Poppies took the opportunity to strike up a conversation with Sal. He started out by congratulating him on winning a pot just before the break. It wasn't a large pot and Poppies had thrown his hand in to set his opponent up. Sal admitted he had bluffed Poppies out and Poppies said something like, "Geez, you sure had me fooled."

The second break came at midnight and Poppies again caved in to an obvious bluff by Sal Tesoro. This time it was for a little more money with about three thousand dollars in the pot. Sal was convinced that he had Poppies number and could bluff him out of a pot any time he wished.

"So what brings you to Reno?" Poppies thought it was time to broach the subject.

"Well, it's not to find stiff competition at poker," Sal was arrogant and insulting. "You guys here don't have enough balls to play the game."

Poppies was inwardly bristling, but externally he was most patronizing. "Well, I have had some unlucky cards, but you have been playing yours extremely well," Poppies almost choked at the words. "But, as good as you are, you don't strike me as a professional gambler. You must be involved in something really important. What do you do for a living?"

Sal was thoroughly hooked by now. He had swallowed enough flattery to begin to believe it and could not resist the temptation to tell this poor poker-playing Californian just how important he was. "I'm from Atlantic City Gambling Enterprises and I also represent the Atlantic City Gaming Association

(ACGA), which I'm sure you know controls gaming nationwide and a few other places as well. I'm out here to negotiate a deal between my company and Harrah's. Also, I have a little unfinished business to take care of. Some joker came out here and screwed up the deal some time ago."

Poppies sensed he was closing in on his objective. "It must have been a real screw up to cause the Atlantic City bunch to send you out here," Poppies was syrupy.

The combination of a few drinks, four hours of mind-numbing poker, and Poppies' flattery loosened Sal's tongue further than prudent and he veritably gushed, "We sent a representative out here several years ago, but the dumb shit got hooked up with a shill who sucked him into a crooked card game. He lost the company's money, got into a fight, and blew the deal with Harrah's. The cops were involved and the bad press has caused Harrah's to stay clear of any involvement with Atlantic City. I intend to work with your cousin Max to turn that around."

Poppies nodded and opened his eyes as wide as he could. "That's terrible. So what happened to the crooks who were running the game and what about the shill?"

"Let's just say that the game folded," Sal smirked. "But I've recently got some intelligence from your authorities in California about the shill. She was and is the only one who really can tell us what happened. I want to know who set up the game, why our guy was fingered, and so forth. Both my company and Harrah's lost a lot of money and took a lot heat in the press over that incident. I figure if I can find her and get the truth out of her, Harrah's will be pleased. I'm sending some guys in next week to pick her up at some jerkwater town not too far from here."

Poppies was devastated, but he had the information he had joined the game to get. It was surprisingly easy. Poppies thought it might take several sessions. He was glad that it didn't because Olivia's days were numbered. The final session of the poker game resumed at fifteen minutes past midnight.

As poker games tend to do, as quitting time drew nearer, the size of the betting increased. Many pots were around twenty thousand dollars. With about thirty minutes to go, the game announced was five-card draw. Poppies had drawn two aces. Sal had drawn two kings. The initial round of betting plus antes had netted a pot of ten thousand dollars. Both Sal and Poppies drew three cards and, without looking at his cards, Sal opened the second round at five thousand bucks expecting Poppies to fold. Everyone else did.

Poppies muttered something about it being his turn to bluff out the competition and raised a modest twenty-five hundred dollars. Sal practically sneered when he said that it would take a hell of a lot more than that for a spineless Californian to bluff out a fearless New Jerseyan. Sal raised another seventy-five hundred and waited for Poppies to crumble as he had done throughout the evening.

Poppies gave his best impression of being shaken and befuddled. "Okay, I'm probably going to lose this but I'm hanging in there," Poppies said in his best falsetto voice. He raised fifteen grand.

For the first time Sal looked at his draw cards—two kings and three threes. A full house. He inwardly gushed with the thought that he had a goose to be plucked. Not only could he bluff this yokel any time he wished, this time he could win legitimately. He didn't want to bluff him out now, just coax a little more out of him. "Okay, your fifteen grand and another fifteen." Now Sal was hoping Poppies would call.

Poppies looked at the pot tote. There was seventy-five thousand plus the ten thousand from the ante and first round bet in the pot—eighty-five thousand total. According to the rules, the maximum bet was an amount to call the bet plus a raise equal to the new amount in the pot. He feigned nervousness, but micro-moused another fifteen thousand to bring the pot total to an even one hundred thousand dollars.

"I'll call your fifteen thousand and raise one hundred thousand," Poppies exclaimed.

There was an uncomfortable silence as Sal glared at Poppies. The most Poppies had bet before that hand was fifteen hundred dollars. Sal had him pegged as a very conservative, bordering on timid, poker player. It was inconceivable to Sal that this itinerant Californian could be bluffing. It was the farthest thing from Sal's mind.

Sal was red-faced and breathing heavily, and his words were laced with acrimony, "Well, you must have hit a barn burner. You haven't stood up to one bluff tonight, so that's the only explanation I can come up with. I've got a real decent hand, but I'm smart enough to know when someone has stumbled into dumb luck. I hate to let this full boat go, but you wouldn't be betting that much if you didn't have a real smoker—at least a high full house or probably four of a kind, maybe higher."

Another long pause and an icy glare, followed by, "I fold."

And with that, the encrypto dealer transferred the largest pot of the night into Poppie's escrow pot.

Poppies never cracked a smile. Nor did he get too far out of his fawning toady character as he watched his hand of two aces and three worthless cards fade from his heads-up screen. No need to do anything to exacerbate Sal. Sal was content in thinking he had folded an inferior hand. He would have been apoplectic to learn a pair had bluffed him out. Poppies had accomplished what he set out to do, and then some. He had found out about Olivia and his net winnings for the night was over one hundred forty thousand dollars. From behind the encrypto dealer master control, Max could see the hands of each player. He announced the last hand for the night and glanced at Poppies with a new respect for his California cousin.

Poppies never revealed much about that night to me, but I got the whole glorious run down from Uncle Max just before we left Reno.

CHAPTER TEN

RETURN TO GRANITEVILLE

Sunday, June 16, 2052
Reno, Nevada

I didn't know until much later about Sal Tesoro's plan to go after Olivia. All I knew at the time was that we were going to return the ACAV to Art and pay a visit to Graniteville where we would try to convince Olivia to come to Nevada. Although I desperately wanted to see Zell, I thought it was risky to go back and said so to Poppies. His explanation was that Art and Camp Resistance needed the ACAV and we owed it to them. I bought into that, mostly because I was thinking of Zell.

The plan was simple. We were to take the ACAV across the border using roughly the same route that Art and his raiders had used two months earlier. Then, we would meet up in Graniteville with Art, who would take the four of us back across the border, drop us off, and Uncle Max would send a gyrocopter to pick us up. I asked what made Poppies think Olivia would be willing to leave now when she was so adamant before.

Poppies just said, "Things are different."

I didn't take time to think about some of the inconsistencies in the plan. For example, why was I needed? Poppies could have taken the ACAV himself. Also, why wouldn't Art and one other come across the border, pick up the ACAV, and return? The answer, of course, was that this was a rescue mission for Olivia and Zell. Also, Poppies didn't want to ask Art to incur any more risk than he already had. The reason I had to go was to be made known in due course.

We left the next night. The moon was but a thin sliver in the mid June sky. Gus had the ACAV primed and ready. He had even found additional laser pods to backfill those that had been expended in the raid. Poppies was a little rusty in operating the ACAV at first, but he quickly regained his prowess. Even though there was no moon, the night-vision capability of the ACAV made traveling over the barren terrain quite easy. I began to wonder how many ACAV's we would need to bring the four of us out, because it was not designed for more than two people. That being the case, we would need all four they had.

The border crossing was uneventful as far as we knew. A few minutes of winding through the mountain ravines and we were headed up the slope to Camp Resistance.

"Aren't we going directly to Graniteville?" I asked Poppies.

It was then that I began to sense that I had not been let in on the entire scheme. Poppies briefed me quickly. "I didn't want to have to tell you this until I was sure. I think something has happened to Camp Resistance. Art was communicating up until this morning and then nothing. I think we must go by there and get a visual on the situation."

My heart started beating a little quicker. As we approached the north entrance, we were astonished. About half of the ACH's had been destroyed and the other half were gone. There was no sign of life, but there was no sign of death either. Poppies hovered the ACAV over where Art's ACH had been. He tried Art on his microcom again. "Something is very wrong here," Poppies voice was grave.

Just then, airborne-based lasers began to tear into the hillside beneath us. Whether they were directed at us was unclear, but Poppies was not willing to find out. With the ACAV's rockets at military power, he jetted away from the laser onslaught. I turned around to see the attack gradually subside. It was then I noticed a laser ray had seared our aft power nacelle. I told Poppies but I think he already knew.

A few minutes later we had climbed the summit to Webber Peak and were descending toward Graniteville. Now my heart was really pounding. Thoughts of Camp Resistance, the laser attack, and seeing Zell again, all bombarded my subconscious. Meanwhile we were losing power according to the rocket-thrust indicator screen.

Olivia was asleep when we arrived, but Zell had thought she heard something and came out to see what it was. I could see her through my night-vision goggles (NVG's) as we hovered over her street. She wore a climate cover that I guessed was mostly transparent and her hair blew wildly behind her face. She still did not know who we were but she showed no fear. As the ACAV rested on the concrete, I jumped out and ran to her.

"I knew you would come back," she gushed with enthusiasm.

We quickly hugged and I told her we were here to take them to Nevada. Question marks began to show in her expression, but by now Poppies had grabbed the two of us by our arms and marched us into the motel. Olivia was awakened by the commotion, and she appeared at her bedroom door with her hand laser ready for business.

"What in the world has brought you back here?" she asked.

Poppies told her to sit down, take a deep breath, and not say anything until he had finished his explanation. I thought at the time that no woman would be able to hold her tongue for that long. I was wrong. Olivia sensed that this was a matter of great urgency and she needed to be informed immediately. Poppies then told all of us about Sal and his henchmen who would be coming. He filled in the details I had been missing. His deal with Art was that the two of them, using a single ACAV, would create a diversion at the border so that the three of us, Olivia, Zell and I, could cross the border on the Humvee.

Assuming a successful crossing, Art would take Poppies across, drop him, and return. The problems began to mount up when Art dropped out of communication. They worsened when someone lasered us, presumably the Chinese, and they had really hit the fan now, because the ACAV was inoperable.

"I'm not sure who will get here first, the Chinese or Sal's goons," Poppies said. "It really doesn't make much difference. We couldn't leave you here to face Sal's guys, so we came to take you out. But now that we have alerted the Chinese, I'm not sure we've done you any favors."

"We thank you from the bottom of our hearts," Olivia said simply. She had once again immediately grasped the essence of the situation and realized that Poppies had come at great risk to save her and Zell. "We can be ready in twenty minutes, can't we, Zell?"

Now it was Zell's turn to speak. I was proud of how brave she had been tonight, beginning from the time she saw the ACAV approach. "If your friend Art is not here and your ACAV is not working, how will we be able to cross the border? The Humvee is no ACAV."

"Good point, Zell," Poppies agreed. "Plan B is to try to take the Humvee a little further north. I saw some possible crossing points when I was studying the terrain maps back in Reno. In the meantime, I will continue to try to raise Art. Even though Camp Resistance was in shambles, we have no confirmation that they were eliminated. It's quite possible they escaped in the ACAV's or in the more modern of the ACH's. While the two of you get your stuff together, Deej and I will go to the museum to get the Humvee ready. We'll meet you there."

The Humvee was exactly as we had left it some weeks before. Poppies grabbed some extra weapons, pulled open the ammunition storage bins, and began loading fifty-caliber ammo by the can. My job was to strap the extra jerry cans of fuel on the rear. We had enough to get to Reno and back five times.

We were just about ready when Olivia and Zell showed up. They had some CSC's and water, hand lasers, and a couple of personal items. Otherwise, they had left the place they had called home for many years just like they were going out for a walk. There were two reasons for that. First, they didn't have time to destroy anything. Second, they wanted Sal's guys or anyone else who came by to think they had not evacuated the premises. Again, good thinking by Olivia.

The Humvee sped along the rugged mountain roadway at about forty km per hour. It was not only much slower than the hybri-cycle, but the ride was much rougher. Through the rear window I could see the dying embers of the ACAV carcass that Poppies had detonated remotely as we rolled out of town. My mission now was to monitor the modar and tell Poppies if anything was approaching. We still were not sure who fired on us at Camp Resistance, and we didn't know who was in closest pursuit, the Chinese or Sal's dummies.

Just after reaching the summit of Webber Peak, but before Camp Resistance, Poppies took the Humvee off the main road. There was a not-too-well-beaten track off to the north, and Poppies hoped it was the one he had studied a few days before. This road was barely two wheel ruts in the weeds and the rough ride got even rougher. The Humvee proved its mettle as it crossed uneven crevasses and climbed slopes of at least 35 degrees. Olivia was the navigator and she was trying to correlate the onboard navigation system with the crude map Poppies had brought along. Zell was in charge of keeping everything tied down as the bumpy ride tended to make a garbage pit of the interior.

After about thirty kilometers, it was so far, so good. I had detected no aircraft on our tail. We had descended to a lower elevation and, although the way was still rough, the extreme slopes had become less so. No one thought we were home free, but our breathing became a little easier. We crossed a north-south road and saw a road sign that read, "Sierraville 8 Km." The moon had set and darkness closed in as we proceeded due east across the high desert plateau.

Five kilometers to go.

The modar first picked up the flying object and gave us an IFF "foe" notification. Coming from our right was an aircraft of some sort on a direct heading to meet us just before the state line. Poppies instructed me on how to obtain more information from the modar. This was a civilian gyrocopter flying at 300 km/hour, but it was armed with lasers and other armament. The next readout said it was a Sikorski 900. Poppies then knew it was not the Chinese, but some of Sal's people.

"I don't know how they managed to cross the border in that vehicle, but we don't have the luxury to point that out to the Chinese," Poppies called out coolly. "They will blow this Humvee back to the last century if we continue on this course."

With that, he pulled the Humvee alongside a rock formation that served as a shelter on the right side only. "Grab whatever weapons you can carry and let's go on foot," Poppies shouted.

We hadn't gone a hundred meters when the first laser shot hit the Humvee. It took the front end out and fried the engine. Poppies and I were slightly ahead of Olivia and Zell. "The good news is they want to take us alive, I think," he said. "The bad news is they want to take us."

152

Zell and Olivia caught up just as we neared the crest of a small rock hill. A scattered array of boulders offered a little protection so we got behind them and tried to become invisible. The Sikorski settled on the ground near the Humvee and two people got out. They approached the Humvee cautiously, but once they saw there was nobody in sight, they returned to the gyrocopter. This time four men got out and began spreading out in four directions. I was surprised to see they did not have night-vision goggles (NVG's). Our only chance was to remain extremely quiet. Even if we were to kill one of the men, the other three would know our position and we were outnumbered and outgunned.

I looked around and Poppies was on his microcom. "Who are you calling?" I whispered.

"I have given up on Art," Poppies whispered back. "Now I'm calling the Chinese border security headquarters."

Poppies was surprised that the Chinese had not responded sooner when the Sikorski had penetrated California airspace. What he didn't know was that the Chinese at security headquarters thought they had killed Sal's gyrocopter back at Camp Resistance.

Confusing the situation even more, Sal had provided enough cash to bribe the local Chinese air security patrol at the border. As a result, local air patrols were not scrambled when the Sikorski first came across the state line. However, when Poppies called the border guard security headquarters, pretending to be a good, loyal California citizen who was complaining about a vehicle in his air space, the situation changed. Headquarters recognized that Sal's gyrocopter was still around. They ordered the border guard station gyrocopter into the air and any bribes became null and void.

Poppies also had no way of knowing that the Chinese were acting on orders from on high to destroy the Sikorski. He was only hoping they could reach the Sikorsky's crew before they reached us. What would happen beyond that hadn't been worked out yet.

The New Jersey hit man closest to us was armed with a powerful head laser. This was a laser weapon mounted to a helmet, so that wherever the head pointed, the laser could fire. Fortunately, he hadn't seen us. But he was close. As he stepped to within ten meters of us, Olivia could stand it no longer. Using her hand laser, she fried the helmeted New Jerseyan.

Poppies would have preferred she wait to buy us more time, but her reaction was understandable. Their intercommunication net immediately alerted the other three that one of them was down. It gave them location, time, and a fix on us. Our best defense now was to spread out. Poppies signaled for Zell and I to move to the rear. He and Olivia stayed in front, but were separated by about ten meters. Within seconds, the goons were on the move. One was headed directly for the rock where Zell was lying. He was five meters away, but still hadn't sighted anyone. Suddenly, Zell was bathed in light. The Sikorski had launched a float-flare, which was an intensely bright flare that floated on a cushion of air about three meters off the ground. The goon wheeled as if to fire at Zell. Whether he would have or not was not put to the test. Olivia dropped him like a hot poker.

The other two would not be so amenable. They took cover and were lighting it up with lasers and anything else they could throw at us. Laser rays zapped the rocks to my left and the ground beneath my feet. It was the closest I had ever been to being shot. Poppies returned their fire. Immediately they turned their attention to him. I couldn't see what had happened, except that overshadowing the exchange of fire between Poppies, Olivia, and the gangsters, was a tremendous explosion. The Sikorski had been wasted. The two goons looked to see the Chinese gyrocopter coming at low angle. It was now looking for other targets of opportunity. Anything that moved was fair game.

The goons moved. We didn't.

In about two minutes, the battle was over. We heard nothing but silence. The Chinese gyrocopter was leaving. After checking the Sikorski and counting the dead gangsters, they were satisfied they had dealt with everyone involved. I wondered later what they thought when they saw the half-destroyed Humvee. Nevertheless, we were alone. No Chinese and no gangsters. The call to the border gate had worked, or so we thought. Sal would be as apoplectic as he was the night of the poker game, and he would be just as oblivious to what happened. We didn't know then that Sal had been on the Sikorski.

Poppies and I called to Olivia and Zell. There was no sound. Quickly we went to their positions. Zell had been hit by a ricochet from the fire. She was unconscious and bleeding. Olivia had been hit by one of the lasers. She was motionless. Poppies took her vitals and tried emergency resuscitation. No response.

She was dead.

CHAPTER ELEVEN

NEVADA MEDICAL CENTER

Poppies and I carried Zell using the two-man carry taught to firefighters. She was not heavy, but we were still at least a kilometer from the border and the terrain was treacherous. We were not exactly sure where the demarcation line was either, so we just kept going. We must have gone four or five kilometers past the border before Poppies said we could take a break. We laid Zell down and I checked her breathing and other vital signs. She was alive, but still unconscious. I checked the timepiece on my cyber bracelet. It was five minutes before midnight, Sunday, June 16, 2052.

Things became a little clearer when I woke up the next morning in the waiting room of the Nevada Medical Center in downtown Reno. I had only a blurry memory of what happened after we made it across the border. I think Poppies made a call to Uncle Max and an ambulance copter came to pick up Zell. We followed in Uncle Max's gyrocopter. I really don't remember arriving at the hospital, but we must have, and I don't remember much about the doctors speaking to us about Zell, but Poppies told me about it later.

It had been the most stressful twenty-four hours of my life so far, even including the episode with the Chinese gyrocopter and the first border escape. Being the target of Chinese lasers, enduring a veritable crash landing in

Graniteville, a hectic rough ride in the Humvee, an attack by gangsters, a counterattack by the Chinese, and a five-kilometer dash across the border with Zell, injured and unconscious in my arms, was enough action for a lifetime, let alone a single night. The entire ambiance of having survived the ordeal was darkened by the thought of Olivia. She was still over there. No way could we even admit we knew her or that we were part of the incident.

Of course we didn't know he was dead, but we thought Sal's wrath would extend to us and certainly to Zell if he knew she were Olivia's daughter. The daughter of the woman who now had cost Atlantic City Enterprises the Harrah's deal, four hired guns, and a gyrocopter would be a target of vengeance if any of them knew. The medical and police authorities were highly skeptical of Poppies' story that Zell was the victim of a fall on the rocks at 4:00 a.m. However, when Uncle Max weighed in, the inherent corruption that existed in both bureaucracies, along with the generous contribution Uncle Max would guarantee, made their skepticism disappear.

Zell was in critical condition. She was unconscious and the best brain-wave technology available was not able to diagnose precisely what part of her brain was damaged. In the past one hundred years, man had found cures for polio, yellow fever, smallpox, cancer, spinal cord injury and many more, but treatment for injuries to the human brain still remained a mystery. Uncle Max sat on the board of the Nevada Medical

Center and could assure us that Zell would get the best of diagnosis and care. That was the good news. The bad news was she was not registering any brain activity. We had little to do but wait.

I spent the next several days doing little else but eating, sleeping, and visiting Zell in the hospital. I was supposed to return to school but Poppies told the school a family member was gravely ill, so I was given a one-week release.

While I was at the medical center, I had the opportunity to speak with a number of doctors and nurses. Mostly I was interested in learning about Zell's condition and prognosis. But one intern in particular, a fellow named Mike Chapman, saw my interest and we developed a curious friendship. It turned out that he had had a compelling interest in medicine after the death of his mother from cancer when he was a small boy. When he learned that my father was instrumental in finding the cure for cancer, he took an even greater interest in me. I think he wanted to cultivate a desire in me to pursue a career in medicine. Even after I returned to school, I would spend my free time at the medical center. In the weeks that passed, Mike, who was studying to be an orthopedic surgeon, taught me a great deal about the history of modern medicine.

Mike was the all-American boy in every respect. He was a three-sport letterman in high school, voted most likely to succeed, and was president of his class. He had the good looks of a holovision actor, but he had higher aspirations. The product of an African-American father and a Hispanic mother, Mike had encountered many challenges through his life. Even in the twenty-first century, pockets of racism and ethnic bias still existed. Mike had seemingly overcome all such obstacles and had parlayed his good looks and keen mind into a scholarship to college and later to medical school. I admired his demeanor and appearance.

Even though I was only fourteen, I thought myself to be reasonably handsome, but I could not conceive of ever measuring up to Mike. I was privileged to know him and to benefit from his tutorials and his friendship. Additionally, Mike introduced me to a wealth of knowledge about advances in medicine.

By the early 2020's, the sight of an amputee with any limb missing had become rare. Advances in functional prosthetics had replaced the benign prosthetic devices of the twentieth century. The combination of bionic tissue and microcomputers embedded in human tissue empowered muscles to contract both voluntarily and involuntarily, just as they do in nature's human body.

Although space travel had progressed, the human body was still the greatest limitation to meaningful exploration of deep space. Doctors had developed a technique to slow down the metabolism of humans during space travel. It was as close to hibernation as humans have attained. An interesting side benefit to long periods of space travel, at velocities approaching half the speed of light, was a slowing of relative time and the aging of space travelers. After several years in space, returning travelers would appear somewhat younger than their earthbound companions of the same age.

Genetic therapy had revolutionized all of medicine. Using cell implantation, doctors found they could cure almost every disease. No surgery was needed for many ailments for which the only treatment previously was through surgery.

Humans were becoming stronger and healthier. Our basic gene pool is better because genes developed in the laboratory have been fused into us. Our bodies have become more resistant to, not only, disease but also radiation, thermal effects, and even gravity. Psychologically, humans are less prone to depression, psychoses, and other mental illnesses.

The general thrust of these improvements was somewhat driven by the desire to develop humans who can withstand the harshness of space and other planets. New fuels and new photon technology had generated space vehicles that could reach speeds of nearly fifty percent of the speed of light. However, the short pole in the tent continued to be the human being. Unmanned probes had great success, but it would take a human of extraordinary characteristics to venture into deep space. Such a being was being created.

The technique of cellular regeneration during suspended animation evolved from experimentation with frozen embryos. In the suspended state, such as existed during long space voyages, scientists could extend life up to two and one-half times simply by modifying the process of cell division. Human cells that normally divide three dozen times before dying were improved to replicate sixty times. Of greater significance though, the time between divisions was elongated. The net result is that in the suspended animation state, the body slowed down, aging slowed down, and the human being involved could live the equivalent of two or three lifetimes.

Paralleling these medical developments was the progress of body-part transplantation. From the rudimentary surgeries to reattach a person's own body parts that had been severed, doctors began experimenting with fingers and toes of different people who had been accident victims. What had begun in the late twentieth century as organ transplants, evolved into body-part donation. It was not unusual for an accident victim in good health to have nearly all the parts of his or her entire body appended to someone else.

Microsurgery to connect nerves, tendons, etc. flourished under the concept of "cell meshing." In this process, tissue at the cell level from one human is linked to another with microscopic transitional membranes. By this method, the problem of organ and tissue rejection was overcome. So it was only logical that replacement of fingers and toes would evolve to hands, feet, arms, and legs. In about 2035, doctors from the Carnegie Institute performed the first successful head transplant. In the now famous case, at age thirty-six, Dr. Edwin Cornell had contracted a degenerative muscle disease similar to ALS. A body-part donor of similar age, size, and body structure had perished in a hydro-skate accident and his donations served as the body for the head of Dr. Cornell. Dr. Cornell survived five years but developed paralysis in his lower extremities and ultimately died of a cerebral hemorrhage.

Full body transplants were attempted numerous times over the next ten years and recipients claimed to have full functionality with their new bodies. However, legislation in 2045 severely restricted the practice. What had been technologically successful had become a social failure. With no restrictions, wealthy people, mostly senior citizens, began competing for younger bodies. Soon, the demand for young healthy bodies outstripped the supply and people, seeking the "fountain of youth," resorted to unscrupulous means (including murder) to extend their lives. With the virtual outlawing of full body transplants, an underground industry similar to illegal abortions of the twentieth century soon sprang up.

"NanoTech" was a word coined out of the miniaturization wave that began in 2000 but flourished in the twenties. Miniaturization to degrees impossible to imagine fifty years ago began to take place in almost every area. Hence the term "NanoTech." Nanocells were developed to align with human body cells to repair tissue, to counteract disease, and to enhance performance. These tiny cells could be injected into an area harmed in an accident and they could replace muscle and bone tissue. Nanomachines were developed in a variety of areas. First, in medicine, nanomachines were made to penetrate the human body and perform tasks such as arterial cleansing, tumor removal, and organ rejuvenation. Second, in man-made devices, nanomachines were used to perform tasks such as rust inhibition in watercraft.

I learned a lot from Mike, and I even was giving some thought to pursuing the study of medicine. But I had lots of time.

The weeks turned into months and Zell's progress plateaued. She was as beautiful as ever to me, but I heard others say how pale and callow she looked. During the days and nights I spent at her bedside, I wondered if she would ever regain consciousness. I wondered if she would remember what had happened. I wondered if she would remember me.

After about eight weeks, Poppies came to my room in the hotel and said, "Deej, it's time to move on. I know you have a tremendous stake in Zell's recovery, but she will either come out of it or not, whether you are here or not.

"I have been speaking with everyone I can reach here in Nevada. Even after the border incidents, which we really can't talk about here because of the gamblers, these folks are in denial. The just don't want to recognize that the Chinese menace is just across the border and, in time, will infiltrate Nevada just as they have California. I am convinced I must seek out other support and I want to go to Colorado. The governor there is an acquaintance of mine plus I want to check in on my mother and stepfather.

"I spoke to Uncle Max and he is willing to look after you while I am gone. However, I am responsible for you and I owe it to your mom and dad to not shirk that responsibility. School will be dismissing in a week or so. I want you to come with me. Will you?"

I was prepared to follow Poppies to the ends of the earth, but he was asking me to leave a person I cared deeply about. Zell was in serious trouble and I felt my being there helped. Why did Poppies have to go? Why now? I was torn to pieces over the decision I had to make. If that is what growing up was about, I didn't want any part of it. Either way, I would hurt.

I had just a few days to decide. Uncle Max assured me that I would be well taken care of, I could continue to visit Zell, and continue my schooling. That option was the more appealing of the two. Two days before school was out, Mike came by the waiting room.

"I understand you are facing a dilemma," Mike began.

I was surprised that he knew anything, but I should have guessed, as there were few secrets on the medical center ward. "I presume you are talking about my staying here or going with my grandfather," I replied.

"So what is it going to be?"

I confided in Mike that I had not decided, and that I was terribly conflicted and guilt ridden about opting for either one. It was then I knew Mike was a wise and true friend. He simply stated, "You should go with whoever needs you most."

Those were words that stayed with me for many years thereafter and I suspect will for years to come. I pondered each nuance of their meaning. Then it came clear. Zell needed doctors, nurses, and medical care, none of which I could offer. Poppies needed to reclaim his family, his state, and his dignity. I was part of that family and I knew Poppies wanted to not fragment it any more. He had stood by me and saved me from numerous pitfalls many times. Besides, I could be a help to him. I never put it to the test but a part of me doubted that he would leave if I had said "no." So I followed Mike's advice.

That night, I caught Poppies by surprise, when I asked, "So, when do we leave for Colorado?" I thought I saw both a smile and a tear as he hugged me tightly.

CHAPTER TWELVE

EASTWARD BOUND

Sunday, August 11, 2052
Reno, Nevada

The border incident, coupled with the rescue of Olivia and Zell, had focused attention on the entire Northern California area. The Chinese had launched a search and destroy mission at Camp Resistance a few weeks after the border gate attack. That is why the camp was deserted and why Art was incommunicado the night of the rescue. They were scattering to the four winds. Again, I was left out of that information loop until much later.

Art had sought temporary refuge outside California, and Poppies arranged for he and Marla to stay in Reno until things cooled off. Art vowed to re-establish Camp Resistance and would do so in due course. In the meantime, the price for his asylum in Reno was the loan of an ACAV. The Camp R bunch needed to keep those vehicles concealed from the Chinese anyway so Art and Marla had used them to scoot across the border shortly after the rescue attempt. They would need quarters, a storage place for the ACAV's, and some money. Once again, Uncle Max came through.

Uncle Max also loaned us his newly acquired Stetson Starflier automobile to make the trip eastward. I'm not sure just what kind of deal Uncle Max and Poppies made because the Stetson Starflier 5000 was a very nice car, but I heard Uncle Max tell Poppies, "There are dozens of Stetsons in Nevada, but until you come back, I'm going to be the only civilian in Nevada driving an ACAV."

So I presumed an amicable arrangement had been struck. The Stetson 5000 was a two-seat, high-performance automobile that could easily reach 290 kilometers per hour. It could be manually driven or hooked to the drive-net that had been placed on all freeways many years ago. That enabled both the driver and passengers to view the countryside or nap as they desired.

As we drove along, I thought about a lot of things. My mind traced the major episodes of the past four months. I thought about the hybri-cycle ride out of California, the first border crossing, our time with Uncle Max, the return to Graniteville, the perilous flight back across the border, and Olivia's death. Most of all I thought about Zell. I felt inner warmth thinking about our weeks in Graniteville, and I got a peculiar feeling when I reminisced about our times at the waterfall.

Finally, I thought about the letter I had written to Zell and left at the Nevada Medical Center. It was dated August eleventh. I had made sure that it would be delivered to Zell when she awoke. Mike had introduced me to Mrs. Bailey, a very efficient woman in nursing administration, who seemed to understand completely when I explained this was very personal and was only to be opened by Zell when she woke up. I trusted Mrs. Bailey to do as I asked. I really didn't have much of a choice.

Driving along, I asked Poppies about a lot of things, partly to pass the time, but mainly to hear his perspective. He knew a lot about a great deal. Most of the subjects were esoteric, but his answer to my question about why the Chinese just didn't attack us with their military consumed about forty-five minutes of the journey, and was most enlightening.

I initiated the discussion. "I'm beginning to understand that the Chinese have invaded our state using a totally new type of warfare. And, if they succeed, they are likely to try to take our whole country. What I don't understand is why the Chinese, or others for that matter, just don't use their military forces as they and others have done throughout history."

Poppies gave me his usual throat-clearing cough and began. "As recently as 2010, nations throughout the world came to recognize the obvious. All-out warfare between major powers involving the use of nuclear weapons or other weapons of mass destruction was self-destructing. As was shown in a few instances where tactical nuclear weapons were employed, the long-term devastation and political wrath from all sides cost the user in every case.

"A small tactical nuclear device was set off in the Palestinian-Israeli conflict of 2015. It was intended for the citizens of Tel Aviv, but its mushroom cloud of radioactivity did more damage to Beirut than to Israel.

"Another device of limited output was detonated in Pakistan during a squabble between India and Pakistan over Kashmir. This was in the early twenties. Again, the fallout affected Pakistan and India equally and nearly decimated the area they were fighting over—Kashmir.

"Even the nuclear attack on Washington D.C. was a failure because the radical perpetrators were turned over to the World Court by their own government. Leaders of nations and even the military have come to recognize there is no way to control a nuclear weapon. Ergo, they aren't to be used. Even the so-called rogue nations have learned to control any nuclear devices they have to keep them from falling into the hands of irrational fanatics. It's a fragile understanding, I know, but it has worked for nearly three decades.

"That doesn't mean that nations don't still have designs on other nations. That doesn't mean that wars will cease. The Petroleum Wars were fought with conventional weapons, and even when the demise of some regimes was imminent, nuclear arsenals remained untouched. So the Chinese have devised another strategy. It worked in Taiwan and it's working in California. The War of Infiltration is this century's contribution to the long list of warfare types that man has invented to control his fellow man." Poppies had once again pontificated on the subject, but I never ceased to be enthralled.

We rolled across Nevada and into Salt Lake City in a little over four hours. Even during the time we spent connected to the drive-net, we still averaged more than 190 kilometers per hour. Poppies decided to stop at Salt Lake and make a quick comparison between the awareness level of people in Utah versus those in Nevada. It would not be comprehensive, but he wanted a sample.

At just after two in the afternoon, we pulled into a resort stop. Resort stops were places that travelers could completely regenerate their body processes. They were quite efficient so a traveler could be completely refreshed and ready to continue in about half an hour. Or one could spend the night and indulge in a number of mind-and-body-pleasing experiences. Even in once-staid Utah, resort stops were very popular. We were spending the night.

Poppies and I decided to try out the hydro-spa on the fifth level. This device had evolved from the hot tubs of the early twenty-first century. The main difference was in size and effect. Several dozen people could use the hydro-spa at one time and the therapeutic benefits were phenomenal. In two minutes my body felt completely relaxed and the aromas of the gases passing through the hydro-spa were intoxicating to my mind. It was a most delightful experience. Off to my left, I saw

Poppies engaged in a conversation with a man who looked to be about forty. I eavesdropped.

"So what do you do for a living?" Poppies asked.

"I work for Humanoid International Corporation," the man stated proudly. "HIC is the leading producer and provider of PR's in the world and we are second to Robots R Us in the space station network. By the way, my name is Francis Alexian Roger Tillman," he said as he reached out his hand to Poppies.

I could tell this pompous person did not impress Poppies. In addition, Poppies never had much regard for people with four names, but I wanted to know more. I knew a little about PR's—that PR was an acronym for personal robot—but in California they were far outside our household budget. I butted into the conversation and Poppies was happy to ease out. After listening to Mr. Tillman for about fifteen minutes, I also excused myself and floated away, but I did learn quite a bit that I hadn't known.

By 2050, the world had advanced to the eighth generation of robots. Most everyone who could afford one had their own personal robot. Much in the same fashion as R2D2 of Star Wars fame seventy years previous, there was an assortment of PR's on the market. It wasn't until the fourth generation, that robots became truly mobile. Generations one, two, and three had wheels but they were no more mobile than the refrigerators of the 1990's. But the fourth generation robot came with, not only two-dimensional mobility, but some were equipped with rocket motors and could travel vertically as well. It was always fun to watch the status-seeking owners of these robots cruising along the airway with their personal robot in tow. It reminded me of dog walking in the twentieth century.

Eighth generation robots had become truly self-sufficient. They came with an intelligence to learn, and they processed instructions and commands in such a way that they were memorized and able to be executed with or without direction from their owners. I appreciated the lesson, but I'm not sure listening to the stuffed shirt, Francis Alexian Roger Tillman, was worth it. The hydro-spa had relaxed my body and dulled my mind so that there was no problem getting to sleep that night.

After I had gone to bed, Poppies took the pulse of a number of people staying at the resort stop. He told me the next day that his assessment was that they were not as oblivious and indifferent as the people in Nevada, but they were just as ignorant. The sophisticated smoke screens sent out by the Chinese in California were effective in Utah as well.

The next day we left for Wyoming. Interstate Route 80 had been straightened out to accommodate the drive-net and the speeds associated with it, but it still remained a fairly desolate drive. As we were cruising along, I teased Poppies about his encounter with Mr.

Tillman. "Why did he have four names and why was he apparently so proud of it?" I asked.

"Well, some folks have to toot their own horn, even if it's only about the number of names they have," Poppies said. "I can tell you a thing or two about why four names is a coming thing. Your children will more than likely have that many."

I settled back for another history lesson.

"After about 2030, the population had grown to such an extent, not to Malthusian proportions, you understand, but enough that names began to be duplicated. As a result, people began to use unique surnames. In the year 2000, for example, one of the most popular boy's names was David. Even if your last name was not common like Smith or Jones, soon there were dozens of *David's* with the same last name as you. Also, as has been the case with naming for centuries, it became faddish to come up with a unique name for your child. So names from ancient times became popular. Xerxes, Aphrodite, Marcus Aurelious and other Greek and Roman notables were fancied. Likewise, contrived names became a hit with the WASP sector of America. Exotic names like Ballonic, Experion, and Zytuminal began to appear on birth certificates. The African-American trend of drawing from old tribal names and variations thereof continued with black babies being named Laterica, Curinca, Laphonso, and Kunte.

"While the popularity of unique names did help distinguish individuals from one another in metropolitan areas, it has made the remembering of a given person's name that much harder. Then, along about 2045, the use of the double middle name began to come into widespread use. No longer was David Wayne Smith acceptable. Now I suppose it has become fashionable, and somewhat practical, to name your son, Igor Sean Zolo Smith. The chances of a random duplicate name are diminished dramatically. I once read that in 2005 there were 750 *Mary Smith's* in the New York phone directory. By 2045, there were only three," Poppies finished with a flourish.

Once again, I had asked for the time and he told me how to build a watch.

We rolled across Wyoming and into Colorado without stopping more than once or twice. The CSC's and the internal personal hygiene expulsion system allowed travelers to remain in the auto as long as they wished. Since the seats were equipped with automatic pseudo-shiatsu massage cells, a passenger received as much stimulus as needed to keep muscles and blood flow normal.

We had dropped south from Cheyenne on Route I-25. The Denver bypass was the only deterrence we encountered. The automatic acceleration capability of the ANS had malfunctioned so each vehicle accessing the net had to do so manually. While most operators had little problem reaching the connect speed, a few were either too scared or too stupid to make the connection. As a result, those vehicles were impeding the way for others needing to reach connection speed. Poppies dropped back until there was enough clearance to reach the needed speed and then he deftly accelerated and connected. Once connected, the rest of the trip was uneventful.

I began to anticipate meeting my great-grandparents for the first time. The more I thought about it, the more I realized I didn't know a lot about them or about that side of my family for that matter. "Poppies, I have a question." I just sort of blurted it out.

"You are full of questions, but that is okay. That's what grandfathers are for—to answer questions from their grandsons. What's on your mind?"

"Well, I have called you Poppies for as long as I can remember. What I am wondering about is, where that name came from?"

Poppies was rarely at a loss for words, but this time he paused for just a minute. "I guess it goes back to my childhood. Your great-great-grandfather could probably tell you in more detail, but as I recall, that was the name I chose to call him. Why, exactly I can't say. Perhaps that was the closest I could come to saying 'Grandpa.' I was just a toddler at the time. Actually, it helped to differentiate between my grandfather on my mother's side and her grandfather who they called 'Papa.'"

"So it was you who started the tradition? I have always wondered about that. What about your grandparents? Did you know them well?"

Poppies reflected back on fifty-plus years. "Yes, I did actually. I called them Grammy and Poppies just as you do. These were my grandparents on my mother's side and they lived close to where I was growing up in St. Louis. Would you like to know more about them?"

I indicated that I would and Poppies began to relate a story I had never heard before.

"My Grandfather and Grandmother Moore, met while he was attending the Air Force Academy, as it was called then, in Colorado. I think they met on a blind date while she was visiting a friend in Denver, but she left the next day to return to California and they didn't see each other for a year or two afterward. Their next meeting was in Southern California when Poppies invited Grammy to come down from Walnut Creek to watch him play football against UCLA at the Coliseum in Los Angeles. That was the first time he met her parents, who you may have heard were called, 'Papa and GoGo.' Their last name was Brantley. I remember 'Go Go' very well. She was a real hoot.

"As I recall, the day following the football game, your great-great-grandparents had their first real date when they went to a theme park called Disneyland, which is the same park you and I visited, although it is now called Disney Space World. They continued their romance by writing letters that were delivered by the United States Postal Service. That service, also called the U.S. Mail, went out of existence in the early teens when electronic transmission made the U.S. Mail as obsolete as the Pony Express of a century earlier. No doubt you've read about both in your history class.

"Anyway, their courtship lasted over four years and, except for a few cross-country visits, it was a long-distance relationship. So it must have been true love. In fact, one visit took place very close to where we were a few weeks ago. Do you remember when we were at the American River near Sacramento? Remember I said this river had some historic significance in our family? Well, according to family legend, it was one evening on the banks of the American River that your great-great-grandfather realized he had fallen in love with your great-great-grandmother. We suspect that, at that point, it was mutual. I don't know the details, of course, but I contrast their peaceful, romantic evening with the violent, chaotic experience you and I had on the same river. I sometimes wonder how close it was to the very place where I shot down the Chinese gyrocopter.

"To continue, they married and had their reception in the same house you and I occupied on Sharmar Court. Do you know how they got the name 'Sharmar'?"

I admitted that I had no idea.

"Well, it is a combination of the first names of your great-great-grandmother, whose name was Sharon and her younger brother, whose name was Marty. Back in the 1950's when her parents built the house, they were the only one on the block and had the honor of naming the street. So they called it 'Sharmar.'

"Your Great-Great-Grandfather Moore was a commissioned officer in the United States Air Force and he and Grammy spent the first twenty-three years of their marriage going from one Air Force base to another as he rose in rank to full colonel. Along the way, they had two children. The oldest was Kristen, who is my mom and who we will be visiting in Colorado. The youngest was John Anthony, better known as Tony, whom you have never met. He is retired now and lives in Mississippi with his wife."

"Did Great-Great-Grandpa Moore fly in the Air Force?" I asked.

"No, he wanted to, but he had a medical problem that kept him from flying, so he became a civil engineer. After he retired from the Air Force, he worked several years for a private engineering company in St. Louis."

"What about your Grammy?"

"She was a teacher when they first married, but after her children came along, she put that career on hold to raise them. That was much more common then than it is now. After her two children were in high school, she returned to teaching and taught for many years in a program for high school dropouts. My mom told me that she helped a great many young people get a new start in life."

Poppies stopped talking but I think he continued to reminisce silently as we drove along. This was a part of my history that I had heard about only in bits and pieces. I treasured hearing about my ancestors and it made me even more anxious to visit Great-Grandmother Kniest.

I looked to my right as we approached Colorado Springs and saw the United States Air and Space Academy. So that's where my Great-Great-Grandfather Moore went. Airships of all types filled the skies as cadets trained for their future jobs as military air and space pilots.

My mind leisurely flitted from thought to thought. The escape, the return to save Olivia and Zell, the days in Reno—but it was rare when my last thought was about anything but Zell.

CHAPTER THIRTEEN

COLORADO

Wednesday, August 14, 2052
Southern Colorado

Great-Grandma and Great-Grandpa Kniest lived south
and west of Colorado Springs. They had a chalet on a
small ranch at the foothills of the Sangre de Cristo
Mountain Range, just south of the town of Westcliffe. I
had seen several holo-photos of the house and the
surrounding countryside and it always looked
beautiful. I couldn't wait to see it in person. The ride
up the mountain roads had to be done manually as the
"drive net" did not exist once we had left I-25. Though
the roads were not much different than they were back
in the thirties, Poppies made short work of the 130
kilometers between the netway and Westcliffe.

As we drove up the winding mountain road to their A-
frame home, I wondered what meeting my great-
grandmother and great-step-grandfather would be like.
I saw my great-grandmother out in the field with the
horses that I had heard about. I guessed that my great-
step-grandfather was in his 30-car garage. I'd heard
from Poppies that Great-Grandpa Tom, as I called him,
loved cars. Sure enough I saw Great-Grandpa Tom in
his garage waxing his cars. He had a very old car that
was from 1999. It took regular gas so he couldn't drive
it very much. I couldn't wait to see this old car. I was

so excited that I felt I could run around Great-Grandpa Tom's garage eight times. When I saw that old car I was amazed. I asked Great-Grandpa Tom why he didn't just get an automatic waxer. He told me that this is the best way to do it.

While I was in the garage, Poppies was talking to Great-Grandmother Kniest. I don't know what they were talking about, but I didn't want to interrupt them because I thought they would be catching up. They would probably be hugging and having fun. When Great-Grandpa Tom and I went back to see Great-Grandma, she had tears in her eyes. When she saw me, she started crying even more. I was wondering if I had done something wrong, but Poppies told me, "This is your great-grandmother, D.J." She hugged me; it was the biggest hug I had ever had. I was so happy I couldn't believe it. While I was looking over my great-grandma's shoulder I saw that Poppies had a couple of tears running down his cheek. That was the first time I had ever seen Poppies cry. I think that everybody was happy.

We would spend well over a year at the ranch on the mountain.

The first few days were spent in becoming acquainted with my great-grandparents. Although she was eighty-seven, my great-grandmother was still a very attractive woman. Her hair had turned a silver gray and her hearing had dimmed, but her face was unwrinkled and she always seemed to have a twinkle in her eye. From the many hours she had spent in front of a computer, her back was not as limber as she would have liked and she limped a little from the culmination of many encounters with her horses. While she was rarely thrown, the mountain trails were fraught with low-hanging limbs, sharp rocks, and shaky footing. The missteps of many rides, along with the repeated upward thrusting on her spine, had compressed her spinal disks to where further riding was out of the question. Still, she went out to the pasture every day to reminisce and talk to her favorites. As I watched her, I wondered if that was what Zell would look like seventy years from now. Zell was never far from my thoughts. Uncle Max kept us informed, but lately the only comment was "no change."

Great-Grandpa Tom was over ninety and, other than a smoker's cough, was in fairly good health. Fortunately, he had stopped smoking several years before cigarettes were outlawed, and he had escaped the ravages of smoke and nicotine that had inflicted many of his fellow smokers. Great-Grandpa Tom still had most of his hair, but it was white as the snow on Pike's Peak. Although he pretended to be oblivious to much of the world around him, he was sharp as a tack. His hands were gnarled from working on machinery and his back bowed slightly as he shuffled along. His hearing was excellent when he wanted it to be. Otherwise, he was stone deaf. He liked to brag that he still weighed the same and wore the same trouser size as he did fifty years ago. He said clean living and a Bud Light beer each day were responsible for his longevity. He could still shoot pool with the best eighty-year-olds in the state and he proved it by winning an "Over Eighty" pool tournament in Manitou Springs.

His one great passion was automobiles. He had collected them for over fifty years and still had one of the original Ford Mustang convertibles that he owned back in 2000. He said it would still run, if he had any gasoline.

After living most of their lives in St. Louis, Missouri, my great-grandparents moved to the mountains of Colorado to escape the congestion of the city. After they had retired, in the late twenties, they traveled extensively throughout the Rockies in search of their ideal retirement location. The chalet and ranch were part of an estate sale they had found out about by accident while visiting friends in Boulder. On a whim they decided to attend the auction. As they passed through the sagging gate to the ranch, they both immediately fell in love with the chalet, the pristine view of the mountains, and the privacy of the ranch. There was room for a stable, a car barn, and a pasture. They arrived at the auction at 1:00 p.m. and by 4:00 p.m. they were the new owners of the property.

Like virtually every home in America in the 2050's, their chalet was heated and powered by solar energy. The roof and siding consisted of the same type of photovoltaic chips that were used on vehicles, except these were larger and had a more intricate circuit board beneath the chip panels. Solar energy could be collected and stored in the state-of-the-art magnesium hydride batteries that had been perfected some thirty years before. Even before the Petroleum Wars, the construction industry was moving toward the use of solar power. Particularly, out in the boondocks, where Great-Grandma and Great-Grandpa Kniest lived, solar was a must.

It was amazing to me that it took so long to develop such a simple concept. I suppose when fossil fuels were available and so cheap, there was little incentive to make the change. I remember learning in school that, as recently as 2015, American homes consumed nearly three quadrillion BTU's of electricity and used some 300 billion gallons of gas for heating and home appliances. By using solar now, there is no pollution, no sound, no smoke, and no carbon dioxide. The only product is power. What's more, it is efficient, renewable, sustainable, and infinitely scalable. Interestingly enough, it was the large oil and gas companies who first saw the need and the opportunity early in the century. Their research into high tech, efficient batteries, solar chips, and delivery systems for the energy they generated paved the way for solar use in remote areas first. But as the price per kilowatt dropped, it became cost competitive with gas by about 2018.

After that, it was just a matter of time until all new construction mandated the use of solar infrastructure and power. Great-Grandpa Tom told me his energy storage capacity was such that they could last for four hundred days without any sun, if necessary. I didn't think it would be cloudy that long.

The ranch consisted of the chalet, a corral, a horse barn, and a car barn. The car barn housed the many antique automobiles Great-Grandpa Tom had collected over his lifetime. It was located about one hundred and fifty meters from the chalet and had been sited near the road so visitors could come and admire the collection. So precious were these autos and the attention Great-Grandpa Tom paid to them, he had an underground tunnel constructed between the chalet and the car barn so he could walk between the two during times of heavy snow.

As we sat down for dinner that evening, I felt as if I had been there forever. The chalet was warm and inviting and my great-grandparents were super hosts. We had real food, including soy steaks, cooked on a barbeque by Great-Grandpa Tom. I learned that they had never converted to eating CSC's and, after tasting the steaks, fresh tomatoes, and corn on the cob from their garden, I understood why.

After dinner, we retired to the deck to look out on the aspen groves and alfalfa fields below. As the sun began to set over the Sangre de Cristo Mountains to the west, Great-Grandma turned to Poppies. "I don't want to get your expectations too high, but I think I have some good news," she said quietly.

As if he knew this was something momentous, Poppies immediately gave her his full attention. "What is it?" he fixed his eyes on her.

"I received a microcom call from a friend of mine who used to work in Seattle. Her name is Crystal and she is now in Northern California, living in a home for retired aircraft workers. By chance, her daughter, whom I also used to know as a little girl, visited her. The daughter works as a linguist in San Francisco and said she had frequent contact with a woman named Jennifer Eagleton."

Poppies was stunned at first and then the questions came in machine gun fashion. "When, where, how is she?" Poppies demanded excitedly.

"I don't even know for sure that it is Jenny," Great-Grandma Kniest continued, "but I'll tell you everything that was passed to me. Apparently this woman, Jenny, arrived there just after Christmas of last year and was held incommunicado for several months. Then, by accident, the Chinese discovered she was fluent in five languages, including Chinese. She has been put to work translating between the languages she speaks, but mostly is concentrating on Spanish and Chinese.

"The Chinese have many Spanish-born translators but they don't trust them to precisely translate the Spanish documents into Chinese. Of course, they also have auto-translators, but they don't trust them either, so they use people of a totally different ethnic origin to give them one more version. That's the job that Jennifer has. Unfortunately, she is not allowed to have visitors or even a microcom, so we can't contact her directly. Also, my friend from Seattle has short-term memory lapses, so that source is not terribly reliable. I am working on getting a direct contact with her daughter, but I fear her microcom is monitored, so we must be careful. But, above all, you must remember this may or may not be your Jenny."

Poppies was silently reflecting on what had been said. "I'm going back. I must, even if there is only a slight chance that it's her," Poppies stated emphatically.

"Well, if I hadn't told you that, what were your plans?" Great-Grandma asked.

Poppies responded, "The first thing I was going to do was to see if Coloradoans were as uninformed as folks in other states about what's going on in California. Then I was going to see Scott Miller, your governor."

"Oh yes, I recall you knew him from school," Great-Grandma still had a laser-quick mind and amazing recall.

"I think he will help me. You know he was originally from California. He only left because he found a job here after school. Then he married a Denver girl, got into politics, and the rest is history," Poppies said.

"So why don't you continue with that strategy and allow me to probe further. I have far less than one hundred percent confidence in Crystal's report. You surely didn't go through everything to get here only to return to chase a rumor from a dingy old lady, did you?"

Poppies nodded, but didn't say anything. That was what he did when he recognized that he had been out-witted. Great-Grandma did not press the issue further. I guess she sensed she had convinced Poppies to stay in Colorado for a while longer.

It was the first of September and the Colorado autumn brought shortening days and crisp cool nights. The golden-hewed aspen groves glistened in the morning sun and then again at sunset. Their rich yellow color, contrasted against the green of the fields, was only surpassed by the deep purple backdrop of the mountains behind them. I watched Great-Grandma twice a day as she walked the hundred meters or so to the pasture below. In the morning the sun caught the smile on her face and her gait and demeanor was that of a woman who was bearing the fruits of having lived a full and happy life. In the evening, her silhouette was framed against the darkening mountain range and, as the sun descended, I sensed she was at total peace.

Such was not the case with Poppies. As winter approached, he was becoming more and more restless with the slow progress of the execution of his "game plan." He had been to Colorado Springs and spoken to businesspersons' groups. He flew to places like Grand Junction, Telluride, Greeley, and Trinidad and made a pitch to local politicians and local leaders. He had been to Boulder several times, thinking the academic community would be better informed and receptive, but none of his contacts there were in any position to take a stand. They expressed opinions, but in the tradition of academia, left action to others.

Poppies had placed a call to Governor Miller shortly after we arrived. He received the polite intercept of the microcom transmission from the governor's computer assistant that promised to deliver the message.

True, the governor was busy with a number of issues, all of keen interest to the voters of Colorado. He could be seen in the media extolling the virtues of irrigating the eastern plains so that more crops could be grown. He had resurrected the idea of forming a Northwestern Water and Power Alliance to bring water down the continental divide from Alaska and Canada for irrigation while harnessing hydroelectric power along the way. He was leading the charge to protect the mountain environment from the onslaught of development that had taken place.

What began as ski-slope resorts and condos was turning into full-fledged suburbia in many locations. The formerly pristine mountain streams were polluted, the craggy landscape was dotted with road signs and debris, and the entire area was overrun with people trying to get away from the overcrowding and dangers of the big city.

Nonetheless, Scott Miller was not a man who would forget his friends. Or so Poppies maintained.

Friday, November 29, 2052
Near Westcliffe, Colorado

But as days became weeks and weeks became months, even Poppies began to doubt his faith in the man. Then one day, as the wind whipped November snow flurries across the eastern slopes, the microcom call came. Actually it came from the governor's computer asking Poppies to engage the visualator at the chalet.

Visualators were the offspring of videophones of the early 2010's. Videophones were mostly used for conferences in those days, but as costs came down, they became popular for individual usage. Once they were miniaturized and made portable, they were even more useful. Visualators were a blend of videophone technology and the holographics that had led to holovision. The visualator in Great-Grandma's house was a flat screen on the wall of the main room and it portrayed a moving hologram of the parties to the call.

It was impressive to see Governor Miller in 3-D sitting in his capitol office with flags of the United States and Colorado flanking his workstation. Although it had been weeks since Poppies first called, it was like the approach was made yesterday. "Hey, Dave," the governor began, "I got your message. It's great to hear from you. What brings you to Colorado? I am humbled that you took time to look me up."

There was no doubt that Scott Miller was a politician. My first thought was WABOS—what a bunch of shit. However, as the conversation progressed, I detected a more genuine side to Governor Miller. Poppies gave him a thumbnail sketch of what had happened in California, what he had observed in Nevada and Utah, and what he thought might lie in store for Colorado if something were not done.

Surprisingly, Governor Miller's demeanor changed markedly in those few minutes. Beneath the political facade was a warm and concerned man. I'm not sure why he felt the need to be such a phony at the start. Perhaps it was the persuasiveness and aplomb of Poppies, but Scott Miller was totally on board by the end of the ten-minute call. Poppies would be going to Denver the following Monday for a meeting on the subject.

To my great surprise, Poppies asked me to go with him to Denver. I had started school again in Colorado, but living in the mountains afforded me the ability to holo-school for all but a few classes.

It had become common as far back as the thirties to use communication technology and high-speed networks to educate children. While the experience was quite different than being face-to-face with teachers and fellow students, the holographic images and interactive ability of the visualator, made my schooling both easy and fun. Plus it was a new experience. Most of the instructors were computer enhanced, but it was quite difficult to tell them from real humans.

I could tell that my California schooling had put me ahead of the level being taught high school freshmen in Colorado. So I coasted for a while. Then I became bored and asked to be put in an accelerated program. After that, I had no worries about boredom, but I could still cover the material in about six to eight hours per day. At any rate, when Poppies asked if going to Denver would impact my learning, I could truthfully say no.

We took Uncle Max's Stetson to the capitol in Denver. Governor Miller had offered to send a gyrocopter for us, but Poppies declined. We took the most direct route to I-25 and then hooked on to the "drive net" for the trip to Denver. I napped while Poppies studied some documents he had brought along. The trip was uneventful and we arrived at the capitol in time for lunch. Although he could not be present, Governor Miller had arranged for us, along with a number of others, to eat in his private dining room. There were about two dozen distinguished looking people there. Some appeared to know each other, but Poppies did not seem to know any of them. After lunch, we were all asked to adjourn to a conference room adjacent to the governor's office. We were seated at a round table with the latest in conference technology at each position.

Governor Miller opened the meeting by welcoming everyone and by saying he wanted to delay introductions so as to get right into the "meat" of the meeting. He also explained, to the disgruntlement of some, the meeting was subject to strict security and everyone would be screened each time they passed through the automatic detection checkpoint.

Scott Miller was a highly impressive man. His voice was as strong as his handshake and he immediately took command of a group, whether it was two people or two hundred. His striking good looks were accentuated by blondish-brown hair, graying at the temples, and steel-gray eyes. His nose was a little too large for his face and bent just a little from a counter-punch he once walked into while boxing in college. His most captivating characteristic, however, was his smile. Actually, it was more of a boyish grin but he could flash it at will and, in his position, he did so widely and often. It had helped get him elected to numerous offices on his road to the Colorado statehouse and it served him well in the meeting of scholarly dignitaries in the room at the time.

He began quickly. "I have asked you here today to help me and my friend, David Eagleton, analyze, validate, and, I hope, solve what I consider to be the most serious problem in the country. Let me start by asking a question. How many of you have been to California in the past two years?" A show of hands revealed only three of the two dozen or so had been there, and one of those was Poppies. I kept my hands under the table and tried to remain inconspicuous.

"How many of you have received microcom calls or other communications from colleagues in California in the past two years?" This time a few hands went up.

"How many of you think there is something strange going on in California?" Scott Miller looked each person squarely in the eye as he surveyed the table of people. In response to this question, all but two hands went up.

"Well, that's why we are here. David Eagleton, from California and an old friend of mine, is here to help bring us up to date on the situation. I'm going to ask David to give you his first-hand assessment of what is going on and how it is affecting us and the rest of the country," the governor yielded the virtual pulpit to Poppies.

Poppies rose from his seat at the table and stood alongside the governor. "Thank you, Governor. I came to Colorado because I was no longer safe in California. The same is true for countless thousands of my fellow citizens. My state has been literally taken over by outsiders, and the institutions we previously thought would safeguard our constitutional rights and freedoms are, instead, being used to subjugate and manipulate our people. I believe they have done the same thing to greater or lesser degrees in other states of our country as well, but I will confine my comments to California, because that is where I know well of what I speak."

Poppies paused and looked at his audience as if to evaluate whether he was being believed or disregarded. No one said a word. I discovered later that most were somewhat aware of what Poppies had said, but now they were about to get a first-hand account.

Reassured that his audience was attentive, Poppies continued. "Before I present the details of what has happened, let me jump to the impact that Governor Miller spoke of. What has happened in California can and will happen in Colorado if something is not done. What's more, it will permeate all of our states and eventually our federal government, as well. America will be defeated and occupied by an outside enemy without ever having fired a shot. Ladies and gentlemen, this enemy is China!"

There was a murmur of understanding and, I thought, agreement that went through the group. Poppies then proceeded to tell of how the Chinese had implanted autism-chips in a large number of Californians. He explained how they had slowly and surreptitiously infiltrated the political and commercial fabric of the state using resources from the Chinese mainland, including money and people.

"Once they had their 'soldiers' in positions of power, the money began flowing in the opposite direction and the citizens of California were either brainwashed, bought off, or knocked off to keep the program going. Extremely sophisticated means were used to deceive and delude Americans in other states and in the federal government throughout the takeover. What you have heard via the media from and about California is fabricated propaganda designed to make you think its 'business as usual' there. It's not. The Chinese are perpetrating myths to buy time."

Then he explained how our freedoms were systematically being compromised, denied, and eliminated. He told of the liquidation of superfluous, non-productive citizens such as seniors and the handicapped. He explained how he had been a victim, how his wife had been abducted, and how he and I had to escape.

At that point he walked over and stood behind me and said, "This young lad has been on a journey through Hell and Purgatory over the past six months. I am proud of the way he has dealt with the danger and adversities, but I regret much more that he was forced to do so. For those of you who have children or grandchildren, I ask you to imagine how you would feel if one of them had to experience what young David Eagleton the Third has experienced."

Then he told of our hybri-cycle ride, the gyrocopter incident, the stay in Graniteville, our two trips into Nevada, and the border carnage that took the lives of

Sal's men. He covered all the pertinent events that had led us to Colorado.

"I would not expect you to take this as gospel from me alone," Poppies softly stated. "There are others still unable to escape, yet still resisting in California. I received a coded message just yesterday from a friend who is just one of many who are forced to live as fugitives in their own state. Although it will be dangerous for him, he has agreed to contribute whatever he can toward your understanding of the situation. So, if you would like, at some part in these proceedings, we can contact him and his fellow dissenters for their assessments."

At that point, I realized Poppies was speaking of Art. It was the first time we had spoken about him in many weeks. In fact, I had assumed he had been killed or taken prisoner by the Chinese and that was why he hadn't made the rendezvous at Graniteville, why he didn't help us recross the border, and why Poppies had stopped talking about him. I would press Poppies for a rundown on the way back to the chalet, but I was glad to hear Art was still around.

"In summary, my purpose in coming here and speaking to you is twofold," Poppies concluded his remarks. "First, I am an American who treasures the liberties that have been enjoyed by Americans for centuries and I don't want those to be taken from citizens of California, Colorado, or any other state. So, like Paul Revere, I am sounding the alarm. Second, I have been personally devastated by the takeover in California. I have lost my home, my freedom, much of my wealth, and most of all, my beloved wife. I intend to return to California to rescue her but I need help. I hope I can get it from folks such as you."

There was a poignant silence in the room as Poppies returned to his seat. I guessed many were astounded at what had just been revealed. How could this happen in America? Others were reflecting on the potential impact to themselves, their families, and their state.

Finally, Governor Miller spoke. "I can't tell you how valuable your personal account has been, David. The people seated at this table have, each in their own way, become somewhat acquainted with the bizarre things going on in California. I, myself, am a California native and my parents were victims of the Chinese oppression. So, as individuals and as a group, we are very sympathetic to your cause. What's more, as I said a few minutes ago, our purpose here is to ultimately devise a strategy to combat this infiltration. We don't know yet what we should or can do, but we do know that to do nothing, is to be swallowed up."

With that the group erupted in applause. It struck me that this was genuine applause for a man who had conveyed a sincere expression of concern and a commitment to act. It was not just a polite clap for the governor.

CHAPTER FOURTEEN

THE RATIONALE

Governor Miller told us that there would be a fifteen-minute break, but before that he asked each attendee to introduce him or herself and give their official position as well as their interest in the problem under discussion.

During the break, the first of many to shake Poppies' hand and congratulate him on his summation of the Chinese situation was the United States Ambassador to China, Mr. Calvert T. Gruenberg. I believe he was sincere in his sentiments, even though he had been their ambassador for several years. His final comments struck a chord.

"How ironic that the Chinese, who venerate their elders and ancestors, should show so little regard for ours. The systematic elimination of American senior citizens is horrible. Even more devastating is the attitude of other Californians who are somewhat aware. I find it alarmingly comparable to the attitude toward the Jews in Hitler Germany over a hundred years ago." As he walked away, the look on his face confirmed the gravity of his words.

The group was slow returning from the break and I could tell the members were still buzzing about

Poppies' remarks. Governor Miller again took control of the meeting.

"Ladies and gentlemen, I think it is important for each one of us to have a broad background on a number of fronts pertaining to this issue. I want you to be at the same level of understanding from a political, economic, military, and psychosocial standpoint.

"Accordingly, I have engaged a number of experts in their field to do that. If it seems like you are back in graduate school, well, consider this a refresher course. Our next speaker is one of the leading economists in the world. I've asked Dr. Conrad Adler to present his views on the economic aspects of this issue. He has agreed to, not only do that, but to give you his views on the world economic situation today. Please welcome Dr. Conrad Adler."

Conrad Adler was a German-born economist from Boston. He was invited to the meeting for two reasons. The first was his expertise. He had amassed a rather large fortune by understanding and investing in world markets. Although, he started with a sizable family fortune, he earned his PhD in economics from Wharton, studied further in Europe and Asia, and returned to Boston where he proceeded to parlay his inheritance from millions to billions. Although he took his investments seriously, he was still more interested in the chase, rather than the catch.

The second reason was that he could clearly see the economic impact of the Chinese infiltration. The American stock markets were suffering, American industry was being sabotaged and skimmed by the Chinese, and the world economic balance was becoming unbalanced. As an investment banker, many of Adler's positions were threatened. He clearly saw the cause as well as the effect. If the Chinese were not stopped, his billions would dwindle to mere millions. He strode to the center of the presentation area and glared at the audience.

"If what I say shocks you, so be it," he began. "It's time this country gets shocked back to reality. For some time now, I have tried to warn our nation's leaders of what I am going to say. I only hope this group will listen better than they have. Let me tell you some things about today's world economy. Financially, America is no longer the dominant force in the world!

"The Chinese intended to be that dominant force by the midpoint in the century. But the AIDS problem and their population burden held them back. They still have the potential, and their leaders intend for this to happen, but they have elected to enhance their gross national product through acquisition, rather than by internal growth. Their spread and hegemony throughout the Orient should have been our first sign. Even in areas where they have not taken over politically, they have financially. The best example of that is Japan. Fifty years ago, Japan was a major player in the world economy. They began to slump in the early 2000's and by 2025, the petroleum shortage stopped their commerce, and without a real alternative like nuclear power, they were powerless (no pun intended) to compete. Today, Japan is still a political entity, but they rely very heavily on China for financial support.

"So, who is the leader in world economics? Well, there are four political entities vying for that honor. The United States is one. Our country took over from the United Kingdom after World War II and held the position for nearly a century. China and its stepchildren such as Taiwan are another. Yet, despite its dramatic rise in economic power, it lacks the sophistication and clout to be called 'Number One.' The Amalgamated States of South America have made great strides in curbing their inflation and binding together, but they have not duplicated the progress of the European Union. So, who is the top economic power in the world today? It is clearly the United Nations of Europe (UNE), formally called the European Union. How is that? I'm glad you asked. Let's look at this in more depth.

"The synthesis of language across the Internet and all communication media facilitated the real unification of Europe. By gravitating to a 'virtual common language' members of the European Union became psychologically, as well as financially, unified by about 2015. The common currency was important, the common leadership and government were important, but it was the identification with the common language that broke down the final barriers to unification. Member states of the EU still have their ethnicity, their traditions, and their loyalties. But these traits are not nearly as strong, nor are individual countries as fiercely nationalistic, as they once were. The result is that school children of the fifth decade in Paris refer to themselves as Europeans first and French second.

"As you know, the UNE government is a loose union of states, much like the Soviet Union of the previous century. However, each state has representation in the central government and each state has membership interspersed through the various cabinets that have been established. The head of state, called the Euro Premier, rotates through an electoral process conducted by a tri-cameral legislature. They are about to adopt a very powerful constitution that will raise their unification to a new level—and their economic strength to new heights.

"America, with its 450 million people, is still a formidable economic force in the world. Also, South America, with its recently unified member states, is becoming an economic threat. They are about where Europe was forty years ago. Their nationalistic forces have not yet been overcome to the extent necessary to create a meaningful block of economic solidarity.

"So, it is Europe with its 800 million people, highly sophisticated workers, technologically superior equipment and methods, and most importantly, all pulling together, that drives the world economy. They have ousted America as champion, but are eyeing both China and South America as up-and-coming contenders.

"Why China picked on the United States instead of Europe is not totally clear to me. I think it has more to do with our favorable political system than anything else. Also, the UNE is getting stronger economically, while the United States is getting weaker. I'll give you the analogy of the lion pack attacking the herd of water buffalo. They don't pick on the strongest bull if there is a sick calf to be had. Not that America is a sick calf, but our economic movement has been downward since the Petroleum Wars and the UNE's has been upward. Couple that with our 'welcome with open arms' political system, and I think the Chinese saw us as ripe for the picking. So far they have been right."

With that, Dr. Adler abruptly ended his remarks and sat down.

"Thank you, Dr. Adler, for your incisive remarks," Governor Miller interrupted the smattering of polite applause that escorted Conrad Adler to his seat. "Next we have another expert to expand your background knowledge."

Earlier, I noticed a newcomer had arrived in the room. He looked to be middle-aged, quite sophisticated, and he apparently was acquainted with a number of the group. I noticed those who seemed to know him regarded him with an air of respect.

"Ladies and gentlemen," the governor began, "Let me present the nation's leading authority on Chinese history, politics, and philosophy, Dr. P. Aidan Moore from Louisiana State University."

Dr. Moore was about fifty, but was in excellent shape. His long brown hair framed a handsome face that had both an air of seriousness and a twinkle of humor. His boyish dimples belied his age and added to his charm. He wore a loose-fitting, custom-tailored climate suit, no necktie, and a broad smile. As he strode toward the front of the room, he stopped to greet many of the people at the table. When he reached the front, he shook hands with the governor and then, to my surprise, embraced Poppies in a bear hug.

The audience was at first astounded, but then amused when Dr. Moore said, "Ladies and gentlemen, for those of you who are wondering, I should tell you that David Eagleton is my cousin and it has taken this challenge to bring us together for the first time in over thirty years." There were more smiles and a round of applause. I was in shock.

Dr. Moore then began his address. "Your governor has asked me to come here to give you a rundown on, not what has happened—my cousin has just done that— but to tell you why it happened. Let's review a little history."

Dr. Moore wasted no time in going right to the subject. The audience had barely caught their breath from the introduction. Now they would be challenged to keep up with a fast-paced tutorial on several decades of Chinese history and its significance on the War of Infiltration.

"The Chinese have always been a strongly nationalistic people. Going back to the days when Mongol hordes fought on the steppes of Manchuria and continuing through the various regional and world wars of the nineteenth and twentieth centuries, China held together. So my point here is, when confronted by a number of potentially fracturing forces, it should be no surprise that China always looked for a way to retain their national integrity. They would do this even if it came at the expense of the United States. Let's explore this in more detail.

"I contend that war has been a way of life for China over the centuries. I mentioned the continuous struggle between the warlords of the first and second millennia, but let us look more recently. I could go back further in time, but I think the case can be clearly made by studying the twentieth and twenty-first centuries. Let's start in 1900—right after the first Sino-Japanese War of 1895 had ended.

"During the first half of the twentieth century, China experienced a revolutionary war that brought down the Manchu dynasty, an imperialistic regime that had held power, as had others, for thousands of years before. Never content, they fought a series of military battles to establish a preeminent leader. Despite the emergence of strong men such as Chiang Kai Shek and Mao Tse Tung, that really never happened then. Numerous competing military commanders, who sought to establish dominance, replaced the warlords. The result was a series of civil wars that ravaged the country.

"Around 1920, the Chinese Nationalist Party, called the KMT, had developed enough strength to defeat the warlords and unify most of the country. However, they could only do this by aligning with the newly formed Chinese Communist Party, called the CCP. They might have succeeded in their goal of unification, but the difference in political ideals, along with the inherent competition between the two parties, broke the tenuous alliance apart.

"Enter Japan. The Japanese seized Manchuria in the early nineteen thirties which lead directly to the Sino-Japanese War in 1937. That was followed by World War II, during which China became a victim of further Japanese imperialism and aggression. Still, the Chinese held together and, although out-gunned and out-witted, they fought a war of attrition. They simply had more people than the Japanese had bullets. The KMT and CCP again agreed to pool their forces to oppose the Japanese. Despite their ideological differences, their loyalty to Mother China was supreme. They formed unholy alliances, they fought unconventional warfare, and they did what they had to do to save their nation.

"Do you hear what I'm saying? When conventional war would not work, could not be won, they resorted to other means of warfare. In the face of superior forces and a formidable enemy, they resorted to unconventional means and they endured. There is a parallel here. Don't miss it.

"In due course, World War II became history. After the defeat of Japan and the expulsion of Japanese forces from China, the fragile alliance between the KMT and the CCP fractured and the two parties took up where they had left off before. Chang Kai Shek and his KMT party were ultimately defeated and banished to Taiwan and the Communists took over Mainland China in 1949.

"So, which side did the United States choose to support? Of course, it was the side that holed up in the comparatively tiny island of Taiwan, not the government that controlled a quarter of the world's population on the giant landmass of Mainland China. We know why we did not choose to back the Communist regime, so it should be no surprise that our action did not endear us to them. It is just one more reason why they would have no scruples about raiding our resources in California and elsewhere today.

"Okay, so much for the first half of the twentieth century."

I thought I detected a sigh of relief from the audience and perhaps Dr. Moore saw it too.

"Let's take a standing break while I catch my breath. If you need to use the facilities, we'll reconvene in about ten minutes." Multiple conversations began among conferees, but I didn't see anyone leave the room.

I had spent a great deal of time during the first part of the conference looking around and trying to figure out who the people at the meeting were and what they represented. Although it was a diverse assembly, with numerous ethnic groups represented, it occurred to me that one fellow just didn't look like he belonged. His title stated he was an associate of Ambassador Gruenberg, but he was of Italian descent and seemed to be uncomfortable during Poppies' remarks. His name was Paulo Moreno. His polite applause at the end of all the speeches and his ever-present scowl caught my attention. I didn't dwell on it until I saw him hastily leave the room at the break when Ambassador Gruenberg was speaking with Poppies.

A few minutes later, Mr. Moreno returned accompanied by two security guards who were admonishing him for having circumvented the security checkpoint that had been established to control entry and exit to the meeting. He feigned ignorance, but the rules had been made quite clear in the earlier briefings. Things seemed to quiet down but I had an uneasy feeling.

Several minutes later, during the in-place break, I felt the need to relieve myself, so I eased out into the corridor and passed through the security checkpoint. I was the only person in the restroom, or so I thought, until I heard a muffled voice coming from the end stall next to mine.

The restroom was typical of those in modern buildings of the mid twenty-first century, in that the user had complete privacy. Stalls were completely enclosed and virtually soundproof. I normally would have ignored the muffled muttering, but something told me not to. I quickly switched my cyber bracelet to "Record" and pointed the receiver in the direction of the adjacent stall. I still couldn't make out what was being said and it only lasted a minute or so. I knew the cyber bracelet recording was much more acute than the human ear, so I could listen to the recording later. I heard the door to the stall open and close and I peeked out to see my Italian-looking friend quickly leaving the restroom.

Although he hadn't seen me, I followed him out into the corridor. I expected him to return through the security checkpoint, but he did not. Instead, he waited until the guards were distracted and started to reenter the room without going through the checkpoint. It took me only a few seconds to get to the guards. I asked if everyone attending the meeting was required to pass through the checkpoint each time they entered or left the meeting. The response was "absolutely," because the automatic detection equipment would know if any privileged information were being taken in or out. Also, it kept a record of who was in the meeting and when.

"So why is that gentleman not using the checkpoint?" I asked, pointing to the Italian.

The guards whirled around and caught a glimpse of Mr. Moreno going through the conference room door. "That's the same fellow who tried to break security a few minutes ago," one guard said to the other.

In short order the guards had entered the conference room and approached the Italian. Their presence and the slight disturbance that ensued brought the meeting to a halt. Even though Dr. Moore had not resumed his address, Governor Miller had returned to the front of the room to quiet it down. Mr. Moreno was irate. Ambassador Gruenberg was embarrassed.

The guards were about to accept the Italian's explanation that he was simply in a hurry to return to the meeting when I began to listen to my cyber bracelet recording. It hadn't picked up all of the conversation, but I had enough to realize that the Italian had been passing sensitive information on his microcom. I moved to the conference audio-visual control panel and spoke to the visualator-center operator.

"I have been asked to have you put this transcript on everyone's visualator immediately," I blurted out.

213

The visualator-center operator was as belligerent as he was lazy and he just looked at me. "I need written authorization for everything I do," he replied with a sneer, "and I certainly don't take orders from snot-nosed kids."

Now I was mad, but I remembered what Poppies had taught me. "Keep your cool and outwit the nitwits you have to deal with."

I calmly replied as I turned to leave, "Have it your way. If you would rather have Governor Miller give you the order, I'm certainly willing to let him know how cooperative you've been." I wasn't brutally sarcastic but the inference was there. Then, I started to move in the direction of the governor. I kept one eye on the fracas with Mr. Moreno and I watched the visualator-center operator with the other.

"Okay, kid, what you got?" I smiled to myself that my bluff had worked. It wasn't exactly a lie but I did what I had to do to garner the support of the numbskull running the visualator center.

"Just download the A/V packet from this device," I said, holding up my cyber bracelet.

The operator took one look at it and effortlessly plugged my cyber bracelet into the panel using a wireless connection. Immediately, on everyone's visualator screen and in everyone's audio system, flashed the words the Italian had uttered in the restroom. The digital read out showed the call had been to California. The identity of the person being called was encrypted, but the treason was obvious.

The message played out, "…and they know about the Chinese movement. I will transmit names of attendees on my next transmission. Governor Miller is in charge, but a man named Eagleton is giving them most of the information. I have to get back now, but I'll provide more updates later. This is trouble and we must do something quickly. Moreno out."

I had left the visualator center by the time the message was finished. Two more guards appeared from nowhere and Mr. Moreno was abruptly escorted out of the room. The chief security agent whispered something to Governor Miller and the governor nodded. It was the last we saw of the Italian. Governor Miller confided quickly with Ambassador Gruenberg and they both nodded their agreement.

Governor Miller again stepped to the helm of the conference. "What you have just witnessed proves the statements by Mr. Eagleton that we are indeed facing a dire situation. Ambassador Gruenberg has assured me that he is shocked and appalled by what has happened. It only demonstrates that in our open society, we can never be too careful. Our enemies can gain easy access. The very nature of our political system and one of the strengths of our government is, at the same time, an inherent weakness when infiltration is involved.

"I told you earlier that we needed security at these proceedings. Now, I hope those of you who scoffed are believers. In any event, we must hope that Mr. Moreno's call did not do extensive damage and we will prosecute Mr. Moreno to the fullest extent.

"For now it is vital that we get on with the meeting and with Dr. Moore's remarks, but first I want to acknowledge the quick thinking and action of young David John Eagleton. D.J., your perception of the situation uncovered a traitor and no doubt has saved all of us a great deal of trouble. Thank you."

At that time the people at the conference stood and applauded. I blushed and tried to ease back in my seat without any further fanfare. I caught Poppies' eye as I sat down and could not escape seeing his proud smile and approving wink. I felt good.

Dr. Moore resumed his address.

"The second half of the twentieth century saw a newly empowered communist Chinese government take up arms against, arguably the strongest nation in the world—the United States. Their surprise entry into the Korean Conflict sent a number of signs to the western world.

"First, here was a gigantically populous nation, flexing its muscles in a show of support for one of its idealistic allies. Second, here was another communist

216

movement, not closely aligned with the Soviet Union, to be reckoned with by the West. Third, while the methodology of warfare they used in Korea looked to be conventional, in reality, it was little more than using hordes of infantry to overrun the undermanned Allied positions.

"Once again, they were willing to employ their armies, and their troops were willing to die for their country and now for a new ideology. This is a powerful motivator and should not go unnoticed. It set the tone for the rest of the century. And, it is one more reason for the War of Infiltration.

"The world emerged from the Korean Conflict, none the worse for wear. The United States felt satisfied that the North Koreans had been thwarted in their attempt to claim the entire peninsula, and we were very happy to declare a truce and resume our business at home. We had saved the world from Communism, at least in Korea.

"China, on the other hand, came away with some bigger prizes and valuable lessons as well. First, they had taken on the West, principally the United States, and held them to a draw. Second, they understood how abhorrent it was to us to pursue a wider war. In the face of centuries of invasions by the Japanese and others, this was a major revelation. Third, they realized that to be a truly dominant world power, they needed a number of things.

217

"They needed modern armies. Their millions of troops could be a liability in a different kind of war. Also, they needed an economy and an industry that would sustain a war, whether it be a war of offense or defense. Mainly, they learned that the key to joining the top echelon of nations was to get a seat at the nuclear table.

"To do all these things would take time. But, inherently, the Chinese are a patient people and they were determined. So they spent the rest of the twentieth century building modern armies, establishing a competitive economy, and developing nuclear weapons. They did this even if it meant befriending an old enemy, such as the United States. Americans rejoiced when President Nixon became the first American head of state to visit China. We embraced the trade treaties that pretended to normalize relations between the two nations. We shuddered when they joined the nuclear club, but we still regarded all their capabilities as archaic. We were content to let them grow technologically and economically, thinking all the time that we could co-exist. Besides, we had other crosses to bear.

"First and foremost among those mid twentieth-century challenges was the Soviet Union. China saw our contention with the Soviets as their best means to buy time. They watched and grew stronger as we struggled and grew weaker. Then, we threw in the Vietnam War as another 'resource depleter.' That, along with uprisings in the Middle East, Africa,

Central Europe, and South America cast the United States as the world's policeman and protector of democratic and pseudo-democratic societies. Ultimately we emerged supreme in our struggle with the Soviet Union, but to some extent we lost sight of the Chinese rise to the center of the world stage.

"Now let's move to the twenty-first century.

"At the start of this century, China had attained the goals she had set fifty years earlier. After having lain docile for over fifty years, she was about to flex her military muscles again and lay claim to Taiwan, but before she could launch her armies, the religious wars erupted in the Middle East. The United States and the Western Allies were so consumed by those conflicts, the fight over oil, and the impact on our economies, that we barely noticed when China began to blockade shipping in the China Sea.

"We were preoccupied when China launched an airborne nuclear test perfectly aimed to direct an electromagnetic pulse (EMP) wave at Taipei in 2018. The nuclear portion of the blast was a non-event, but the EMP was devastating. The satellite-launched blast and subsequent pulse fried computer systems throughout the city, shutting down the government, transportation, and most of the economy for weeks. The already weak Taiwanese leadership was ripe for a coup d'etat. They myopically were expecting overthrow from within for months and had lowered their exterior guard.

"All of those conditions gave China the courage she needed and she moved into Taiwan in 2020. It wasn't an armed invasion; it was more like a move in. This was an important signal to the Chinese leadership. After having gone through the agony of conventional wars throughout their history, they concluded that walking in and taking over, in what amounted to a bloodless coup, was a far superior option. I think that actually gave them the idea to use 'bloodless' warfare again. Of course, as you know, the first thing the Chinese did was to rename Taiwan. It is once again known as the island of Formosa. I wonder if they plan on renaming California?

"Whether they consciously planned to 'invade' the United States as they have or not, is subjective. Two things probably impacted that decision more than anything. The Petroleum Wars were the first factor. Not only did those wars remove an energy source for the United States, it did so for China as well. And they could afford it less than we could. Their solar and other energy options were not nearly as far along in 2035 as were ours. In one sense, they blamed us for having destroyed the world's petroleum.

"However, I contend that there was a second factor that was equally important in their decision-making. That was the AIDS epidemic that threatened to decimate their people in the mid 2020's. Before we get into this, I propose we all take another break."

Dr. Moore, or Uncle Aidan, as I would soon begin to call him, realized that he had just saturated a number of very good minds with his history lesson and explanation of what led the Chinese to stage their infiltration invasion. This was his way to give them a chance to reflect and get their minds positioned to accept the challenge he was going to give them in his finale.

Hesitantly, I approached Dr. Moore who had just begun talking to Poppies. Before I could clear my throat, he turned to me and said, "I'll bet this is the brave young man I have heard so much about. Are you D.J. the third?"

I rarely was caught off guard these days with all that had happened, but this was one of those times. I could only stammer that I was, indeed, David John Eagleton III and it was an honor to meet a new relative. Both Poppies and Uncle Aidan laughed.

Uncle Aidan said that he was supposed to fly back to Baton Rouge that evening, but he would cancel his flight because he wanted an opportunity to spend more time with Poppies and me. I was thrilled. I had learned more about China in the past hour than in my past fourteen years. I was beginning to understand why the Chinese had come. Now I wanted to know what we Americans were going to do about it.

After calling the group back to order in the conference room, Dr. Moore resumed his lecture.

"Of course, the Chinese motivation to infiltrate and invade the United States can also be attributed to the AIDS epidemic. As you will recall, just prior to the turn of the century, AIDS had claimed the lives of over 22 million people, worldwide. In the next two decades, over 60 million died of AIDS in Africa alone. While there was a leveling off of infections in the United States and Europe, the spread of the virus in the most underdeveloped countries exploded. China was among countries such as Botswana, Zimbabwe, and even Russia, where new cases of HIV infection began doubling every year. Worldwide, the scourge had become the fastest-growing epidemic in ancient or modern history. By 2040, Africa had lost another 100 million to AIDS and the continent had become a pariah among the nations of the world. Visitation to the sub-Sahara had all but ceased and, had it not been for strict measures taken in Egypt and the northern rim countries, all of Africa would have become a human wasteland.

"The spread in China continued unabated until the first early vaccines began to show promise in the early forties. Still, it was estimated that there were a half a billion people with the virus in China alone in 2041. That was one in four.

"Our ratio was much better, but it still was a drain on the United States economy. We had led the world in research and treatment, but in the face of scarce resources, we treated our folks first. Further, we set up a quarantine system to protect us from the outside. The United States had implemented a comprehensive program to preclude a Chinese or any HIV-infected immigrant from coming into the country as early as 2011, but the need to treat the afflicted masses in China, led Premier Chan We Chung to seek out technology and financial resources. He first looked to Europe, but they were suffering as well. Obviously Africa and the sub-Sahara were off limits and the Middle East was virtually destitute once their oil was gone. He had little recourse but to undertake the assault of California, other wealthy locations in the United States, and elsewhere."

The assembled group of leaders and scholars were nodding their heads as if to signify their understanding of what was said. Uncle Aidan took a breath and began his wind up.

"Ladies and gentlemen, the Chinese believe they were forced to take on California and the United States. Just as they were forced to fight a war of attrition against the Japanese a hundred years ago, they became convinced that America was their enemy and should be opposed.

"Moreover, they became convinced that America was the cause of their problems because we ruined the oil deposits and we didn't do enough to solve their AIDS situation. In their minds, we owed them. In addition, we were the logical targets because, (1) we are their ideological opposite, (2) we killed many of their ancestors in the Korean War, and (3) we had the money and technology they needed. Furthermore, as they had learned from their bloodless takeover of Taiwan, they could fight and defeat their enemies in a new and different way.

"These reasons and this historical rationale are why we have lost California and possibly other states and why we are here today. I submit that the direction of history is not yet set. It can be diverted and in some cases, it can be reversed. California is only lost if we allow it to be. I further submit that if we allow things to progress as we have, their appetite for power and resources will increase. I don't know what state is next on their list, but I assure you Colorado is on it somewhere.

"I'm going to turn the lectern over to Governor Miller now, but I want to leave you with one challenge. Our great nation began with the resolve and action of a few patriots sitting around a table in Philadelphia almost three hundred years ago. Our great nation can begin again with the resolve and action of a few patriots who are sitting around a table in Denver today. We know the enemy, we know why, now we must determine how to react. Thank you for your attention."

The group rose to their feet and applause filled the room. Uncle Aidan took a seat next to Poppies. Governor Miller took the helm. He thanked Uncle Aidan profusely for his insight and for clarifying the issue before the group.

Then he issued his challenge. "There will be more speakers tomorrow. I am asking you to remain here in Denver as my guests. All expenses will be covered by the State of Colorado. What I want you to do is to put together an action plan to counter this act of war by China. I realize it is insidious and surreptitious, so much so that we are being defeated without realizing it. Well, now we do realize it. I challenge each of you to reach back into your considerable minds and experience and come up with a road map we can use to beat these folks and reclaim our nation.

"I have asked my lieutenant governor, Jim Martin, to be the leader and coordinator of your efforts. He, not only can serve to channel your ideas, he is in a position to cut through any red tape you might encounter. Thank you and good luck. All our futures depend on it."

The meeting had taken virtually the entire day. Cocktails and dinner were arranged for the members who would remain and, though they were invited, Poppies and Uncle Aidan were not part of the "think tank" that had been organized. We stayed a short while for cocktails, nibbled some hors d'oeuvres, and departed about dusk for the chalet. Poppies and Uncle Aidan had thirty years to catch up on.

CHAPTER FIFTEEN

FAMILY REUNION

I was half dozing as we cruised down I-25 from
Denver to Colorado Springs. Again, I watched with
admiration and awe as we passed the U. S. Air and
Space Academy. The air was filled with craft of all
kinds as each cadet received their own personal
gyrocopter once they had completed their "doolie"
year. No one in the family had entered the military
since Great-Great-Grandfather Moore had attended the
Academy when it was first getting started. Maybe
military life would be good for me, I thought. Then I
drifted off to sleep with visions of wearing the
incredibly handsome flying suits, and boring up
through the stratosphere at mach ten, thus saving the
nation from enemies, real and imagined.

I awoke to hear Poppies and Uncle Aidan flitting from
subject to subject as they attempted to reconstruct the
past thirty years for each other. We zoomed along
Route I-25 attached to the auto net, and Poppies and
Uncle Aidan were covering the thirty years at
breakneck speed. Uncle Aidan said he had not visited
my great-grandparents in years.

As I listened to their conversation I found that he had
traveled extensively pursuing answers to questions
most people had not thought of. He was more than a
historian. His numerous other degrees and fields of

study had interwoven to make him the foremost advisor to corporations, international combines, and even heads of state. Those seeking to profit from and control world markets and destinies sought his insight into economics, political science, and international relations. He was also more than an intellectual; he was a pragmatist with a gift to predict how the various global forces would work together to bring about change.

Following his graduation from LSU, Uncle Aidan had taken a job in Korea. He worked directly with the United Nations Arbitration Board that was charged with facilitating the reunification of the two Koreas. Although the board chairman received most of the credit, it came out later that it was young Philip Aidan Moore who envisioned and orchestrated many of the key aspects of that union. Apparently, it was those successes that whetted his appetite for more of that sort of thing. He had never married, which wasn't all that unusual these days.

I woke up just as we pulled into the chalet driveway. Great-Grandmother Kniest was waiting inside the airlock. Poppies had called her shortly after we left Denver to let her know there would be one more family member for dinner. We had covered the 250-kilometer trip in just over an hour. She ran out to meet us and threw her arms around Uncle Aidan. He stood about 191 centimeters, but she pulled him down to her level for a big hug. He was her only nephew and she called him Philip.

Although all three of us were extremely tired from the fast-paced day, her warmth and the smell of home cooking rejuvenated us. She had whipped up her specialty, lasagna. Uncle Aidan said it was like old times when he used to visit her and Great-Grandfather Tom in St. Louis, Missouri. He was still in college at LSU, but frequently found time to make the journey up the Mississippi to visit his grandparents. Great-Great-Grandpa Moore and his wife, Sharon, lived just outside St. Louis in Illinois. While he was there, he would always spend some time with his aunt and uncle too. They still worked for Boeing Air and Space Corporation, and the infrastructure needed to create weapons systems was another of Aidan's varied interests. So Great-Grandfather Tom arranged plant tours that showed Uncle Aidan how Boeing planned, designed, and built air and spacecraft.

Uncle Aidan's father and mother had retired some twenty-five years ago to a posh senior citizen center in Gulfport, Mississippi. Great-Uncle Tony had been quite successful in the finance business and had risen to CEO of a finance company in Baton Rouge. He and his wife, Suzanne, were spending their golden years playing golf and traveling around the world. They developed a liking for cruise ships, but they would never take any of the space cruises on the satellite network. They were content to venture out on the ocean only.

Uncle Aidan could only spend the one night, as he had to fly to Chicago to meet with someone in the Department of State the next afternoon. I learned later that it was John Spencer, the Secretary of State himself, that Uncle Aidan was meeting. The government was sending an official gyrocopter to the chalet to pick him up for a connection at Peterson Field and Spaceport.

Before he left, he and Poppies had one more serious conversation. "There is one more thing you should be aware of that I couldn't disclose yesterday," Uncle Aidan lowered his voice. "There were federal government reps in attendance and one never knows who can be trusted and who can't these days, but that is particularly true with the Feds. One fellow at the meeting was from National Security and reports almost directly to the Office of the President. I was surprised that Scott Miller brought them in, but I guess he knew he would need their help sooner or later.

"At any rate, President-elect Chae may not be a totally reliable ally. She has held political offices at many levels over the years and her credentials look impeccable, but there are a number of Americans who are wary of her. As you know, she is of Korean extraction and is a second-generation American citizen. Nevertheless she is Oriental and just may have leanings toward the Chinese. I can't substantiate any of what I am saying now, but I'll keep you posted if anything changes."

President Yun Mi Chae was the first Oriental woman to be elected President of the United States. Although there had been two female presidents before her, both were WASP's and neither had distinguished herself as a great statesperson. So, that was one reason the nation was stunned when Mrs. Chae won the election with votes to spare.

This was the second election held without the involvement of the Electoral College, which had been legislated out of existence just prior to the election of 2044. Why Senator Frank Nunn, the Democratic candidate and front-runner until a week before the election, did not win was still being analyzed in Chicago.

After Uncle Aidan had gone, Poppies received a microcom call from Denver. It was Scott Miller. I could only hear Poppies' end of the conversation, but I got the drift. Governor Miller was telling him that the ad hoc group had finished their work and had developed both a plan and a list of action items to be done. One of those items was to do what Poppies had been doing for weeks—spread the word to the people. Governor Miller wanted Poppies to spearhead that effort in Colorado and in Chicago. There would be a small staff of support assigned to him to arrange transportation, set up the schedule, and handle administrative details. In addition, Poppies would not have to beat the brush to find groups to address. The Governor's office would handle that.

It was exactly what Poppies knew had to be done, and he wanted to do it, but he wanted to get back to his hunt for Grammy too. He was torn. Ultimately, he told the Governor he would do it for no more than six months. Then he would need to return to California. Scott Miller replied that, in six months, he hoped a phalanx of people would be going to California.

CHAPTER SIXTEEN

THE CHALET

Poppies left the next day and I didn't see much of him for many weeks. He came back to the chalet for Christmas, but the rest of the time I was privileged to be alone with Great-Grandma Kniest and Great-Grandpa Tom. I had plenty of schoolwork to keep me busy plus the winter snowfall had filled the pastures and hillsides around the chalet. We spent a great deal of time indoors and going to and from the barns to tend the horses and the cars that Great-Grandpa Tom thought needed as much care as the horses.

On the rare days that Great-Grandpa Tom could make the walk, we'd stroll down the path and walk around his car barn. This wasn't as much a barn as it was a museum. True enough, the outside looked like a simple barn. Inside was a different story. Great-Grandpa Tom had decorated each stall to mesh with the vintage automobile he had collected. His pride and joy were Ford Mustangs of around the turn of the century. He had cared for each one personally through the years and now they were his legacy to his family and anyone else who had the interest to come and see them.

He took me to each of the thirty-plus stalls and gave me a short history on how and when he acquired each car, what it cost, what it was worth today, how fast it would go, and so forth. But I knew he would never sell one. In the past, he had entered many of his treasures in car shows. And, according to Poppies, he nearly always won first place. I didn't know much about car history, but I could tell Great-Grandpa Tom did. One day I asked him to tell me more about the history of the automobile and how it had evolved over the years. I sat back and listened keenly.

Great-Grandpa Tom said, "I don't have enough time on this earth to give you the whole story, but I'll try to give you a thumbnail sketch of what has happened since I first got interested in cars. That was back in the late nineteen hundreds. At least that was when I could afford to have my first car for show. I'll never forget it. It was a 1989 Mustang. Red, dual exhausts, not a scratch, except for one time when your great-grandmother decided to take it in and have a security system installed as a surprise birthday gift. I loved her for doing it, but I hated the scratch that the yokels put in the paint."

He stopped in front of an old 1999 Mustang and sat down on the bench. The stall was filled with memorabilia from that era. A CD player still played old songs of 1999. On a shelf sat a laptop computer, long since unable to compute. "Car and Driver" magazines of that era graced a coffee table and an old time color television, also not working, was in the corner. The screen was only thirty-five inches and I was told there was no three-dimension capability at all.

"This was the first car that I bought new after we were married. Your grandfather was only about eleven at the time. It won a lot of prizes too. But let me get back to your question."

Great-Grandpa Tom closed his eyes as if to better visualize the past and began to talk. "In my day, cars were it. They were the way people got around. Highways and something called freeways were everywhere, and you could go from coast to coast by car if you wanted to. Gasoline stations were plentiful and gas only cost a little over a buck a gallon. That was before the metric system became the standard of the land. Anyway, highway departments built roads like crazy. I drove to work every day and your great-grandmother took her car too. No one thought it would ever end."

He stopped as if to let a few years drift by. "By 2029, the Petroleum Wars had virtually exhausted the supply of affordable gasoline. Fifteen years earlier, the hybrid automobile began to flourish, first as a gas-electric hybrid, and later as a hydrogen-electric vehicle. The advances in gas-electric cars had raised the gas mileage to 200 miles per gallon (back in the days when they still used English measurements instead of metric). But even that was insufficient to make continued use of a gas-driven internal combustion engine economical.

"The price of gasoline had risen to $75 per gallon, but the future of that fuel was doomed as each year, fewer and fewer barrels of oil were refined. Part of the shortage was because the supply of fossil fuels simply ran out. However, a bigger part was the total waste of those supplies before and during the Petroleum Wars. I can remember back in the days when gas-powered automobiles consumed a gallon of gasoline for every twenty miles driven.

"People kept building cars and roads like there was no oil shortage and by 2011, the ratio of cars to people in most developed countries was one to one. In the United States, the personal car had replaced the family sedan for most of the driving, although it was commonplace for a family to have a car for each member plus a van or sports utility vehicle for family trips. The Petroleum Wars did not diminish the desire for that standard of living, but how the 'need' was met changed considerably."

"I always had seen pictures of people going on long vacations in cars, but we never did. Why?" I asked.

"Well, cost was one reason, but there were many other factors. But let me continue." Great-Grandpa Tom felt most comfortable tackling one subject at a time. "The PC, or personal car, began to develop as a result of traffic congestion. Manufacturers and traffic authorities got together and found that a smaller, narrower car would permit double the vehicles on a given lane. So traffic lanes began to be designated for PC's only. Two abreast on a normal twelve-foot-wide lane could be easily and safely done. That, along with the auto-directional navigation systems, informally called the "drive net," allowed an even higher traffic density.

"The auto-directional navigation system (ANS) was designed for commuters, but was later extended to the open road. The system contained a transmitter and interlock device that permitted the driver to turn the steering, braking, and overall operation of the PC to a computerized traffic system. By voice-dialing in the origin and destination, the PC would be 'remotely driven' by the system. The driver could snooze or simply enjoy the scenery. A few minutes before reaching the destination, the auto-nav system would alert the driver and verify that the vehicle was ready to return to manual operation.

"It was quite similar to the aircraft autopilot system of the twentieth century, except that it was much more sophisticated. For example, PC's would be staggered no further than ten meters from each other as they paraded down the freeway at speeds of one hundred forty kilometers per hour. When a PC needed to be switched to manual operation, the ANS would transfer the PC to a transition lane where lower speeds and greater vehicle spacing were required.

"PC's with hydrogen-electric engines were totally emission free and could be used as a source of electricity for other uses. For example, they could be used to run power tools at a remote location or supply power to your home in an emergency. They used solar-hydride batteries that, not only received charge from the sun (the entire automobile surface was a series of solar panels comprising a mosaic), but also from the braking operation.

"It was called regenerative braking. During braking, the electric side captured energy previously expended by the propulsion side in accelerating the PC. Acting much like an old-time generator, the electric motor would activate whenever braking was employed. The motor helped slow the car, a sort of downshifting, and it stored the kinetic energy from the PC's forward momentum, using it to recharge the batteries.

"A far cry from the old gas-guzzlers of the twentieth century, the PC's of 2040 were as close to perpetual motion as man had advanced thus far. The combination of the highly efficient, low weight solar-hydride batteries used for the electric motor, the solar panels making up the car exterior, and the solid-state high density hydrogen pellets used for the hydrogen engine resulted in a car that could go for fifty thousand kilometers before new pellets were needed. The batteries needed little or no attention, unless the regenerative braking system had malfunctioned, in which case, solar alone would not maintain the charge. That happened rarely."

"But people still have cars," I piped up. "Uncle Max loaned us his Stetsen 5000 to come back here."

"Yes, but do you know what a Stetson 5000 costs these days?" Great-Grandpa Tom asked, knowing I didn't.

I admitted I had no idea and was summarily rebuked as a wet nose kid by Great-Grandpa Tom as he said, "Well, Deej, that little jewel lists for 560 thousand. So, I guess your Uncle Max has a pretty decent job there in Reno."

"What makes them so expensive," I asked.

"Back in my heyday, you could get that same car for around fifty grand. I remember a Lexus your great-grandmother owned that cost about that much. We didn't realize how cheap that was. Of course, as time went by, luxury accessories and mandatory safety features drove the cost up.

"For example, cars of fifty years ago didn't have the virtual cocoon envelopes (VCE's) around each passenger the way they are today. Fifty years ago, the best we had were something called seat belts and air bags. Cars then had computers to perform menial tasks but the evolution to today's 'smart' car didn't really begin until about 2020. Computer-controlled systems keep your wheels on the road under the worst conditions so skids are non-existent. Heads-up displays keep you abreast of all systems when you are driving manually. All controls are voice-activated. Can you imagine the old days when we had to reach down and dial in a radio station? Automobile accidents used to kill thousands of people every year. Today, it's almost impossible to get into an accident. The computers won't let you. Even if you do, the VCE will keep you from getting a scratch."

I sensed Great-Grandpa Tom could wax eloquently on this subject for hours, but he tired easily and I had learned about all I wanted to learn about car history for that day.

I hoped that spring thaw would come a little early in 2053. I had managed to get through most of my first winter of cold and snow. I got through it, but I didn't like it. I suppose I would always be a warm-blooded Californian at heart.

Poppies had continued his visits to the various groups designated by the governor's office. But, I could tell he was becoming impatient. Moreover, he was encountering elements that were resistant. Before, people were either receptive or indifferent. Now he was finding this was no longer the case in some enclaves. He wondered why. Could it be that the tentacles of Chinese influence were reaching Colorado? In late January, he was asked to go to other states and present the message. Kansas, Missouri, Iowa, and Oklahoma were the first to be visited. Later, most of the other Midwestern states were added.

Friday, February 14, 2053, Valentine's Day
Kniest Chalet, Colorado

I was coming back from the car barn after having completed my chores. I wanted to make it a special Valentine's Day for Great-Grandma Kniest. I had gotten up a little early because I had a personal Valentine's Day gift to prepare for her. I had been working on a special project to sort out old family albums and convert them to holographic images. Some of them dated back to the mid nineteen-hundreds. How quaint people looked back then. The girls wore dresses called poodle skirts and the guys all had funny ducktail haircuts. They were all excited about something called Rock and Roll, but I couldn't find any rocks or rolls in any of the photos. I had taken the albums and compact disks and a couple of other media forms up to the small office in the barn. Since neither she nor Great-Grandpa Tom ever went there, that was where I was working to complete the gift.

I finished it about 9:00 a.m. and left the barn headed for a late breakfast. As I approached the chalet airlock, I sensed something was wrong.

Even though the airlock was closed, there was some debris between the inner and outer doors. Nervously, I called out as I passed through the lock. My fears were substantiated as I entered the dining area. There was Great-Grandpa Tom lying on the floor, eyes closed and breathing heavily. I thought at first he had fallen and I called to Great-Grandma Kniest loudly. Then I noticed

241

the laser wound beneath his left temple. I again called for help. Great-Grandpa Tom began to stir, but only barely. I was relieved that he was alive, but I had no idea of what to do next. He had a weak, rapid pulse, a raspy cough and a bad case of incontinence, but he was still breathing. He tried to whisper something to me, but I was so flustered, I didn't grasp what he was trying to say. After a few seconds, I cranked up my microcom and asked for the Colorado Springs Med Evac with as much clarity and coolness as I could muster.

I really don't remember how long it took, but the Med Evac copter showed up rather quickly and went right to work on my great-grandfather. My feeling of relief was totally shattered when the medic asked if there were any others living here. It was then I realized that Great-Grandma Kniest was gone.

It took Poppies less than an hour to get there. He arrived on the heels of the medics and immediately took charge of the situation. The first order of business was to get Great-Grandpa Tom stabilized and into the gyrocopter. As he was being taken through the airlock, Poppies turned to the next priority. "Where is your great-grandmother?" he asked.

I replied that I had not seen her. Immediately, we joined the two cops, who had arrived in the copter, in a room-to-room search. In less than five minutes, we confirmed what I had realized before. She was gone. No doubt, the same people who had lasered Great-

Grandpa Tom had abducted her. Poppies turned to the police and demanded they contact the FBI, as well as all of the state law enforcement authorities.

"What do you mean, you will report this as a missing person?" I heard him yell at the cops. "If you do that, no one will do anything for thirty-six hours, while you boys sit on your asses and fill out paperwork. That's what the California police told me when my wife disappeared. I want every agency that can think, seek, and shoot on this." With that, he microcommed Governor Miller. Both policemen were a little smug when they heard him make the call. Their expressions turned to astonishment and then to trepidation when the governor asked to be put on the visualator on the wall behind them.

His impressive form with the two flags behind him filled the entire screen. Glaring at the two policemen, he said, "I'm directing you two to begin the investigation immediately and I'm going to have your boss and his best people down there in an hour. This is not just any eighty-seven year old woman that's missing. This is the mother of one of the most important men in the nation and he has an important job to do. And that job won't get done until you guys get his mother back. Any questions?" Governor Miller could be very persuasive when he wanted to be. Governor Miller turned his attention to Poppies and expressed sorrow and chagrin that such a thing had happened. The visualator session ended with his offer to do anything that was needed. Poppies could call him day or night.

"Thanks, Scott," said Poppies as he terminated the session. Both policemen had their heads down and were occupied counting the buttons on their shirts.

I know it took longer but it only seemed like a few minutes had passed until the air was filled with gyrocopters. State police, FBI, the local deputy sheriff, and a couple of others all showed up. Poppies demanded to know what law enforcement organization really had authority over the case. They caucused quickly and all agreed that, since an abduction was involved, the FBI would be the lead agency. The FBI would collect the evidence and call for help from the other agencies when needed. Otherwise, they were to remove themselves. The two cops who had been redressed by Governor Miller were only too glad to get out of there.

After the medics and extraneous cops had left, Poppies turned to me and said, "Where were you when the abduction and the shooting happened?"

I told him about being in the car barn working on the Valentine's Day present, but that I had a strange sense that something was wrong even before I saw the airlock and Great-Grandpa Tom on the floor. I told him that I was in the barn for an hour, no more.

Poppies said it was okay and that he needed to get to the hospital to check on Great-Grandpa Tom and to change his schedule for the next few days. I told him to go ahead and I would be fine in the chalet with the two FBI agents that had set up camp in the dining room.

The excitement of this day rivaled that of the gyrocopter "shoot down" and the border crossings put together. I hadn't eaten anything since breakfast and it was nearly eight in the evening. My stomach and my mind were both swirling. I had no appetite. I said good night to the FBI agents and went to my room to go to bed. Despite being bone tired, I couldn't sleep. What had happened? Why? How could someone or some group have come and gone without me hearing anything? I tossed and turned for several hours playing the scenario over in my mind.

Then it hit me. Great-Grandpa Tom had tried to tell me something before he lost consciousness. I didn't understand what he was saying, but perhaps my cyber bracelet had picked it up. The bracelet captured both video and audio continuously and fed it to a downlink. Moreover, it had the ability to filter out noise and to synthesize voice transmissions into data that could subsequently be transmitted wirelessly to any screen and replayed in written or audio form. I jumped out of bed and commanded the bracelet to retrieve all the audio from the previous twelve hours and download it in written form on the screen in the room.

The screen began spewing all kinds of verbiage and I realized I had been talking to myself in the barn. It picked that up, along with the comments I had made aloud while working on the albums. That was good. At least I hadn't disengaged that feature on the cyber bracelet. I commanded it to fast forward to the time I came back from the barn. I was astounded to hear voices that were not mine in the background. I directed the bracelet to filter out the foreground noise and amplify the background. It sounded like someone was saying, "They left us." I transcribed it to the screen. That is exactly what had been said. I checked the corresponding video, but was unable to determine where the voices were coming from.

I continued to listen. Soon my excited breathing and gasping at finding Great-Grandpa Tom was audible. That was followed by my scream of surprise as I rushed to his side. In a few seconds, Great-Grandpa Tom's words were heard. Again, I could not make them out. I adjusted the volume, filtered the competing noise, but they were still garbled. As a last resort, I tried the transcriber.

There it was, clear as day. Great-Grandpa Tom had said. "Kristy–taken to barn!"

I ran from the bedroom to the dining room where the FBI agents had set up their base camp. Both were there, but they were stiff as a board. Someone or something had fried their brains with mind stoppers and then hit them with a nerve destroyer agent. They were alive in body only. I tried not to panic. That meant whoever was responsible for their deaths probably had lasered Great-Grandpa Tom and abducted my great-grandmother. The thought that they were still on the ranch, the FBI agents were dead, and I was the only one around, crossed my mind briefly. My shaking hands got a little relief when I concluded that they must not know I was there. If they did, then surely I would be in the same condition as the two G-men. "Okay," I said to myself, "that is an advantage for me."

I quickly looked around the chalet for any signs they might still be inside. I turned my cyber bracelet up to pick up any extraneous sounds such as breathing and was relieved to find none. Since the previous communication said, "They left us," I concluded there were at least two of them. They probably had returned to the car barn. That is probably where Great-Grandma Kniest was, if she were still alive.

It was obvious these thugs had little regard for human life. They had shot Great-Grandpa Tom with a laser and killed two FBI agents, so if they found me, they wouldn't hesitate to include me in their violence. Still, if my great-grandmother were alive, I had to do something. I tried to remain calm but my knees were shaking and I couldn't catch my breath. I had to assume they had microcom intercept capability and I had to assume they had other means of detecting movement. So I didn't dare make a microcom call. Apparently, whoever brought them to the ranch abandoned them in the middle of the attack and abduction. I didn't know why, but that wasn't important right now.

I took a laser pistol from one of the agents. He wouldn't miss it.

The path to the barn was well lighted, both from the moon that was nearly full and from the security lights that were strategically placed all over the ranch. I hoped the intruders hadn't found the underground passage we used in cases of heavy snowfall. I dared not turn on lights so I went to Poppies' room and pulled out the night-vision goggles he had used to cross the border.

Quietly, I headed down the stairs to the snow tunnel. I guess the flow of adrenalin overcame the cold and my fears because I didn't remember shaking any more. At the other end, I had to raise a trapdoor to enter the barn. It was located just inside the regular entrance, but fortunately it was screened by some of Great-Grandpa Tom's junk. Although there was an automatic opener, I manually pushed up on the hatch until a crack of light beamed through. I could see the entry door, the 2023 Mercedes SL, and the pile of junk, but no thugs. I used my cyber bracelet to search for any audio. At first there was nothing. Then I thought I detected a sound. It was snoring. It sounded like more than one person. I opened the trap door hatch and quietly crawled out.

I wasn't sure where they were, but I thought they were on the ground floor. Carefully, I crawled up the staircase to the second level where I had spent much of the previous afternoon. A catwalk had been constructed along the entire length of the building so visitors could view the displays without having to walk among them. I crawled along the narrow walkway, looking over the rail periodically to see where they might be. About halfway across, I looked to my right. There was Great-Grandma Kniest, bound, gagged, and apparently drugged in one of the storerooms. The door was wide open. She had been tied to a chair and was in a distorted position, but even in the dark, she looked to be alive. My first reaction was one of gratitude and jubilation. My second was how much I hated the people who would treat an old lady that way.

I tried to focus on the problem at hand. I crawled along for about twenty more meters. My knees were getting sore, but I dared not stand up. Then I saw the enemy. There were two of them. One was fast asleep, snoring in the back of a 2009 Mustang convertible. The other was supposed to be standing guard, but he was sitting and dozing, although he cradled a laser rifle in his arms. He appeared to be Oriental, but I couldn't tell about his friend in the back seat.

I had never fired a laser pistol at a human being before. I wasn't sure I could do it then. Still, at that moment, I didn't have the latitude to sort out the ethical and philosophical aspects of the situation. I pointed the laser pistol over the catwalk rail, took aim, and sent a ray of two thousand volt-lumens into the seated sentry.

He was dead before the rifle he was holding hit the concrete.

I then turned my attention to the back seat of the Mustang. The second kidnapper was obviously a sound sleeper. Even though the laser was silent, the sentry had let out a gasp when he was struck and his weapon made a scraping noise as it scooted along the concrete floor. I swung my leg over the rail and dropped to the floor. It was a three-meter drop, but my adrenalin was still flowing and I barely noticed the impact. With no regard for stealth, I ran to the Mustang, arriving just as the man in the backseat began to stir.

I think I said something like, "If you value your life, you will do exactly as I command."

He was still groggy, but quickly coming back to reality. He raised his hands, and I directed him to slowly get out of the car but to keep his hands in the air. "Get face down on the floor and keep your hands on top of your head," I ordered.

"You are just a kid," the man shot back as he began to realize my voice still had an octave or so to go before I could pass as an adult.

I wasn't sure how to respond, so I didn't. I watched in the dimly lit car barn as the man slowly and deliberately dropped to his knees as if to comply with my direction. Then he rolled to his right and came up with something in his hand. I couldn't tell what it was and I was in no position to ask. One burst from the laser pistol caught him in the thigh. Whatever he had in his hand went flying as he grabbed his leg.

"You sonofabitch, you fried my leg!" he exclaimed in obvious agony. Then he passed out.

All at once a wave of relief and weakness came over me. I leaned back on the hood of the Mustang and reflected on what had happened. I was about to be sick when I realized there was much more to do and I couldn't be certain the second man was totally incapacitated.

My microcom call to Poppies caught him en route back to the chalet. I didn't tell him all that had happened just then, only that I had found Great-Grandma and we needed to get her medical attention. He told me to sit tight and he'd be there in fifteen minutes. I wanted to go to Great-Grandmother Kniest but I didn't dare leave my wounded adversary. I thought about tying his hands but the idea of approaching him seemed foolish. He looked to be unconscious, but he could have been playing possum. I kept the laser pistol pointed in his direction and kept my distance.

I tried not to look at the man I had just killed.

CHAPTER SEVENTEEN

RECOVERY

It seemed like an eternity, but it was only a few minutes until Poppies came into the barn. He looked at the two men lying on the floor and then he looked at me. "It looks like you have been busy," was all he said but I sensed the concern he felt from the stern look in his eyes.

Poppies went immediately to Great-Grandma Kniest after I told him where she was. I was both pleased and chagrinned that he left me to ride herd on the two attackers. It felt good to have gained Poppies' confidence, but the impact of the evening was beginning to sink in. I felt my body tremble even more than when I was coming toward the car barn.

In short order, Poppies came out of the upper-level storeroom with Great-Grandma Kniest in his arms. She was barely conscious and not coherent. The stress of having been gagged and bound to a chair had taken its toll on her nearly eighty-eight-year-old body. Poppies said he had called both the police and the medics. Their summoning to the chalet was beginning to get old.

I slept soundly after I got to bed. The man I had shot in the leg never moved while I was guarding him and the other man wasn't going to move again. I gladly turned my weapon and my responsibility over to the sheriff's deputy who was the first to arrive. Curiously, that night none of them asked for details of what happened. I just told them I was the one who did the shooting and that seemed to stop them in their tracks. I suppose they thought this was not the time to press for a full explanation.

Poppies spent most of the next day with his mother and the medical people who were dispatched to the chalet. The doctors determined she had suffered no great physical injury but the emotional and mental strain could not be measured. They would treat her in the chalet for a day or so until she had regained her strength and then take her to the Colorado Springs Medical Center for mental and emotional rehabilitation. She was still not coherent when the air ambulance took her away the next evening.

After several hours of repeating the harrowing attack and rescue story to FBI, local police, state patrol, and agents from the Department of Homeland Security (HLS), I was beginning to wilt. Still, the big picture of what had happened had some big holes in it.

The consensus was that the attackers came in by some sort of stealth vehicle, which meant the operation was well funded. The vehicle was probably an advanced gyrocopter of some kind that operated very quietly. It had to be or I would have heard it from the car barn. The vehicle left no signature footprint of a landing, so the attackers must have been dropped off near the front air lock. For reasons unknown, the aircraft left before the job was done, leaving the two thugs in the middle of their skullduggery. It's possible that my return from the car barn spooked the copter, but if it did I was unaware of it.

At any rate, apparently as I was coming in through the front airlock, they were going out the back with Great-Grandma Kniest.

Why they stayed in the car barn, why the copter didn't return, and why they came in the first place were questions to resolve.

After all of the locals had gone, Edgar Fiorello from HLS sat down with Poppies. "Governor Miller filled us in on what you've been doing and why," Fiorello began. "We think you are the reason your parents were targeted two days ago. The two attackers have been identified as henchmen for the New Jersey mafia, but they were up for hire by anyone who would foot the bill. Have you ever known anyone or had contact with anyone in the New Jersey mafia?"

At first Poppies was about to say no. Then he remembered Sal Tesoro. "Well, actually, D.J. and I have had quite a relationship with the boys from New Jersey." Then he related the story of both the poker game with Sal, the rescue mission for Zell and Olivia, and the ill-fated attack by the New Jersey gang at the border.

"Well, we hope to get something out of the guy your grandson nicked with a laser, but so far he's as tight-lipped as a preacher whose organist has alum on her boobs."

I liked Fiorello immediately. He had greenish-blue eyes surrounded by clear, olive skin and wore a moustache. He looked to be about thirty-five. His smile and interested expression convinced me he was totally sincere.

The next week was spent in making visits to Great-Grandpa Tom and Great-Grandma Kniest in Colorado Springs and in briefing sessions with the lawmen involved. It turned out that HLS and the FBI were jointly in charge, but Fiorello became the de facto chief. I wondered why the Colorado authorities had fallen back. Poppies explained that it was a kidnapping, but moreover, it was the possible foreign agency involvement that put the crime in the hands of the Feds. At last, something had finally brought the Chinese to somebody's attention.

Poppies and I had not spoken about the two hit men, the shooting, or my part in the fracas since that night in the car barn. After the Feds had retired, Poppies put his hand on my shoulder. "Deej, I just want you to know something. That was an incredibly brave thing you did in the car barn. Even though it has been a few days, I suspect it will take a few months before it all sinks in. My advice is don't let the other night bother you, but if it does, you know you can talk to me about it. Above all, if you have misgivings, guilt feelings, or anything of that nature, don't hold them inside. You saved your great-grandmother's life and who knows how many others. Be proud of yourself and know that I am proud of you too."

I listened closely and tried to absorb the full meaning of Poppies' words because thoughts and memories of that traumatic night had begun to bother me.

On the seventh day after the attack, Fiorello asked Poppies to join him in Denver with the governor and others. I was not invited, but Poppies gave me a full rundown when he returned to the chalet. The second gunman, whom I had wounded, finally cracked. He belonged to a professional strong-arm gang that worked directly for Atlantic City Gambling Enterprises (ACGE). He and his buddy were "on loan" to a Mr. Chan Lang Fang who was owed a favor from ACGE. The nature of the favor was unknown but it had something to do with a shot-down gyrocopter in California.

Mr. Lang Fang shuttled between Chicago and Sacramento working as a paid lobbyist. He was believed to have ties to both Luis Santiago, the governor of California, and United States President Yun Mi Chae. Lang Fang provided the aircraft, the weapons, and the plan. One of the reasons the gunman was willing to talk was that he felt he had been set up. Apparently, he believed the gyrocopter left without reason. Whether it was true or not wasn't important, because as long as he believed it, he was willing to sing. However, having done so, his continued survival, even with police protection, was dubious. He had implicated the New Jersey mob, Chan Lang Fang, and possibly others in very high places.

My great-grandparents were making progress, but it was painfully slow. Great-Grandpa Tom had suffered some brain damage from the laser shot to his head. His speech was slurred and he was somewhat paralyzed from the waist down. He was able to get around in a wheelchair, but doctors said it would take months of therapy to regain muscle strength and stability. At ninety-plus years of age, they were not terribly encouraging.

Great-Grandma Kniest was doing much better. She had recovered from her drug-induced incoherency and had gone from being silent to being adamant. She couldn't understand why they simply didn't go get the bastards that had invaded her home. She also couldn't understand why they had invaded. Poppies started to explain that it was because of his presence, but she would have none of that. Whether she was in denial or simply didn't want Poppies to know that she understood everything, was always something I wondered about. She was a smart and tough old lady and she loved Poppies dearly. The last thing she would want would be to add to his guilt over the attack.

It had been several weeks since my encounter with the mob hit men, but I still remembered the details as if it were yesterday. Particularly, I couldn't erase the vision of the man I had killed with the hand laser. Great-Grandma Kniest helped me a great deal one day when she saw me looking pensively out the window.

"You know, D.J.," she began, "I never have thanked you for saving my life."

I was only half listening when she started talking, but her warm words brought me out of my trance. I looked toward her. She knew something was bothering me and she guessed what it might be.

She continued, "During the weeks that I've spent in this hospital, I had time to think. I thought about my life and all the trials I had been through in my eighty-seven years. I started feeling sorry for myself for a while, but then I thought of you. You are my favorite great-grandson, you know."

I felt special until I remembered I was her only great-grandson. The smug expression on her face told me she was pulling my leg.

"I thought of what you must be going through, and it occurred to me that you have been through more trials and tribulations in the last two years than I have in eighty-seven. I can't tell you how proud I am of you for what you did for your great-grandfather and me last Valentine's Day. Even more than proud, I am grateful. You know there are times in life when you must choose between shades of gray. I know you didn't want to shoot that man. I'm sorry you had to, but I'm glad you did.

"Who knows what might have happened if you hadn't taken over. They had already murdered the FBI agents. Poppies would have returned and been ambushed. Assuming I wasn't already dead from the duct tape, they would have killed me. And certainly, the first time they realized you were still around, they would have done the same to you. These were evil men and would have brought more evil on this world had you not stopped them. Try not to worry about your actions that night. It is kind of like David having to slay Goliath. We humans have a tendency to judge after the fact. I say we live our lives as best we can and leave the judgment up to God."

I remember her words of thanks and affirmation every time I think about that night. I still get a sick feeling in my stomach, but her reassurance helps. It will take a long time.

During the month following the attack, Poppies and I continued to stay in the chalet. The daily visits to Colorado Springs eased into three a week as we could see this was going to be a long process. I continued to do my schoolwork via holo-teach, although my mind was not totally focused. I worried about my great-grandparents. I worried about Poppies because he was concerned about a second attack, my safety, Grammy's situation, and the hornet's nest he had stirred up. In addition, he felt terribly guilty at having brought this on his parents. He had a lot on his plate, and I wished I could do something to help.

Finally, I worried about Zell. It had been seven months since I had seen her and during those seven months she had emerged from her coma, but had little recollection of the past. She remembered bits and pieces, but large chunks of time were missing entirely from her memory bank. Also, those chunks varied from day to day. One day she would remember an event from her past, but the next day she would have no idea that she had remembered it, nor would she be able to duplicate the recollection. The doctors were quite baffled. I had tried to communicate with her, but she seemed confused about who I was. Mrs. Bailey, the nurse I had known in Reno, said she thought it best not to press the issue for the time being. I felt a terrible sadness and a quiet desperation at being apart from her. I fantasized that if I were there, I could bring her out of her funk.

Tuesday, March 18, 2053
Colorado Springs, Colorado

On March eighteenth, we celebrated Great-Grandma Kniest's eighty-eighth birthday. She was still in the Colorado Springs Medical Center, but we ordered cake, ice cream and lasagna for the staff and a few well-wishers who came to the party. Great-Grandpa Tom was able to get around with a cane now, and he surprised her by walking in the door. It was the first time she had seen him walk in six weeks. In the middle of the party, Fiorello gave Poppies a microcom call. Poppies was needed in Chicago the next day.

Edgar Fiorello, Scott Miller, and Poppies left at 9 a.m. for a 10:30 meeting with President Chae and selected members of her cabinet. Although no one was specifically named, the three travelers felt assured that news of the attack, Poppies' barnstorming speeches around the Midwest, and the recommendations coming from the ad hoc committee in Denver had caught the attention of many in the administration. Again, I was not present, but Poppies told me about it when he got back. I remember sitting on the balcony of the chalet in the chilled night air and listening to him tell about meeting the new President in the Oval Office.

The meeting was delayed because the President was late getting back from another obligation. Jeff Hornacek, the head of Homeland Security and Fiorello's boss, orchestrated the meeting. Apparently, Edgar Fiorello had convinced him that what was going on in Poppies' life was a matter of significant internal security and Hornacek was responding. President Yun Mi Chae had been elected the previous November, so she had only been in power two months. Hayden Leftwich, the Attorney General, was present, as was Emile Rodriguez, the Secretary of the Interior. There were a few others in the supporting cast, but Poppies wasn't sure who they were or what organization they represented.

Hornacek explained to the President and the group that the recent attack on the Kniests was really an attack on Mr. Eagleton. His office had investigated the matter and had come to the conclusion that there were certain subversive factions who objected to Mr. Eagleton's message and were intent on stopping him. Secretary Hornacek continued, "Whether the attack on his family was intended to intimidate him or whether it was intended for him, we don't know. The important point is, if what Mr. Eagleton is saying were not credible, then why would they want to shut him up?"

Next, Governor Miller was asked to tell about his ad hoc committee and what they found and recommended. Poppies said Scott had done a superb job of giving a capsulated version of the problem, its potential consequences for all states and the nation, and the committee's recommendations. At that point, President Chae appeared to be a bit uncomfortable, particularly when the governor said the recommendation was to take back the State of California by whatever means necessary. Poppies said President Chae cut off Scott at that point and turned to Jeff Hornacek. "Is there any more?" she asked.

Secretary Hornacek took an inordinate amount of time to respond as if he were weighing two courses of action. Then he spoke, "You're damn right there is, Madam President." And then he proceeded to tell about Chan Lang Fang and his connection to California and his frequent journeys to the Chicago White House.

"Now I'm either in charge of homeland security or I'm not, but I see what's happened as a grave threat to our country and I believe Governor Miller is right. We must retake those states that have been infiltrated and are now aligned with a foreign power. I also agree Mr. Eagleton has, at great risk to himself and his family, spoken out on this subject alone long enough. It's time for this administration to take a stand. We came into power knowing that our nation had undergone some power shifts. We knew some states and even the District of Columbia had been taken over by groups that had agendas other than the preservation of our way of life. That is part of why we moved the capital out of Washington during President LaPhonso Jackson's administration a few years back. Our foreign enemies have used our own democratic processes to undermine our government. It's time to put a stop to it."

All the cabinet members and others present enthusiastically indicated their agreement. But President Chae was not so vocal. She simply said, "I'll need some time to think about this. But right now I have another commitment." They all stood up and the meeting was over.

Poppies speculated out there on the balcony that there was more going on with President Chae than anyone knew. Fiorello had told him that Lang Fang had known President Chae long before the election, and he suspected there was more to their relationship than just lobbying when he came to Chicago.

264

On Wednesday, April 2, both Great-Grandma and Great-Grandpa Kniest came home to their chalet. The round-the-clock surveillance and bodyguards would continue indefinitely. The little command center the Feds had set up in the car barn had been so well equipped they could detect a gnat coming in at twenty thousand meters.

April second was also exactly one year to the day Poppies and I had boarded the hybri-cycle in Walnut Creek. It would not have been possible to predict some of the things that had happened in that one short year. It's almost impossible to believe they actually did. As the sunset formed a crimson gold rim over the Rockies, I looked to the west and thought of Zell. I did that often. I hoped she was getting better. I hoped she could remember more. I hoped she could remember me.

CHAPTER EIGHTEEN

THE NEW CHALLENGE

Saturday, May 10, 2053
Kniest Chalet, Colorado

Governor Miller's private gyrocopter landed on the south pasture at precisely noon. The message from his assistant said he was coming down just for lunch. I think Poppies knew better. Nevertheless, Great-Grandma Kniest was thrilled. I asked her if she would be serving CSC's and she nearly threw me out of the kitchen. Although, she had help from a local caterer, Great-Grandma Kniest wanted to prepare the entrée. The governor would be treated to her specialty, lasagna.

After the meal, Scott Miller and Poppies retired to the balcony. The spring breeze off the mountain was beginning to warm a little so they could sit out without needing their climate suits. I probably shouldn't have, but I positioned myself inside the door and pretended to be studying. Actually, I was eavesdropping.

"David, I want you to think about something. I don't want an answer today, or tomorrow. I only want it when you have mulled over all the ramifications to you and your family. Then, I'll accept your answer with no further comment or urging. Are you with me?"

Poppies nodded that he was and, though I couldn't see it, I suspect his face showed a twinge of anxiety. Governor Miller continued, "David, my ad hoc committee has become a task force. They are through with thinking about the issue. They are done with putting out recommendations. The want to DO something."

Governor Miller paused either for effect or to allow Poppies to respond, but there was only silence. He spoke very slowly and deliberately. "The task force and I have explored any number of ways we could go after the Chinese thugs who have taken over California. We could exhort the federal government to send in military forces, declare martial law, and set up some sort of a military regime, such as General MacArthur had in Japan after World War II. That seemed dumb and highly over reactive. Plus, I'm not sure if that regime would be preferable to the one already there.

"We considered using a sort of vigilante operation where we would send in our own thugs to intimidate and perhaps eliminate the key Chinese operatives who have gotten into positions of power. Again, that option had so many downsides, it was rejected before it was thoroughly thought through. And that's okay with me. I could tell you about numerous other strategies that we dreamed up, considered, and rejected. But let me tell you the one we want to use."

Poppies stopped Scott Miller at that point to say, "Before you get too deep into this, there are a couple of things I need to articulate. One is that I have responsibilities to my folks, to D.J., and to my wife and I need to get on with those. Being the spokesman for the cause has taken me away from my family. So I am telling you now, the attack and these past few weeks have been a real wake-up call. The attack has convinced me that running around the Midwest, sounding the alarm is something I have to stop. Secondly, I have to get back to California. I feel terrible that I am here and Jenny is there. We think we know where she is, but we're not sure, nor do we know what her circumstances are. Even if it means my life, I can't bear to not make the effort."

Governor Miller waited a minute as if to give Poppies an opportunity to express other points. When none came, Scott Miller said, "I don't blame you for wanting to do both of those. What I am about to outline is totally compatible with both of your points. The strategy we want to use is to beat them at their own game. We want to use money to fund campaigns; we want to send in a sizable cadre of people who can identify local candidates and who can perhaps fill positions themselves.

"In short, we want to oust the Chinese infiltrators city by city, county by county, and ultimately take over the statehouse. I have about half of the people we will need already signed up, and by summer, I'll have the rest. You, David, are key among the rest. The task force recommends, and I heartily agree, that you should run for governor. We have the resources; we have the will. All we need is your nod."

I listened so hard for Poppies reply that I almost fell out of my chair. There was nothing said for a long time. I thought perhaps they had walked out of earshot. Ultimately, Governor Miller began again.

"The two points you stated earlier are compatible with the strategy. The safety of your parents can be guaranteed by the surveillance and protective measures we've established here at the chalet. If you move back to California, I would think there would be a reduced threat for those left here in Colorado. That is simply because I think the New Jersey attack was to get you. They failed at that and whatever else happened was only collateral damage. Secretary Hornacek was right. It's time for others, besides you, to inform the masses.

"To your second point, what better way for you to explore your wife's situation and location than by going back as a candidate? The national visibility you will have makes you virtually bulletproof from the California Chinese. The last thing they want to do is bring attention to themselves in places where they have not yet infiltrated, that is, the rest of the United States. There is no way they could assassinate or impede a gubernatorial candidate and not become front-page news in every corner of America."

Again, a long stretch of silence.

Finally, Poppies spoke. "I am going to do as you asked and that is I'm not going to say anything now. I probably won't say anything for several weeks. The greatness of this honor is only exceeded by the greatness of the responsibility associated with it. I admit you have made some compelling arguments. There are some other loose ends I am very concerned about. For example, why wasn't Mr. Lang Fang indicted? Also, what is his connection with President Chae? If she is not on board with the task force or with her own cabinet, then it tells me she is on board with the Chinese. Despite her Oriental name, her background would suggest she is purely American. But if she has any sentiment, any ties, any feelings whatsoever for the Chinese, she is a danger and does not have the best interests of this country at heart. We need to find out for absolutely certain what side of the fence she stands on."

There was a little more chitchat, but I never heard Governor Miller say he disagreed. Perhaps his political nature was keeping him neutral. After all, like him, she was a Republican. At least that was the ticket she ran on.

CHAPTER NINETEEN

THE DECISION

The next few weeks were more relaxed. Poppies was at the chalet most of the time and we spent more time together as a family. Great-Grandma Kniest was completely well now as far as I could tell and Great-Grandpa Tom was very close. He still had some stability problems and a little difficulty speaking. But he never did talk much.

There was one day though when just Great-Grandma Kniest and I were in the chalet. She asked me about Zell. I had been quite close-mouthed about our relationship, but I suppose Poppies had filled her in some time ago. "I understand you are quite fond of a young girl back in California," she began softly.

I was caught by surprise and being somewhat flustered, I blurted out, "Yes, Great-Grandma, I have strong feelings for her. Her name is Zell." Normally, I would have been more circumspect in my reply, but she had caught me with my guard down and the truth came rolling out.

"Tell me about her," she asked with a soft compassion that told me she knew quite a bit, but she wanted to hear it from me.

"Zell and her mother befriended us when we were trying to escape the Chinese at a place called Graniteville," I said. "We spent several weeks with them and left only when Poppies thought it was safe to travel. But after making it across the border into Nevada, Poppies found out that Zell and Olivia, her mom, were in great danger. So we went back to get them. Only we were attacked at the border and Olivia was killed and Zell was wounded. She is still in the Nevada Medical Center trying to recover her mind and her memory. Uncle Max checks in on her from time to time, and occasionally I talk with a nurse who is taking care of her. She is a little better, I think."

"I understand you didn't want to leave her when you had to come to Colorado."

"Yes, and I second-guess myself nearly every day when I think about that decision."

"Have you ever asked yourself what you could have done for her had you stayed? Have you thought of what might have happened here if you hadn't been around to rescue me? Have you considered what a help you have been to your grandfather over the past year? It seems to me you made the right decision. But tell me about Zell."

"Well, Zell has long, dark, reddish-brown hair and she is very pretty. She is just my age although I think she looks at least a couple of years older. She is quite athletic and is very smart, but her best quality is that

274

she is genuine. She doesn't wear gaudy makeup, she isn't stuck up, and she makes me feel great when I'm with her. I really miss her."

Great-Grandma Kniest smiled that knowing smile I'd seen many times before. "Well, I can't wait to meet this girl. I'm sure she is all you have said and more. If you want my advice, you should continue to keep tabs on her through the nurse you spoke of, and someday you will return to California and you will see her again."

"But what if she doesn't remember me?" I was almost pathetic in my frustration.

"That will depend on a great many factors you don't control. Only be concerned about factors you can affect and leave the rest up to God. But, if I'm any judge, I'll bet she'll come out of her illness and she will recognize and remember you. If she has any sense at all, she will. Otherwise she would be missing out on knowing someone who cares for her very much. I can tell you do and I can tell you're hurting over this. Just have faith and I can almost assure you things will work out."

I thanked her for her kind words, and from then on, I felt I could go to Great-Grandma Kniest with any problems I had, particularly if they involved Zell.

It had been six weeks since Scott Miller and Poppies had chatted on the front balcony. Poppies had been more relaxed than I had seen him for some time. He was enjoying the family get-togethers at the chalet. He and Great-Grandpa Tom would sometimes walk out to the barn and just talk. Other times I would see him sitting on the corral fence enjoying the Colorado summer breeze. But lately he seemed a little more intense. I sensed he knew his time was about up to give Scott Miller an answer.

On the Fourth of July, Poppies asked me if I would like to take a short trip. I presumed he meant to Colorado Springs or Denver, but he said it would be to Baton Rouge. I had never been there plus I was always eager to go with Poppies. I asked why we were going and he said he needed to pay Uncle Aidan a visit.

Tuesday, July 15, 2053
Baton Rouge, Louisiana

Poppies and Uncle Aidan met on the LSU campus at Baton Rouge just after lunch. I was surprised to be asked to tag along on the trip and even more surprised to be included in the meeting. On secure microcom, Poppies had previously outlined the offer Scott Miller had presented and asked for Uncle Aidan's advice. Poppies also had made him aware of his reservations regarding President Chae. They agreed that meeting face-to-face in a secure environment was essential.

Uncle Aidan had reserved an inconspicuous conference room that had been rendered totally secure from electronic eavesdropping. After several hours of discussing strategy, Uncle Aidan changed the subject to the one he knew most concerned Poppies.

"Let me give you a summary of some additional research I have done on our new President," Uncle Aidan began.

"Yun Mi Chae is a second-generation Korean-American who grew up in New Jersey, attended American public schools, married her college sweetheart, and settled in for what was supposed to be, a white-picket-fence lifestyle. But, in between college and the fence, she became interested in politics. Her campus support of New Jersey Republican gubernatorial candidate, Lee Phong, in the mid twenties led her to more politicians, more campaigns, and eventually she was compelled to run for office herself. At age twenty-five, she was elected alderwoman of Ocean City, New Jersey.

"Ms. Chae was smart and savvy and she picked up on what it took to curry favor with the voters and with the party. She went from alderwoman to mayor and from mayor to state representative, where she earned a reputation as a tough fighter for her constituents and for her state. After twenty years in state politics, at age forty-five, she decided to run for the United States House of Representatives. She won in a landslide and distinguished herself in a number of areas, not the least of which was her stand against scientific experimentation on humans, which earned her national recognition in the early forties.

"But, even with those credentials, her meteoric rise to national prominence and the top spot on the ticket in 2052 was nothing short of a miracle. The Republicans were not expected to compete that year. The incumbent Democratic President, Hector Negroni III, had the Hispanic vote locked up. As that now represented nearly forty percent of the registered voters and guaranteed him the large states of California, Florida, Texas, and New York, he seemed unbeatable. Moreover, the Republicans had fielded a number of lackluster candidates, and they spent most of the days before the primary sniping at each other.

"Suddenly and surprisingly, just before the Republican Convention, a new voice was heard. Ms. Yun Mi Chae ignored her Republican rivals and began to attack President Negroni. He had numerous areas of vulnerability. His handling of the economy in the aftermath of the Petroleum Wars had been abysmal and had cost the United States dearly. Also, his stand on international relations was hopelessly naïve. People called him GW because he seemed to be following a policy of isolation, much like that of the first president, George Washington. That, as much as anything else, paved the way for the Chinese and others to infiltrate our borders and to erode our hegemony overseas. He rolled over to the Muslims when he simply gave back the oil fields of Iraq and Saudi Arabia. True, there wasn't much oil left, but we had been able to pump enough to make the few special lubricants that required natural petroleum. That didn't keep the Middle East from reverting to a pre-World War II economy, but it typified his spinelessness.

"The real surprise and never-answered question was where did Mrs. Chae get her campaign funds? Up until October of 2051, she wasn't even a candidate. She had raised no money. She had no political action committee (PAC) resources. Then out of nowhere, holovision ads bombarded the American public. Supporters came out of the woodwork in what was proclaimed to be a grassroots movement.

"She fit the bill nicely. She was unknown nationally and, therefore, the opposition had little to criticize. She was of Amerasian descent, a woman who had climbed the ladder the hard way, and she spoke well. What's more, she was charming and attractive. Her fifty years of life were not apparent. She could easily pass for being in her late thirties. Even though she was divorced, that was no big deal because over seventy percent of the voters were either divorced or never married. There were no scandals in her past or skeletons in her closet as far as anyone knew.

"The elimination of the Electoral College also played a significant role. The antiquated concept had been replaced by a new formula that weighed popular vote far more heavily, but still left the more populous states with the biggest hammer.

"She came out of the convention with the nomination. Her holovision blitz hit Negroni like Hitler hit Poland

and, before the Democrats could figure out where to counterattack, she had 'blitzkrieged' her way to the White House.

"However, now I will tell you the rest of the story.

"Yun Mi Chae's grandmother was a nightclub dancer in Song Tan, South Korea in the 1960's. She met and married a G.I., Staff Sergeant Phil Chalmers, and he took her back to the States. Their daughter, Cho Li, was born in Fairfield, California just before Sergeant Chalmers left the Air Force. She grew up in Fairfield and attended college at UC Davis. Her first job after college was in San Francisco, and she was a cheerleader for the San Francisco Forty-Niners before she married a wealthy California businessman named Jack Campbell. That marriage did not last, and Cho Li left California and Jack, not knowing she was pregnant with his baby. Yun Mi was born in Elizabeth, New Jersey in 2001.

"Yun Mi Campbell never knew her father. She was raised by her doting mother, who had become totally Americanized and, other than her Korean name, passed none of her Korean heritage on to Yun Mi. Yun Mi met Charles Chae in 2020 at a political rally in St. Louis during college. He had come from Stanford and she from Princeton. The Young Republicans were gathered to plan the youth movement for the Republican slate in the coming election, but once Yun Mi and Charles met, there was little planning done.

"He was immediately smitten and began courting her on the spot. He had money to burn and impressed her with sightseeing trips down the Mississippi on an old paddle wheeler, a tour of the Arch and the Lewis and Clark Museum, and a visit to the St. Louis Art Museum in Forest Park. She was impressed that a California boy would have such couth.

"Along with his obvious wealth, Charles charmed Yun Mi by emphasizing their common heritage. He was also a second-generation Korean-American. His grandfather had been a tailor in Seoul in the 1970's, but had saved enough to send his children to the United States for college. Charles' father returned to Seoul and began an import/export business that featured the export of celadon and other Korean artwork. After making his fortune at an early age, he immigrated to the United States and married a girl from Palo Alto. That marriage resulted in the birth of Charles in 1999.

"After the St. Louis convention, Charles returned to Stanford and began preparations to transfer to Princeton. That was no small feat, but with enough money—and his family had it—mountains can be moved. They completed their final two years of college at Princeton and moved in together during their last semester. Charles wanted to be married. In fact, he had wanted to marry her from the time he had met her in St. Louis. Yun Mi was not as eager. However, ultimately, the lure of a financially secure life persuaded her to say 'yes.'

"For Yun Mi, it was not a marriage made in heaven. Charles was a loving, caring, and smothering husband. He had his idea of what a wife should be and do and he was insanely jealous. Yun Mi was strong willed and, though she hadn't decided exactly what path her life would take that year after college, she was pretty sure it wasn't going to be a stay-at-home mother of the five children that Charles wanted. The more she pulled away, the more adamant he became. The marriage lasted five years.

"She had renewed her interest in politics, much to Charles' displeasure. She had refused to get pregnant, despite Charles' insistence. The final straw came when Yun Mi's mother, who had moved back to California, became ill, and Yun Mi went to Fairfield to take care of her. Charles was furious. He would pay for the best doctors, he would pay to have Cho Li moved to New Jersey, but he didn't want his wife out of his control. That incident and his reaction finally convinced Yun Mi there was no hope for her to live her own life or to pursue her own dreams with Charles as her husband. In August of 2028, Yun Mi Chae filed for divorce.

"In the ensuing years, her political career began to take off as I have said before. Her social life seemed to languish with one or two exceptions. Several years after the divorce, she was visiting her mother in California and met a Chinese businessman, whose name was Chan Lang Fang. He operated a number of retirement and nursing homes, and Yun Mi was looking for a place for her mother to live. Cho Li was not in good health, and it was time she stopped living alone. By chance, Lang Fang had a new establishment opening up in Grass Valley. Yun Mi and her mother visited Grass Valley, became enchanted with the surroundings, and were impressed with Mr. Lang Fang. A deal was struck. Cho Li would move into the new complex upon completion and would be guaranteed a place to live in either the independent, the assisted, or the full service nursing home wing for the rest of her life. Yun Mi felt relieved.

"However, with the passage of new laws throughout the country, and particularly in California, regarding euthanasia, Yun Mi became concerned that Cho Li would become a casualty. Lang Fang assured her that his political connections, along with his common heritage to the Chinese administrators, would give him all the control he needed to honor his commitment regarding her mother. Initially, she was grateful and believed he was simply doing the honorable thing. However, even as a low-ranking member of the House, she noticed that Lang Fang's attention seemed to be expanding from the simple subject of care for her mother.

"On one occasion, he had solicited her vote to give wider latitude to organizations caring for the elderly. On another, he had lobbied her to vote against appropriations for federal oversight of institutions such as his. He explained that, in addition to running a nursing home business, he had become their spokesman and lobbyist at a number of levels of government. She didn't particularly like it, but she accepted his explanation.

"Chan Lang Fang was another second-generation American. Born of Taiwanese parents who had immigrated to California, Chan was studious and introverted, growing up in San Francisco, where his parents ran a hole-in-the-wall chop suey place just off Market Street. Probably, the biggest reason he had few friends was his appearance. Slight of build, his hollowed out cheeks accentuated his slanted, beady eyes. To say he resembled a toad would be an insult to the toad.

"Despite his unappealing looks and demeanor, he had worked his way through school and, when his parents died, he invested his inheritance in real estate. How he became connected with prominent California political figures is somewhat of a mystery, but rumors of operating a ring of call girls in Chinatown still lingered long after Lang Fang had moved on to more legitimate businesses involving care of the aged.

"Immediately after being elected and even before her inauguration, Lang Fang contacted President-elect Chae, ostensibly to congratulate her, but his motives became quite apparent. Now that she was in a position of great influence, he was going to use his relationship to further the cause of, not only elder care, but also the new government functions in California. He never stated, but strongly suggested, that he was the only person who was standing between her mother and euthanasia. Further, the reason for that was that he was politically aligned with the new governor and other prominent legislators and officials. It wasn't blackmail, but it was the closest thing to it. She was in a dilemma.

"A few days before, she had been elected to the most powerful office in the land. Now she felt powerless. She would have to find a way to get her mother out of the California elder-care system, but for the time being, there was no choice but to play along with Lang Fang.

"Yun Mi's troubles did not end with Mr. Lang Fang. As I said earlier, the millions in campaign funds that appeared from nowhere actually did come from somewhere. A great deal of it came from the gaming industry supplied by organizations such as the Atlantic City Gaming Association (ACGA). The industry had called in its chits from casinos and gambling organizations across the country to buy this Presidency. Not only did the more sleazy of the casinos contribute, but even those with a reputation for honesty kicked in, including Harrah's. While she was somewhat insulated from the providers of the money by the Republican Committee chairman and the Committee to Elect, in the aftermath of the election, it was clear they and the gaming industry expected to have their people named to cabinet and other appointed positions.

"The banquet at the inaugural ball had been a compliment of Dom Orosco, chairman of the ACGA. He took that opportunity to remind President Chae of their generosity and that he would never reveal the source of the funds because some folks might think that she was supported by ill-gotten money. It was another semi-veiled threat, but one that was very real in her mind. Unfortunately politics is replete with such stuff.

"In short, I believe Ms. Chae is a conscientious and loyal American. However, she has attracted some baggage that is swaying her neutrality and giving her bias. I am convinced that, absent these distractions, she would be one hundred percent behind the initiative proposed by Governor Miller's task force and Secretary Hornacek. We must do two things. First, verify my conviction. The only way to do that is to talk to her. Second, we need to eliminate her baggage. I can handle the gaming industry, I believe. But you must deal with Mr. Lang Fang."

The two men had pretty much agreed that the first step was to approach Ms. Chae. I wondered how they could pull it off. After all, it wasn't like they could invite her over for dinner. I had underestimated Uncle Aidan. He made a couple of microcom calls, cashed in a few chits, I suspect, and the two of them were on their way to Chicago the next day.

I was left in the care of Uncle Aidan's assistant at LSU. I had the run of the campus and of his condominium, but I preferred the campus. It was there I encountered Professor Otto Krueger, a hardheaded German and head of the Religious Studies Department.

Professor Krueger was old. I think he not only remembered World War II, I think he served in it. Of course, that is impossible for that would make him well over a hundred years old, but he grew up in its aftermath, and his father and uncles all fought for the Nazis. Of course, they were on the Russian front. He wore a full beard and that was the only hair otherwise visible. His deeply wrinkled brow overlooked his taped-up spectacles that barely hung on the bridge of his nose. He had lost most of his German accent, but he had replaced it with a little Cajun flair, so one had to listen very closely or it came out as garble. Still, he had an inimitable charm and I was attracted to him immediately.

I was in the library using their study equipment to keep up with my schoolwork and also just browsing around at subjects that caught my interest. Not everything in the LSU library had been converted to digital format so they still had some paper bound volumes from the olden days. I was climbing on the ladder to retrieve a book on the history of modern religions when I got off balance and dropped the book—squarely on the head of Professor Krueger. I thought at first I might have killed him because he went down like he had been shot. After a crowd gathered and some students helped him to his feet, he looked around and asked,

"Vell, to whom do I have ze honor of thanking for zis collision?"

I almost said nothing, but I knew that was the wrong thing to do, so I spoke up, "It was me that dropped the book, sir. It was an accident and I am very sorry. I hope you are all right." I spat the words out without taking a breath and prepared to take my verbal punishment from the crotchety-looking old man.

To my surprise, he simply looked at me and said, "Ze book you dropped was ze one I haf been looking for. You could haf just handed it to me, but othervise, danke."

With that awkward introduction, I again expressed my regret and asked if there was anything I could do to make amends. He waved it off and said something like, "It vill take more zan a book to ze head to kill me off," and then asked why I had wanted the book. I explained about my school assignment and he said, "Vell, since ve both are in need of ze same reference, I suggest ve share. Vould you join me in a cold drink and ve can do zat." That began a most pleasant friendship and learning experience for me.

In my studies, we were assigned three major religions and required to trace their evolution from 2000 to the present. I had been given Protestantism, Catholicism, and Islam. I quickly learned that I really didn't need the book. Professor Krueger was a walking encyclopedia on the subject, and he gave me much more than I could have garnered from the study net or the books. This is the essence of what I wrote for my assignment.

In the year 2000, the Protestants and Catholics represented much of the Western World and the Muslims represented the Middle East, South Asia, and a few other areas in Asia and Africa. Even though the three religions were theologically compatible, their followers found many ways to be contentious. Professor Krueger, who was neither, suggested that the contention was more economically than religiously motivated.

All three religions believed in the sanctity of life, doing good works, and treating others as you would treat yourself. Islam had a Koran that outlined their credo, and Protestants and Catholics had a Bible that did the same. The prophet Mohammed began Islam and the spiritual leader of the other two was Jesus. Each proclaimed to be the true means to eternal life and the path that humans should follow. Those following Islam seemed to be more pious than the followers of Jesus, but on the other hand, the Muslims tended to be very un-Godlike in many respects.

At any rate, in the years before and immediately following the turn of the century, splinter groups from each religion began to stir up the main bodies. Zealots in the Muslim faith belonging to these splinter groups began a campaign of terrorism. This was primarily directed against followers of the Jewish religion, who had confiscated holy land in Israel, but it also was directed against the followers of Jesus in America. Although there had been a number of minor incidents, the act that mostly incensed the American Protestants and Catholics was the strike against two skyscrapers in New York in 2001. Actually, most mainline Muslims were also appalled, because wanton death and destruction were not part of their tenets. Nevertheless, when it came time to take sides, Muslims lined up with Muslims, Protestants lined up with Protestants, and the Catholics did likewise.

The final blow came, however, in 2013 when factions representing a number of anti-Semitic groups floated a low-grade nuclear bomb up the Potomac and into Washington, D.C. The death and destruction was considerable, but miniscule compared to the long-term effects. Residual radiation had made an area with a radius of twenty kilometers uninhabitable for years. The government and all its trappings were moved to West Chicago, and the wrath of the United States against all of the Muslim zealots was swift and conclusive. Unfortunately, collateral damage resulted and many innocent citizens were also killed.

While this angered the affected nations, they also had a "come to Mohammed meeting" with themselves. In a surprising move, many major Muslim states sided with the United States in rounding up and eliminating the renegade groups. They had finally realized that these groups represented a severe danger to mainline Muslims as well as to other religions and nations.

Their continued existence simply wasn't worth World War III and annihilation.

The first decade of the twenty-first century saw both sides at odds as the drive to eliminate the zealot terrorist factions took place. But by about 2015, they were cooperating and most terrorist groups had been neutralized. There was a renaissance in Islam during that time as well. Partly because of exposure to western ideas, and partly in reaction to the archaic beliefs of extreme fundamentalist factions such as the Talaban and al-Qaida, mainline Muslims reinterpreted the Koran.

In the next decade, the interchange between the three religious groups increased. Muslims from the Middle East traveled to Europe and the United States, and there was a similar visitation of western Catholics and Protestants to countries embracing Islam. Their coming to the United States helped shape our policy toward them and their religion, and the reverse was also true.

A significant resurgence of religion took place in the third decade of the twenty-first century. The Islamic features that had stood the test of time for centuries were reinvented again, partly because of the Petroleum Wars and partly because of the exposure to the West.

Protestantism and Catholicism also were heavily transformed. The multiplicity of protestant denominations began to merge. However, they did not merge into one of the original denominations such as

Methodist, Lutheran or Pentecostal. They gravitated to a newer more modern concept called "Light." This denomination still espoused many of the same principles as protestant factions of old, but much of the dogma was dropped. The organization of the church changed from one of autocracy to one of democracy. Obsolete traditions just died out. For example, terms like elders, deacons, priests, and the like were replaced by less formidable terms such as "religions leader." Rituals such as baptism by immersion, confession, and the wearing of robes and pointy hats were among those phased out. In their place were one-on-one sessions between the religions leader and the parishioner or small group discussions. Formerly sacrosanct institutions, which constituted unneeded management entities, simply died out for lack of support.

Church services changed dramatically. No longer was there the repetitive pattern of scripture, anthem, sermon, benediction and whatever else the minister or priest chose. Worshipers still congregated but evolution had made this a highly participative and informal activity. There was no preacher to rain down fire and brimstone from a pulpit. There was no pomp, and no pious ceremonies bored or intimidated the congregation. There was no boring litany of scripture readings and sermons that were difficult to understand. It was a plainspoken session where people were free to contribute or not, and one free of all the unnecessary ritual. Yet, at the same time, the church service gave those participating a new fresh outlook and filled the deep religious need that humans have always felt. Only now it was done without the extraneous ritual.

By the middle of the century, it was obvious that, despite predictions to the contrary, in the hearts and minds of people everywhere, God refused to die. The modern world cried out for a modern religion and it was delivered. Those faiths and churches that failed to understand and move in that direction were left to wither on the vine. It is not over by any stretch, but a new, common, charismatic religious worship has captured the imagination of millions. True, Muslims still believe in Mohammed and Protestants and Catholics still believe in Jesus, but both Islam and Christianity have largely discarded the superfluous trappings of the old and have embraced the no-nonsense, plain speech, and reverent participative services that meet basic human needs.

I spent two days with Professor Krueger while I waited for Poppies and Uncle Aidan. Also, I received a top grade on my assignment.

I had desperately wanted to go to Chicago, but even though I tried to invite myself, I was politely told this was not a meeting for on-lookers. Poppies and Uncle Aidan would be meeting with the President in a private and virtually secret session. Only the Secret Service people on duty would know. It was listed on her schedule as a meeting with "personal friends." Although I was not present, both Poppies and Uncle Aidan filled me in over the next few weeks and months. I was fascinated. The trip to Chicago went like this.

Poppies and Uncle Aidan took a private flight from Baton Rouge to Chicago. It was provided by one of the deep-pocketed backers of Governor Miller's task force.

About halfway there, Poppies asked Uncle Aidan a question. "There is something I don't understand. When I met President Chae before, I certainly didn't ingratiate myself with her. In fact, just the opposite. So, how is it you were able to arrange this meeting? And on such short notice?"

Uncle Aidan turned to Poppies and gave him half a grin. "You really don't know, do you? I had hoped to keep some things 'close hold' but I don't know any way to explain it except to lay it all out to you. I think you need to be as informed as you can be, if you are going to have a chance of pulling off this gubernatorial election thing.

"I know President Chae personally. I have known her for years. How do you think I knew so much about her personal life when I was giving you a rundown the other day? The short version is that I also attended that Young Republican Convention in St. Louis in 2020. Charlie Chae wasn't the only one attracted to Yun Mi. Only he got the girl. I guess I didn't have enough money or credentials to compete.

"I lost track of her for a few years and then we ran into each other after I had come back from Korea on the unification job. I was addressing a group in Miami and she was in the audience. She came up afterward, we renewed acquaintances, and we have been friends ever since. She had just divorced and I admit I was very fond of her. But the combination of two ambitious careers and her sour attitude toward marriage, kept anything from developing.

"That was okay with me I suppose. I went my way, but we kept in touch. I served as her friend and behind-the-scenes advisor whenever she needed me for over twenty years. I mentioned that her social life was nil, except for a couple of brief affairs. Well..." Uncle Aidan paused.

Poppies was flabbergasted. "So you are telling me that you and the President of the United States were...?" The implication was obvious. "So that is how you were able to get us this meeting. That is how you know so many intimate details about her. I'll be damned. So, is she really a straight shooter?"

"If I didn't think so, I wouldn't be on this flight," Uncle Aidan became more serious. "But, it is more important that you think so. The real purpose of this meeting is to smoke out what can be done to solve her problems with Lang Fang and Dom Orosco. Of course, it's also to make you comfortable that the highest office of our federal government is behind you."

With that insight in his pocket, Poppies was able to better understand the subtleties of the conversation at the meeting with President Chae. It was held over a light dinner in the President's private dining room in the Chicago White House. Only the Secret Service and the food servers were present, and they were out of earshot most of the time.

It was obvious that Yun Mi Chae had a special feeling for Uncle Aidan, but it was concealed so well that anyone "not in the know" would be oblivious. They discussed the dilemma she was in with Lang Fang, why he simply could not be arrested, and what options they had to deal with him without harming Cho Li. The same was discussed regarding the ACGA and Dom Orosco.

President Chae said, "I think I have something that would put both of these guys away."

Then she produced some highly classified air traffic transmission disks that were proof that both Lang Fang and Orosco were involved in a gyrocopter shoot down back in June of 2052. The transmissions and other documents clearly told the story of Dom's conspiracy with Lang Fang.

President Chae continued, "As you heard, Orosco called Lang Fang and advised him of the time and location the gyrocopter would cross the Nevada border. He also mentioned that ten million dollars would be transferred to Lang Fang's account the next day. Apparently some poor slob named Tesoro had gotten on the wrong side of Orosco and that was Dom's way of feeding him to the fishes." President Chae had summarized the transmission disk perfectly.

Poppies sat there in amazement. What neither President Chae nor Uncle Aidan knew was that he and I were involved in that shoot down. That explained a lot. Poppies mind was reeling. That is why we were attacked as we came into Camp Resistance. The Chinese were not after us. Based on Orosco and Lang Fang's tip, they were after Tesoro. Then later when we were about to be zapped by Tesoro, the Chinese actually came to our rescue—inadvertently, of course. The Chinese had taken them on and eliminated them as originally planned. Lang Fang got his ten million as agreed and as verified from bank records President Chae produced.

"So the connection between Dom Orosco and Chan Lang Fang directly implicates both of them in the murder of the Tesoro bunch and Olivia?" Poppies injected.

"Yes it does, but who is Olivia?" President Chae asked quizzically.

Then Poppies told the story of how we were in the middle of the whole fracas and how Olivia and her daughter had become casualties.

It was obvious to President Chae and Uncle Aidan that Murphy's Law was working overtime here. There were way too many coincidences.

Finally, Uncle Aidan spoke up. "We have everything we need for a conviction. What we don't have is a way to keep them from exerting their leverage while we are waiting for the wheels of justice to turn. Until we solve the Cho Li problem and isolate President Chae from the dirty money of the ACGA, we can't move legally."

Uncle Aidan looked squarely at President Chae and said, "Can we agree not to expose any of this until we have solved both of these issues? I have a couple of ideas. When we have safeguarded your mother and neutralized Orosco's threat, I'll let you know. Until then, go along with both of them, but try not to give away the Supreme Court. I'll let you know when you can sick the FBI on them."

President Chae agreed and offered one big unsolicited assurance. "If you can pull off those two chores, you will have my full support and that of the federal government as you try to retake California," she said. "Of course, whatever we do must be within the law."

And on that note, she thanked them for coming, wished them good luck, shook Poppies' hand, and gave Uncle Aidan a kiss on the cheek. But, as Uncle Aidan said later, it was a "Presidential" kiss.

The next day after returning to Baton Rouge, Poppies called Governor Miller. It was the shortest conversation he ever had.

All Poppies said was, "Let's do it."

CHAPTER TWENTY

THE CAMPAIGN BEGINS

July 2053 was moving along fast, but the activities of Uncle Aidan and Poppies were moving even faster. We didn't return to Colorado for several weeks. They had set up a headquarters of sorts on the LSU campus in an abandoned communications center that Uncle Aidan had commandeered from the university. Supporters flew in from Colorado and other parts of the country. I could only guess they came because they were recruited by the Governor Miller task force or by Uncle Aidan. I found out he had made quite a number of connections over the years and was now cashing in on some of those contacts.

What thrilled me most was that, I was not only allowed, I was recruited to help. I worked in the command post doing whatever needed doing. My first priority was to attend to my studies, which I did most enthusiastically because I wanted to get back into the action. As a result, I was privy to a great deal of what took place.

Thursday, August 14, 2053
Baton Rouge, Louisiana

By mid August 2053, the operation was in full swing. Uncle Aidan served as campaign manager and organizer. Poppies began boning up on his opponent,

Governor Luis Santiago. He wanted to know him better than he knew himself. Poppies remarked that he thought that was the key to the election. If he could uncover every weakness, every character trait, every unsavory deal that Governor Santiago had been involved with, he could use them once he got back to California and on the campaign trail.

It was during these days that I got to know Uncle Aidan much better. I had been in awe of him since our first meeting in Denver and I continued to be amazed at his many abilities. I could tell he had a special fondness for me though and, over time, I was able to overcome my shyness. He and I were alone in his condo one weekend. After dinner we began talking about a variety of subjects, and I asked him what gave him the greatest pleasure in life.

He thought about it for a minute and said, "I suppose it is during the negotiation process when I am successful at making the opposing sides believe that what I want them to do is their idea."

"Can you give me an example?" I asked.

"Well, I got my first real experience at it during the Korean reunification sessions," Uncle Aidan stated.

"So how were you able to accomplish the reunification of North and South Korea?"

Uncle Aidan smiled thoughtfully and then said, "I tricked them."

Obviously there were question marks all over my face, so he went on. "You may or may not know from your history of the Koreas, but each side was fiercely nationalistic. Yet, underneath that loyalty was a loyalty to their ethnicity. They had sprung from common ancestors. These were ancestors that had stood together against the Japanese, the Mongols, and other would-be aggressors. They had as much respect for each other as they had fear. I tried to capitalize on both.

"South Korea had a much smaller military than the North, and once the American forces withdrew, their fear of a military attack quadrupled. The fact that the United States had promised to support them if attacked gave them little consolation if there was nothing left to support. South Korea's economy had reached 'major power' proportions. They had replaced Japan as the leader of the next tier of economic powers. The top tier consisted of the United States, Europe, Russia, China and South America. Right behind were South Korea, Indonesia, India-Pakistan, and Australia.

"North Korea had a two-million-man army and had enough conventional weaponry to take on any country in Asia, including China. When they built and exploded their first nuclear weapon in 2008, their stature among world military powers increased dramatically. However, their economy continued on the same road as it had for decades. North Korean dictators beginning with Kim Il Sung and continuing with his son, Kim Jung Il, had never grasped the essence of economic growth or reform. As a result, North Korean initiatives such as free trade with its neighbors (except South Korea) failed. It failed because, once a neighboring country began trading a commodity with South Korea, Kim took that commodity off their trading list. It didn't take long for the list to dwindle.

"Still, North Korea struggled to compete with the South in trade and banking. Time after time, they came in second. As a result, the North Korean people lived in poverty, starvation, and squalor, and the government couldn't improve their lot as long as the military was the first priority.

"The trick was pretty basic. We suggested to the North Koreans, that South Korea was about to launch the equivalent of a price war on commodities with which they were in competition. For example, military equipment and supplies North Korea was receiving from China would be purchased by South Korea at prices far above those North Korea was paying. On the flip side, rice and the few manufactured goods exported by North Korea to Japan, would be offered at one-tenth the price by South Korea. Deprived of revenue from exports and physical items needed for defense, North Korea could see degradation of its military and potential internal revolution.

"On the South Korean side, we suggested that North Korea was at its economic wit's end and was about to launch a military invasion. We pointed out that North Korea had seen how successful the Chinese had been in their acquisition tactics and were about to do the same. The logical area to acquire was South Korea. It had the economy and resources to bail out the deeply depressed North Korean economy and, after all, they were the same people. It was only logical and fair that they be united under the one true political philosophy, Communism.

"Once each side had seen the logic of the argument, the level of concern grew without much prodding. We allowed it to fester for a few days and waited for them to ask how to avoid the calamity. We drug our feet for a few more days to raise the level of anxiety and then outlined a plan of unification that gave each side half a loaf. However, we did it in such a way that convinced them they had devised it. Not only did they not lose face, they gained credit. In addition, when we analyzed 'their' respective plans, we strongly hinted that the North Koreans were getting the better deal, when we spoke with the North Koreans. When we spoke to the South Koreans, it was just the opposite.

"The unified country still has some sorting out to do, but they have made great strides and, so far, they share the commitment."

Once again, I went to bed with a new and greater respect for my Uncle Aidan.

One evening a few days later, Uncle Aidan called several of the key players together and announced he had completed the campaign game plan. "Here is the document that I want you to read, memorize, and safeguard with your lives. Actually, this disk is only symbolic. The real plan is encrypted in the campaign computer and those few of you with the password can access it. The reason we are here tonight is that there are some parts to our plan that will not be documented. We will talk about them, so you will understand the overall plan, and to help you if we do something not covered by the plan. Let me give you the big picture.

"We can't go into California until we have established ourselves as a very well known entity. That goes for every candidate we are sponsoring. Since we can't physically be in the state while we do that, we will use fronts and insiders who are already there. For example, we will set up a campaign headquarters for Mr. Eagleton in Sacramento that will look for all intents and purposes like 'the' campaign headquarters. However, the real one will be here. The one in Sacramento will look reasonably credible, but when the Chinese come to inspect, they will report back that it is only a naïve bunch of kids who are trying to make a statement. I believe the Chinese will actually welcome the apparently inept challenge because it will add legitimacy to their position when they win fair and square.

"Mr. Eagleton will run as a Republican, but others of our group will run as Democrats. We will do that to be able to counter the incumbent Chinese stooges, regardless of party. I have to give it to them. They were smart. When they began running for office, their candidates ostensibly adopted the party that was strongest in the city or county they were in. Any real allegiance to either the Democrats or the Republicans was a sham. The Chinese Communist Party, the CCP, solidly drove their politics. Once elected, the front party, be it Democratic or Republican, was given lip service but their real loyalty was to the CCP. Our plan is to beat them at their own game.

"Before Mr. Eagleton sets foot in California, his name will be a household word. The same will be true for most of our candidate slate. Part of the strategy is to have the media blitz build him up as larger than life while he remains elusive and mysterious. As I said, Governor Santiago is a Democrat, so we'll run Mr. Eagleton as a Republican. It looks legitimate to both parties, to the voters of California, and to the national audience who will be following every turn in the campaign trail. The 2.2 billion dollars we have in the war chest will guarantee it.

"After the media blitz, but before Mr. Eagleton returns to California, we must deal with Mr. Lang Fang. That's where an old cohort of Mr. Eagleton, at a place called Camp Resistance, comes in. While the forces from Camp R are detaining Mr. Lang Fang, Mr. Eagleton and his staff will make a grand entry into

California. The holovision and other media coverage will be much too intense for the Chinese to try anything physical. Plus, we are counting on them to continue to underestimate the threat.

"This will not be an overnight event. We expect it will take many months of exposure to gain the confidence of the California voters. We must overcome the oppression and the strong-arm tactics during that time also. It doesn't make any difference if we persuade a voter that Mr. Eagleton is the best man for the job, if the voter is intimidated to go the other way, he or she will.

"There are a great many other details in the plan and I insist you develop a great familiarity with it. If you have any questions after you've read it, feel free to ask. If you have any questions now, ask away." Uncle Aidan was as captivating then as he was at the task force presentation in Denver. There were no questions.

Chan Lang Fang was moderately piqued at the political stirring that had begun. Even before Governor Santiago's top assistant had summoned him to Sacramento, he was aware of the opposition movement that was under way. He had assured the governor's staff there would be no interference from the federal government into California's internal affairs. He further assured the governor that this upstart movement was totally self-contained inside the state.

However, as the media coverage intensified, it became apparent there was a greater force involved. Moreover, whatever it was, was very well funded. Even though the Chinese had gained partial control of local holovision, it was impossible to harness the entire industry. Additionally, the ubiquitous national and international channels were beamed by satellite all over the world, including California. So, if the national "press" was touting opposition candidates, the local populace found out and the local media began broadcasting the stories too.

Lang Fang would need to get his "personal enforcer" to bring pressure on somebody. He wasn't sure who that somebody was, but he would turn that detail over to President Chae.

She sensed that it was time to move when he strongly hinted that Cho Li was in jeopardy. He further hinted that, if something wasn't done to stem the media saturation, he could no longer persuade the California Department of Senior Citizen Activities to look elsewhere. They would be inspecting his retirement center very soon.

President Chae suggested he meet her in Nevada in a few days. Then she called Uncle Aidan.

Art Morris had reorganized Camp Resistance and had kept it alive and well over the months since the border crossing. He had also kept in contact with Poppies via the secret communication system they had devised.

Additionally, he had formed numerous clones of Camp R and they were all fairly well equipped.

Not all of his camps and supporters were physically in California. A small cell, led by Arturo Viani, was established on the outskirts of Reno. Arturo Viani was a former U.S. Army Special Forces captain who had distinguished himself in the Petroleum Wars by single-handedly going into Arab capitals or tribal strongholds and kidnapping the top leader. He spoke several Arab dialects and one of his exploits was to capture Prince Il Fassil of Yemen.

Disguised as an Iraqi diplomat looking to make an arms deal, Viani convinced Il Fassil to meet him in Riyadh following a conference of petroleum-producing states. Although security was extremely tight, Viani drugged the prince and smuggled him out of Riyadh in a surface-to-air-missile container. The next day he delivered him to coalition headquarters on the flight line of Aviano Airbase, Italy. There were fighter aircraft, attack gyrocopters, and other weaponry on and surrounding the flight line. The prince was so dazed, he thought he was back in Yemen and, gazing at the plethora of weapons, he marveled at the deal he believed he had negotiated.

When Chan Lang Fang stepped off the flight from San Francisco to Reno, he was met as usual by a valet who would gyrocopter him to his hotel. Arturo Viani had made arrangements to pinch-hit for the valet that night.

Chan Lang Fang woke up several days later somewhere in Northern Nevada. He was in an underground compartment consisting of a bedroom, bathroom, and living room. There was no contact with the outside world. All services were computer driven and there were no humans within fifty kilometers of the place, but one could have walked right over it and not been the wiser.

The California press mentioned his disappearance in passing, only because of his alleged association with the President. Governor Santiago made no public comment, nor did any of his staff. Lang Fang's family members were so busy pouring over his will to see what their shares would be that, before he was missed, he was forgotten.

Monday, September 15, 2053
Sacramento, California

The next day after Lang Fang's disappearance, Poppies and his entourage re-entered California. It was mid September, and he had just over a year before the election.

Poppies' first order of business was to rescue Cho Li before the Chinese could put two and two together. He spirited her out of Grass Valley and had her safely with Art at Camp Resistance before nightfall. The on-site manager at Grass Valley resisted at first, but when Poppies produced authorization from Cho Li's daughter, the President of the United States, along with a complimentary payment of ten thousand dollars for administrative inconvenience, he not only agreed to let her go, but he turned over her entire file and removed her from their electronic database. It was as though she had never been there.

Poppies' next priority was to present a visible presence to the media and to Californians. He needed to establish that he, indeed, was there and would be for the long haul. It would take months to do that, but he was resolute.

Although third in the game plan, it was Poppies' first and most important priority. He must find Grammy. The game plan called for that venture to be kept very low key. Uncle Aidan felt that the chances of finding Grammy alive were better if there were no mention of her until they actually found her.

As much as I wanted to accompany Poppies to California, I was only able to share the campaign experience from my post at the LSU headquarters.

On October 1, 2053, I returned to Colorado and the Kniest chalet. I spent the remainder of 2053 there and was only privy to a few of the specific incidents associated with the campaign. I had more time to concentrate on my schoolwork and I threw myself into it. I had had an education during the past two years that would be the highlight of my life, but there were other things I needed to learn. Plus, I would need to do well in the formal class work of high school if I expected to get into college.

My schooling had continued via holo-teach ever since I left California. Actually, public schooling had evolved considerably over the past forty years. The advances in communication technology, coupled with the tight budgets faced by schools, forced educators to find a different way to educate the youth of America. One solution was holo-teach. Well over sixty percent of students across the nation were enrolled in holo-teach and in many ways it was better than physically attending school. The computer-generated instructors were more gifted than their human counterparts, and almost as real. Plus, each student received one-on-one attention for as long as the session took. My personal instructor was named Angelo.

I had a number of favorite subjects, but I particularly liked astronautics. One day Angelo was teaching me about other worlds and the possibility of finding life there. Angelo's lecture went like this: "Space exploration that had begun in the late twentieth century, continued even though the world was at war for most of the first half of the twenty-first century. Unmanned probes visited all the planets in our solar system, except Pluto.

"Samples of rocks and soil were brought back to earth from most of them. Scientists were thrilled when the sample returned from Uranus was found to contain life-forms. Unfortunately, the tiny microorganisms were parasitic and attacked plants of all species with ravenous vigor. Herbicides and insecticides of all types were tried, but because these organisms measured less than two hundred nanometers, they were able to resist all forms of earth poison. These little animals had endured the harsh extremes of climate in Uranus, so it wasn't likely that Earth's moderate environment would be any challenge.

"Finally, biologists studying the smallest life-forms on earth were brought in to study the problem. At that point, several hundred acres of plant life had been infected by the Uranus nanocrobes. The only way to contain them was to dig a totally sterile ditch twenty meters wide around the infected field. That stopped their voracious spread, but like most parasites, they continued to live on the host plants. Meanwhile, any plant life that might be left in the ditch would create a bridge for the Uranian pests to move to the next area.

"Ultimately, they were contained by the sterile ditch technique, but eradicating them proved to be a more sinister challenge. More by accident than anything, biologists stumbled on a way to combat the unwelcome guests. By extracting similar size organisms from the depths of Earth's volcanic pits and from superheated geyser pools at places such as Yellowstone, they found that Earth's nanocrobes were parasitic to those from Uranus.

"It took several years but eventually, enough Earth organisms were harvested and implanted in the

Uranian-tainted areas, and the Uranian life-forms were destroyed. The irony of all this is that scientists learned the lesson of 'be careful what you wish for' the hard way. For centuries, man had yearned to find life in any form on another world. It came, not in the form of little green men in spaceships, but in extremely little nondescript nanocrobes, and they nearly caused our destruction."

I had heard about the discovery of life on another planet, but I had not known about the problem it caused. I suppose that was because, once resolved, the important thing to teach school children was the significance of finding life outside our world and that, if it were on Uranus, then other forms of life were almost certain to exist elsewhere in the universe.

I vowed one day I would visit another planet.

Great-Grandma and Great-Grandpa Kniest were getting along, but I could tell they had lost a step. No doubt, the attack and kidnap incident contributed. I often wondered about that. The motive behind the attack and many of the details had never been revealed.

Uncle Aidan stayed behind in Baton Rouge. He still had one task yet to be done. President Chae had kept him informed of Dom Orosco's demands since the day of their meeting in the Chicago White House. The ACGA had become increasingly insistent that certain individuals be appointed to key positions in the government. In particular, they were interested in federal judges who were either soft on gambling or those whom they could intimidate.

Further they wanted legislation to reduce taxes on gambling profits and another bill to put a ceiling on the total tax owed by any given casino. For the large casinos, it would be a license to steal. Dom had consistently reminded President Chae of the ACGA's great financial support and that his requests were for favors already paid for. Lately, he insinuated that if they didn't get the results they wanted, the media would get the story of who really financed President Chae's campaign.

Monday, October 27, 2053
Atlantic City, New Jersey

Uncle Aidan, and three of his friends, showed up in Atlantic City before lunch on October 27. He had used these fellows before in scams, but this was to be the biggest, and the most dangerous. Two of them posed as Secret Service agents and the third posed as a White House attorney. Uncle Aidan was the ombudsman in the entourage. Upon arriving in Atlantic City, they ostensibly were to make a surprise visit to ACGA headquarters and Mr. Orosco. Through another scam artist, they were able to tip Dom off that the Feds were in town. So when they showed up at ACGA that afternoon, Dom was already quite smug thinking that he knew they were coming. As a result, he paid little attention to their fake credentials when they flashed them.

Their "purpose" was to investigate casino contributions to politicians across the board. Of course, by the time they arrived, Dom had had time to prepare. The White House lawyer told Dom this was just an advance group to provide the notification required by law and that dozens of accountants and other fact finders would descend on ACGA offices on Monday. They busied themselves with other preparatory matters, and Uncle Aidan was able to catch Dom Orosco's ear.

"Can I have a minute in private, Mr. Orosco?" Uncle Aidan was about to play the good cop in this "good cop/bad cop" scenario.

Don Orosco's ego was as big as his stature was small. It probably was a lifelong compensation for his 152 cm height. Dom had black slicked-down hair and a pencil-thin moustache. His olive skin and hairless body betrayed his Italian heritage. He liked to wear hats, even in the summer, perhaps because it made him feel taller. His voice was permanently raspy and his quick temper had gotten him in trouble more than once. Over the years, he had learned to control his temper most of the time, and he had adopted a pseudo-sophisticated manner that would impress most of the women in a New Jersey bowling alley. He thought well of himself and responded favorably to anyone who said they agreed.

Dom took Uncle Aidan to his ninety-fifth floor penthouse and they met over a glass of merlot. "I am here as a representative of the White House, but not a member of the White House, if you know what I mean. My real objective is to see if we can find a middle ground to all of this." Uncle Aidan began.

He took a sip of wine and continued, "What would you think if we could make this audit go away indefinitely?"

"I'd say you could have just about anything the ACGA has to offer," Dom replied. "What do you want? Money, girls, drugs, what?"

"Nothing that complicated or expensive, Mr. Orosco. The situation is this. The White House is still getting its feet wet and needs more time and opportunity to get its ducks in line. The media, as well as the Congress, won't stand for some of the judicial candidates the ACGA is sponsoring. The fact of the matter is, if the White House appoints them, they will not be confirmed. In the process, the President would have egg on her face and you wouldn't see any change. It's a lose/lose proposition. So I have another deal."

Dom Orosco was not a gullible sort, but his interest had been piqued. Uncle Aidan seized the opportunity. "I have two aspects of this issue to point out. Number one. You have some exposure and certain members of the White House do as well. Although it would do greater damage to the White House if campaign financing sources were revealed, it will be unfavorable publicity for the ACGA, as well."

"Hey, there is no way the damage would be equal," Dom started to rant. Uncle Aidan deftly cut him off.

"Number two. What if we were to throw in a gyrocopter attack and murder as well as the attack and kidnap of private citizens in Colorado?" Uncle Aidan spoke the words dispassionately. "The government has indictable proof that implicates you personally and the ACGA in both of those. Right now, there is no intent to pursue the judicial process. In view of the two aspects I just mentioned, I would hope we could negotiate a deal that would keep the status quo."

Dom began mumbling and cursing to himself as he could see his leverage over President Chae eroding. He wasn't prepared for the second aspect. He believed he was free and clear of both incidents.

"I'll have to think about it and let you know." Dom's wine glass began to shake a little.

"Okay, I can stop the accountants up until 9:00 a.m. tomorrow. Otherwise, I can't be responsible." Uncle Aidan stood up to leave.

"Wait a minute. How do I know this is legit? What proof do you have?"

Uncle Aidan threw the disk version of the selected transmissions surrounding the gyrocopter shoot down on the table. A second one contained the confession of the hired goon whom I shot and captured in the car barn.

"I think these will be all the proof you need. I'll be waiting for your microcom call. Thank you, Mr. Orosco. Good afternoon." Uncle Aidan let himself out of the penthouse, leaving Dom Orosco standing in the middle of the room with his mouth wide open.

Once he had heard the disk conversations, it was a "no-brainer." Dom Orosco called Uncle Aidan's microcom that night. The deal was done.

Although I wasn't present on the scene, the next several months of the campaign went about as Uncle Aidan and Poppies had planned. The media saturation soon reached every Californian from San Diego to Yreka. The Chinese initially started out to squelch the broadcasts. Then, when that didn't work, they tried to counter them. That didn't work either because they continually underestimated the amount of money Governor Miller's task force could throw at the media.

Meanwhile, Poppies was giving many Californians hope there might be an alternative to the Santiago administration. Over the months, Poppies' message had transitioned from one of making himself and his principles known, to one of attacking Governor Santiago and his programs. One such issue was

Santiago's treatment of the Black population. In the inner cities, preferential programs favored the Chinese and Latinos across the state. The Black community had truly become California's "most oppressed minority" under Santiago's tenure as governor. Poppies was determined to exploit that and garner the Black loyalty as well as their vote.

By design, nothing was said about the CCP or any of the ties this puppet regime had to the Chinese. At least, not then. It was February 2054 and the election was still nine months away.

Saturday, February 28, 2054
San Francisco, California

It was a relatively simple matter to locate Grammy. Great-Grandma Kniest had given Poppies the information he needed to start. He dared not personally begin the inquiry because virtually every word he said was recorded and published in the media. Again, Art came to the rescue.

As a member of Poppies' campaign staff, Art gained new freedom to move about the state. His first contact was with Crystal's daughter who still worked in San Francisco. Her name was Tammy Rodriguez and she was most willing to talk. It seems as though her mother, Crystal, had been identified as a candidate for the euthanasia program administered by the California Department of Senior Citizen Activities. She had died of "natural causes" a few months earlier.

Tammy was bitter, but also fearful of recrimination, so she could not speak out. Plus she had no real proof. She told Art that her mother was at a nursing home in Sonoma County that once had been a thriving winery. It was now a compound of several buildings and housed several thousand seniors. The place was called Sonoma Cutrer.

It took Art and two of his lieutenants less than an hour to make the trip from San Francisco to Sonoma. Once he got there, he approached the site management with a request to visit Jennifer Eagleton. Meanwhile, his two companions were scouring the buildings and grounds searching for her. The idea was to try both methods simultaneously. If polite inquiries didn't work, they were prepared to take more intrusive action.

The CCP had done their homework and a background check of David John Eagleton showed him to be a dissident whose wife had been conscripted for translation work. They had quickly issued the order to have her moved to a secret location. They had moved fast, but not fast enough.

After twenty minutes of stalling, Art's patience was at an end. He walked through the reception area directly into the site manager's office. Although Art was in his early sixties, he weighed 110 kg. Plus, after many days at Camp Resistance, he was fit. As he burst into the manager's workplace, he pretended that he was just an old friend (which was true), who had been given the runaround by the manager's staff. He commented that if that is the kind of service they provide here, he might register his observations with the Department of Senior Citizen Activities and send a copy to the governor.

The intimidation worked. In less than a minute, Art was en route to the building where Grammy worked and lived. He found her in a three-by-four-meter room. One side had a bed and nightstand. The other side had a console of translation equipment. There was nothing else. She didn't recognize him at first, but when he mentioned Poppies' name and the work they did twenty years earlier, her face brightened.

"I knew he would come," was all she said.

Art had alerted the two assistants on his way to Grammy's room. They had the gyrocopter in place at the end of the building. As Art and Grammy made their way down the hall and out the south entrance, security forces from the complex were coming in the north alcove. No shots were fired, but the escape was narrowly made. Art flew low over the deserted Sonoma Cutrer vineyards until he felt he had eluded any who might be in pursuit. Then he charted a direct course to Eagleton Campaign Headquarters in Sacramento.

I wish I could have been there to see the reunion of Grammy and Poppies. She was still dazzled by all that had happened. Her two-plus years of virtual captivity had dulled her senses, but not her love. They embraced for a long time without a word being uttered. Art told me later that, of the several people there, none were dry-eyed.

It was not safe for Grammy to remain at Eagleton Campaign Headquarters. If the Chinese or the press located her, it would be hard to explain the "abduction." Poppies and Grammy had about an hour together, which they spent in private. During that time Poppies did his best to explain what had happened, but eventually gave up, saying, "Just trust me. All this will come clear in time."

After having been apart for so long, Grammy wanted Poppies to come with her, but she sensed his resolve and finally acquiesced. The promise of his return to Colorado in a few weeks helped, as did the fact that her favorite grandson was there waiting for her. She would come to the chalet and stay with Great-Grandma and Great-Grandpa Kniest until this California thing was settled. It was with joy and relief, but not without trepidation, that she boarded the gyrocopter for the flight out of California.

In early March 2054, I received a communication from Uncle Max. Zell, now fully recovered, was moving to Southern California to live with a foster family. The name of the family was not releasable, but he assured me that, at his last visit to her, she had recovered much of her memory and smiled broadly when he mentioned my name. It wasn't much, but it formed all the hope I had.

Once Chan Lang Fang and Dom Orosco had been neutralized, President Chae was free to do her part. One of the reasons, Poppies was less encumbered by the Chinese, was that a torrent of federal officials began probing every activity in the state. Everything from spotted owl protection to mistreated dockworkers quickly came under scrutiny of federal investigators, inspectors, and fact-finding groups. The net effect was to bog down the administration so they couldn't thwart Poppies' campaign. A bonus was that, in numerous instances, the inspectors uncovered bona fide violations of federal law and other practices that pointed very unfavorable fingers at Governor Santiago and his administration. Again, by design, the linkage to the CCP was not made public.

Poppies shuttled back and forth between California and the chalet in between grueling days of campaigning. Grammy had recovered nicely from her two-year-long ordeal, and she was enjoying the solitude and beauty of the ranch. She also had ridden horses as a girl and was eager to help with the care of the three still in the corral. I settled into a daily routine of helping Great-Grandpa Tom with the chores, doing my studies, and getting to know my grandmother again. In the winter, I learned to ski and found it to be a most exhilarating sport. Once I had my license, I was the designated driver into the village for supplies, and, occasionally, I made a trip as far as Colorado Springs.

I had grown in both mind and body during those years and, at age seventeen, I stood 195 cm and weighed 98 kilograms. Shaving and puberty had come at the same time when I was fourteen and now the shaving part was routine. My hair had turned a couple of shades darker and my voice no longer cracked. My shoe size was 13. Poppies said it was a direct inheritance. I had little contact with other teenagers except that I occasionally went to youth events at the church. There were a number of cute Colorado girls there, but I thought of them only as friends.

Approximately eight months before the election, it became obvious to the CCP that they were in danger of losing ground in many of their strongholds. They began pumping over three billion dollars into the campaign for Governor Santiago and his group. They increased the intimidation tactics already common by police and other authorities. They turned some minds, and they frightened some voters, but, by and large, Poppies was holding his own.

In addition, the effects of the autism-chip implants were wearing off on a substantial number of Californians. These folks were becoming more and more disenchanted with the Santiago regime. At the six-month point, Poppies was trailing in the polls by less than three percentage points. Uncle Aidan concluded it was time to unleash "Plan Clincher."

Chan Lang Fang had been "detained" in Nevada for a good long time. During his solitary residence, he was given brainwashing drugs and was bombarded with psychological messages, some subliminal and some not. It was time for him to return to the scene.

Wednesday, July 1, 2054
North of Reno, Nevada

Early that morning Mr. Lang Fang was given a memory-altering medication in his coffee and taken to the Reno Airport, where he had been some nine months before. As he staggered into the concourse, he was immediately arrested by the FBI and charged with the murder of Sal Tesoro and the attack and kidnapping of Great-Grandma Kniest.

The combination of his return to the world, his arrest, and the apparent solution to two crimes made front-page news in media across the nation. Luis Santiago and Dom Orosco conferred via microcom. Both were totally bewildered at what this mysterious reappearance meant. They would find out soon enough.

Mind-altering drugs and messages had influenced Chan Lang Fang for nine months, but he was lucid enough to realize he had become the patsy for Santiago, Orosco, and the CCP. He was a broken man in many respects, but he was more than willing to tell his story. His appearance before Senator Ross Grimshaw's Judicial Subcommittee was compelling.

"Mr. Lang Fang," Senator Grimshaw began the proceedings, "Will you tell this subcommittee what your business is?"

"I am a businessman, retirement center owner, and lobbyist."

"For whom do you lobby?" the senator inquired.

"For the Association of Retirement Communities, Atlantic City Gaming Association, and for the State of California."

"Will you tell this subcommittee what else you do for the ACGA and the State of California? I am referring to the gyrocopter attack incident on June 16, 2052."

"Yes sir. I was asked to alert the California border patrol that an aircraft would be crossing the Nevada-California border."

"And who asked you to do that?"

"Mr. Dom Orosco, Chairman of the ACGA."

"How did you do that?" Senator Grimshaw was deliberate and closing in.

"I passed the request to Governor Santiago. He authorized the response, and my role was to give them the time and location."

"Did you know the intent was to shoot down the aircraft?"

"Yes, sir, I did."

"So, is it your testimony that you passed a request from Mr. Dom Orosco of the ACGA to Governor Luis Santiago to have a gyrocopter shot down?"

"Yes, sir, it is."

"Do you know why Mr. Orosco wanted it shot down?"

"A man by the name of Sal Tesoro had double-crossed Mr. Orosco and was trying to oust Mr. Orosco from the ACGA. He was on the gyrocopter and that was a convenient way to exterminate him."

"Why was Governor Santiago willing to go along?"

"Ten million dollars. Technically, the gyrocopter had intruded into California airspace and was flying without permission. But the standard procedure for such an intrusion is to force the aircraft to land, not immediately shoot it down." Chan Lang Fang neglected to mention his ten-million-dollar payment, but he had provided names, crimes, and motives.

Dom Orosco and Luis Santiago watched the holovised proceedings in horror.

"Let me get this straight. There were two gyrocopters involved. What did Tesoro want in California?" Senator Grimshaw appeared confused.

"Actually there were three air vehicles and one Humvee ground vehicle. Tesoro wanted to abduct a woman who was living in a small town because he thought she had information he wanted. He bribed the border patrol station sergeant to allow him to cross. What he didn't know was that Orosco had paid Santiago even more to not let him get back.

"Thinking it to be Tesoro's gyrocopter, the Chinese allowed another air vehicle to cross the border. But when it went directly to a known camp of renegade Californians, the Chinese opened up on it. I'm not sure who or what that vehicle was, but it was not Tesoro's. In the meantime, Tesoro's gyrocopter was headed for Graniteville. Apparently, when they got there, they found that the woman and some rescuers had already left in a Humvee. They gave chase and were in the process of destroying the Humvee when the Chinese discovered they had not destroyed Tesoro's copter, but the vehicle of the rescuers. I can't explain how they knew, but the Chinese showed up a few kilometers before the Tesoro copter reached the border and wasted that copter and all souls aboard."

Senator Grimshaw and the members of the subcommittee sat for a moment in stunned disbelief. Then he continued. "Turning to another incident, tell this subcommittee what you know about an attack on the parents of David Eagleton, currently running against Mr. Santiago for governor of California."

Chan Lang Fang looked directly into the camera. I was incensed by what I heard. "The attack on the two old folks in Colorado was initiated by Governor Santiago. He had become aware that Mr. Eagleton was spreading the word about certain activities in California. He wanted to keep his hands clean and, since he could not leave California jurisdiction, he asked Mr. Orosco to repay the favor for the Tesoro gyrocopter shoot down. Mr. Orosco was to provide two trained men and a stealth gyrocopter pilot to eliminate Mr. Eagleton. The gyrocopter aircraft came from California."

"And what happened?"

"The mission was botched from the start. They showed up when Mr. Eagleton wasn't home. They went into the house and only found an old couple. They shot the old man with a laser and were going to take the old lady hostage, thinking she could lure her son to come after her. The gyrocopter pilot was spooked by someone coming to the house and decided to leave the scene. He waited for an all-clear call from the two in the house but the call never came. He presumed the mission had failed and returned to his base. One of the men stuck in the house was killed and the other was wounded. That's all I know."

So, now it was coming together. I finally understood what had precipitated the confusion during the rescue

331

of Olivia and Zell. The chalet attack was also coming into focus. I was sure Poppies knew he was the target of the attack. That is why he felt so guilty about the injuries to Great-Grandma and Great-Grandpa Kniest.

On the other side of the coin, arrest warrants for Dom Orosco and Luis Santiago would be out within hours. Whatever Dom might say about ACGA financing of President Chae's campaign would be much less credible now. Out West, the credibility of Luis Santiago had been shot to hell.

Tuesday, November 3, 2054
Sacramento, California

The holovision broadcasts on that November Election Day of 2054 were breathtaking. Reports from throughout the country were beamed continuously, but no state got more coverage than California. From the early returns, it was clear the CCP puppet politicians were being unseated. At eleven o'clock Pacific Standard Time, Governor Santiago conceded the election. My grandfather, David John Eagleton, would be the next governor of California.

CHAPTER TWENTY-ONE

EPILOGUE—AUGUST 2055

California had been saved. The state with the "worst case" situation had overcome its oppressors. Equally important, the mold for the salvation of other states that had been infiltrated was cast.

Grammy and Poppies were in their eighth month in the California statehouse. The Chinese power wielders and the few Chinese stooge politicians who were not thrown out of office had quietly resigned and left the country. The truth about the War of Infiltration was beginning to be known at all levels in the state. Local politicians called the election a resurrection of California life and freedom. School children were free to express their views and sang the praises of the new governor. Some of the more corrupt CCP "soldiers" were brought to justice. Others simply disappeared. Poppies and Grammy were together and truly happy for the first time in years.

Uncle Aidan returned to his professorial life at LSU in Baton Rouge. He maintained close contact with Poppies and advised him on many matters. Other states that had experienced the infiltration were calling for Uncle Aidan's advice. He had enough work to last another five years.

Uncle Max retired from the gaming business and took his considerable wealth back to Oregon, where he and his wife bought a beach house overlooking Cannon Beach. He spent his days hiking the trails of Acola State Park with his grandchildren.

Great-Grandma and Great-Grandpa Kniest moved from the chalet to an assisted-living complex at the base of Pike's Peak in Colorado Springs. They spent their days reminiscing about their time at Boeing in St. Louis, their retirement years on the slopes of the Rockies, and fell asleep most evenings looking out on the mountain sunsets. Great-Grandpa Kniest never passed up an opportunity to tell one of their fellow residents about his automobile collection. Great-Grandma Kniest never passed up the opportunity to tell how proud she was of her son, the governor of California—and my Poppies.

President Chae could not overcome her association with the ACGA and Dom Orosco. At her party's behest, she declined to run for re-election. She would retire at the end of her term to New Jersey to care for Cho Li and to pursue her memoirs.

Scott Miller kept the task force alive and turned its attention to Florida and other states where the Chinese infiltration was most evident. He split his time between the task force effort and being governor. In 2055, he decided to run for President on the Republican ticket. It seemed most likely that on January 20, 2057, he would be inaugurated the 55th President of the United States.

Chan Lang Fang was placed in the witness protection program after having testified against Dom Orosco and Luis Santiago. He allegedly returned to the Orient, but was tracked down by the CCP and suffered their most extreme corporal punishment.

Dom Orosco was sentenced to life imprisonment and is currently residing in a two-by-four-meter cell with amenities quite different than those of his Atlantic City penthouse.

Luis Santiago committed suicide before he could be sentenced.

One hundred years and five generations have passed since my great-great-grandfather, the original Poppies, graduated high school. On May 30, 2055, I received my high school diploma and my acceptance into Stanford University.

Monday, August 9, 2055
Kniest Chalet, Colorado

Under a crystal clear Colorado morning sky, I put my gear in the old Stetson given to me by Uncle Max and headed west to California. I retraced the route Poppies and I had traveled some three years earlier. Most of the time, I stayed hooked up to the drive net and just dozed or mused over the past three-plus years. It has been quite a journey. It was almost over, but not quite. There was one more thing to do.

I climbed the slope past Mount Webber and reflected back on Camp Resistance. I looked to the north and recalled the night we were attacked by Tesoro's gang and the Chinese. I winced as I recalled Olivia's death. As I had done many times, my thoughts turned to Zell. Despite efforts to maintain contact, because of my involvement with Poppies' candidacy, my studies, and helping to take care of my great-grandparents and Grammy, I had lost track of Zell.

The Stetson picked up speed as I steered down the incline toward Graniteville. It was like an old horse returning to the barn for some oats. I slowed as I entered the outskirts, and I was happy to see some people had returned. A few shops were open, a restaurant or two, and I was pleased to see the motel we had lived in for those six weeks had reopened. I parked in front.

The path to the pond and waterfall was much the same. Smooth stepping-stones, carefully placed, transitioned into a pine needle trail leading to the rocks at the waterfall. It was six o'clock in the evening. I had double-checked my cyber bracelet watch a dozen or more times since coming into the town. I had told myself repeatedly not to get my hopes up, not to expect anything, but my heart was racing.

I paused to survey the scene. It was like nothing had happened. The permanency of the stone array and the incessant soft roar of the water splashing into the pool made the events of the past three years pale in comparison. It was as beautiful as I had remembered. I climbed to the spot where we first kissed. The vision seared my memory and tears welled up. All alone, I let them come.

I sat there for quite a while. I wasn't sure just how long until I checked my watch. Fifty minutes had gone by since my arrival at six. The shadows were beginning to lengthen and the fading sunlight caught the cascading water just right to display a rainbow. The sunset and spectrum of color would be my last memory of this place. I turned to go.

I reached down on the ledge to jump from the rock and, to my surprise, found a crumpled piece of paper. Although the light was waning, I recognized it immediately. I trembled as I unfolded each crease. I could tell it had been unfolded and refolded many times. In the golden California sunset, I read:

August 11, 2052

My Darling Zell,

I am sorry to leave you, but I hope one day you will get well and understand. Most importantly, I hope you will get well.

I will try to keep up with your progress through Uncle Max and Nurse Bailey.

I hope we can stay in touch after you get well even though I am in Colorado and you are in California.

If not, one day I will return to California. When I do, I hope to see you.

If you and I should lose contact and, if you agree, I propose we meet at our favorite spot on the third anniversary of our last meeting. That would be at six o'clock on August 11, 2055. I'm sure you know where I mean. It is the most beautiful place in the world for me because you were there. I hope you will be again.

With love, your friend,

D.J.

I gasped aloud. She was here. But when? I was specific in the note. I said six o'clock. I grabbed the note again. I had said six o'clock but I didn't say whether it was a.m. or p.m. I was aghast. I was in pain. I was about to panic. Had I just missed her by twelve hours? What could I do now?

My eyes burned with the tears of distress. My lungs pumped air to satisfy the oxygen demanded by the instant adrenalin rush. My heart pounded to keep up with both. I folded up the note and was about to run from the glen, when I looked up. Coming up the path was my Zell. No longer a beautiful girl, she was now a beautiful woman. I was frozen to the spot for what seemed like an eternity and then I moved to meet her. Without a word, we embraced and I caught the scent of her hair and felt the beat of her heart. On cue, she looked up and I gazed down to see tears trickle down her cheek toward her smile. I had no words, nor did she. We communicated all that needed to be said through our eyes and our touch.

My journey with Poppies was over.

THE END

Printed in the United States
73759LV00001B/2

9 781410 762481